Copyright © 2024 by LK Wilde

Cover Design by Jarmila Takač

ISBN 978-1-0686792-0-9

All rights reserved.

No portion of this book may be reproduced in any form without written permission from the publisher or author, except as permitted by U.S. or U.K. copyright law.

The Happy Place
LK Wilde

For Joe and Tom,
my very own Berties x

Chapter One

An ordinary evening: stirring spaghetti hoops while craning my neck to check on Bertie. My precious boy sat in his usual spot, glued to the Xbox screen, building a Minecraft home from colourful blocks.

'Dinner will be ready in five minutes. Bertie, did you hear me?'

Bertie grunted a reply, and I popped two pieces of white bread into the toaster and took the pan off the heat. If Rob found out I was feeding Bertie pasta hoops and white bread for dinner, he'd have a fit. This one small rebellion made me smile. I turned the radio up and tapped my foot as Taylor Swift's latest song blasted out. I smiled again, twirling around as I wondered what my in-laws would think if they could see me now. To them, I was *Olivia*, the Oxford-educated lover of classical music and Radio Four. To Bertie I was *Liv,* lover of cheesy pop music and kitchen discos.

The toast popped up, and I smeared an extra thick serving of real butter onto it. Not the plastic, baby-sick-coloured healthy spread Rob kept in the fridge.

I slopped the hoops over the bread, catching a dribble with my finger and licking it. The taste took me back to a cramped dining room in a small house. A family of four squashed at the table, eating own-brand tinned food, which was all they could afford while the parents scrimped and saved their way through university. Those were the days.

I left the cavernous kitchen to fetch Bertie. He was sitting cross-legged, leaning back against the plush white sofa. White Dove carpet, Pegasus furniture, Fresh Kicks walls. I shuddered at the memory of my mother-in-law beating me into submission in the home decor store with her lecture on the one-hundred-and-fifty-thousand shades of white. Living in our house was like being in a warm version of Lapland, the decor highly unsuitable for an eight-year-old boy.

I pulled the headset away from Bertie's ears and leaned over to kiss his bushy black hair. 'Dinner's ready.'

Bertie reached up and brushed my kisses away, causing his hair to spike up like a helmet.

'Come on, Bertie. Your food is getting cold.'

'Is it vegetables?' asked Bertie, wrinkling his nose.

'Nope. Spaghetti hoops.'

Bertie held a hand aloft for me to high-five.

'Thanks, Mum. I won't tell Dad.'

'Good boy,' I said, smoothing down his hair as he walked past.

Bertie shovelled fat spoonfuls of dinner into his mouth and chewed like a cement-mixer. 'You'd better remember your manners when we go to Grandpa's at the weekend. No eating with your mouth full there.'

'Not Grandpa's, please.'

'You know they love seeing you.'

'They hate me.'

'Of course they don't.'

I'd become an excellent liar since becoming a wife and mother. Hate may be too strong a word, but Rob's parents oozed dislike for their grandson, burying their feelings beneath a polite stream of questions about his schooling and extra-curricular clubs. Despite their forced interest in Bertie's life, their tight smiles, winces, creased foreheads, and occasional sighs told my emotionally intelligent son all he needed to know.

After gaining permission, Bertie jumped down from the table to return to his game and his friends. I cleared away the plates, rinsing out the can, crushing it beneath my boot, and hiding it at the bottom of the recycling bin so Rob wouldn't find it.

'Mum? Can I have a yogurt?'

'Only if you come and eat it in here.'

'I promise I won't spill any.'

'You know how your dad feels about eating in the living room.'

'Stupid Dad.'

'Bertie...' My rebuke was pointless, for the headset was clamped over his ears once more.

With Bertie's rebellious meal tidied away, I turned my attention to the fridge. Among the olives, hummus and rainbow of vegetables Rob put in his smoothies, I found two tuna steaks, and all the condiments I'd need to make the complex garlic and herb sauce Rob loved. At least the pain-in-the-butt sauce required the use of a few brain cells, unlike any of the other tasks I had performed that day.

After chopping, crushing, sautéing and stirring, I could leave the pan for long enough to send a message to Rob.

Dinner will be ready at 6.30 x

My phone beeped, and I swallowed down an ever-growing lump of resentment at my husband's reply: *Forgot to say. Out with the lads. Back late. Stick it in the fridge and I'll heat it up when I'm home.*

It was too late to stop cooking, so I pressed on, taking out some of my frustration on the bottom of the pan as the sauce threatened to stick. Unable to leave the temperamental creamy goo, I prayed Bertie was still on Minecraft, and hadn't sneaked Rob's copy of Grand Theft Auto into the console.

I savoured my solitary meal. After spending a significant chunk of my evening preparing it, it seemed a crime to gobble it down in a fraction of the time. Wednesday was supposed to be one of my alcohol-free evenings, but the large glass of pinot worked its chilled, mellow magic and as I finished the last mouthfuls of tuna steak, I felt relaxed enough to consider putting on my lace nightie at bedtime.

By the time I'd bathed Bertie and read him three chapters of *The Hobbit*, Rob had arrived home and was ensconced on the sofa. Before greeting him, I pulled one of his low-calorie beers from the fridge. With so little challenge in my life, the least I could do was score top marks on the wife front.

'How was your day?' I handed Rob the beer and sat on the sofa beside him, curling my legs beneath me.

'Same as ever. The board is being a pain-in-the-arse. Usual crap.'

'And the drink with the lads was fun?'

'Yeah, although Chris went on and on about his bloody stag do. He wants to go coasteering in Wales. Why can't he go to Prague or Amsterdam like a normal bloke?'

'He's always been outdoorsy.' I waited for Rob to ask about my day, but the question never came. 'Hey,' I said, running a finger up and down Rob's gym-toned arm. 'Maybe we could have an early night?'

'Yeah, maybe,' said Rob, not taking his eyes off the TV. 'But I want to watch *Football Feedback*.'

'Sure.' I knew *Football Feedback* wouldn't finish until eleven, and that might count as an early night if you didn't have to wake until eight, but I knew I'd be up at six with Bertie. 'Back in a minute.'

Upstairs, I changed into the silk and lace nightwear I wore on special occasions. It smelled a little musty, so I squirted Chanel No 5 liberally across the silk, promptly scrubbing with a tissue as the perfume left greasy marks on the fabric.

After running a comb through my thick, straightened hair, I brushed my teeth and slicked gloss across my lips. Back downstairs, rather than going over to Rob, I draped myself against the door-frame, in my best attempt at sexy.

'Rob?'

'Huh.'

'Rob.' I tried to purr, like I'd heard women do in films, but it came out gravelly, like a leery builder. I cleared my throat. 'Rob?'

My husband forced his eyes from the television screen and looked at me. 'Why are you wearing that?'

'I thought we were going to have an early night?'

'I told you, I want to watch *Football Feedback*.'

'Right.' Heat rushed to my face. I tried to nonchalantly turn, but the lace of my nightdress caught on the door handle, and Rob laughed at the ripping sound which followed.

Back upstairs, the bedroom door closed with a quiet click and I leaned against it, blinking hard to dispel the threatening tears. How many weeks had it been since Rob showed any interest in me? Not weeks. Months. Failure wasn't in my vocabulary. Ever since the teachers at my grotty comprehensive had picked me out as Oxbridge material, everyone had me pegged for success. I couldn't fail in my role as a wife. Apart from motherhood, it was all I had.

I pulled off the torn nightdress, scrunched it between my hands, and threw it in the bin. From beneath my pillow, I pulled out my flannel pyjamas, slipped them on and climbed into bed. The need to restore some dignity was strong, so I pulled the newspaper from my bedside cabinet and folded it on my lap. Pen clamped between my teeth, I worked my way through the cryptic crossword, grateful I could get something right.

Chapter Two

A six o'clock start should have allowed plenty of time to get out of the house by eight. I crouched down in front of the washer-dryer, trying to force open the door.

'What's going on, Mum?'

I looked up as my bleary-eyed boy shuffled into the room. 'Just this stupid washing machine not behaving itself.'

'Will my uniform be ready in time for school?'

'Of course.' I cursed under my breath, yanking at the door.

'Why don't you turn it off and on?'

'Good thinking.' I switched the machine off at the plug, counted to ten, and switched it on again. The light turned green, and I opened the door, pulling a soggy shirt out and silently cursing once again.

'I can't go to school in a wet shirt. Everyone will laugh.'

'Don't worry, I'll have it dry by the time we leave.'

'How?'

We both looked at the window, mottled with fat drops of rain. 'I'll hang it on a radiator, then finish it with a hairdryer.'

'OK. Can I have breakfast? I'm starving?'

'You're always starving.' We walked through to the kitchen and I filled a pan with oats and milk.

'Can't I have coco-pops?'

'Not on a school day. You know what Dad says, porridge is brain food.'

'It's gross.'

'Not if I put berries in it,' I said, reaching into the freezer.

By half-past seven, the shirt was still damp to the touch. I crept into my bedroom to retrieve the hairdryer, although I could've stomped through in hob-nailed boots and not woken Rob, who lay sprawled on his stomach, snoring loudly.

I'd had the hairdryer going on full heat for ten minutes when Bertie appeared at my shoulder, making me jump. 'Mum?'

'What is it?' I asked, blowing frizzy hair from my face and brushing a sheen of sweat from my forehead as the hairdryer blasted out hot air.

'My tummy hurts.'

'OK. What have you forgotten?'

'What do you mean?'

'Bertie, we both know a sore tummy is code for *I forgot to do my homework.*'

Bertie had the good grace to look sheepish. 'Maths.'

'Sit at the kitchen table and get it done, then. You've got twenty minutes.'

'But I don't understand it.'

'Fine. I'll help you. Get set up and I'll join you in a minute.'

Five minutes later, hairdryer in one hand, pencil in the other, I helped Bertie work through the endless list of maths questions even I struggled to understand. The school gave out a stupid amount of homework. Rob insisted on paying out a fortune for Bertie's private education, but it seemed the school palmed off most of the teaching for parents to do at home.

'What?' Bertie yelled at me over the squeal of the hair dryer.

'I said, subtract this number from this number and you'll get the answer.'

'What?'

I turned off the hairdryer. The shirt was still a little damp, but it would have to do. 'Look,' I said, writing out the answer to the maths problem on a piece of scrap paper.

'But, Mum, that's cheating.'

My free hand bunched into a fist beneath the table, and I clenched my teeth. It wasn't even eight yet, but already the day felt unbearable. 'Do you want to finish your homework before we leave in five minutes?'

Bertie let out a dramatic sigh and copied my answer down into his book.

'What's all the racket going on down here?' Rob walked into the room stark naked. My husband had a fine physique, but his insistence on displaying it at the breakfast table baffled me. Beside me, Bertie rolled his eyes, waggling a finger in imitation of Rob's genitals, and making a throwing up motion with his other hand. I suppressed a giggle.

'Sorry for the noise. I've been trying to get Bertie's shirt dry in time for school.'

'Shouldn't you have seen to that yesterday? My uniform was always pressed and folded ready for me the night before.'

'I'll bear that in mind. Can you call the repair man again? I don't understand why he hasn't come to fix the tumble dryer yet. Oh, and don't forget it's parent's evening tonight.'

'Yeah, it's in the diary. I'll try to make it.'

Try? What did that mean? It wasn't like Rob had a boss dictating his schedule. 'Come on Bertie, we're going to be late if we don't get a move on.'

The journey to school was irritating and uncomfortable. We crawled along in heavy traffic, rain water soaking through my trousers thanks to a hole in the roof of my

Mini convertible that Rob still hadn't got around to fixing. Turning into the long drive of Bertie's exclusive school should have come as a relief, but as I pulled up beside a collection of showroom-sparkling four by fours, I caught sight of my reflection in the mirror. Thanks to the hairdryer incident, and subsequent drenching on our way to the car, my usually straightened hair now frizzed up in a mass of dark, unruly curls. I'd had no time to put makeup on, and knew as soon as I stepped out of the car, everyone would see the large wet-patch covering the rear of my white jeans.

I grabbed Bertie's bags from the back seat and shepherded him into the building. Yummy mummies swanned around the corridors, shiny, groomed, their faces plumped and filled to perfection. I nodded to the less scary women, but avoided all conversation, keen to get in and out of the building as soon as possible.

With a quick kiss on the cheek, I shoved Bertie into his high-ceilinged, light-filled classroom and rushed back to the car.

'Olivia?'

Damn it. I'd almost made it to the door when a voice made me turn. It was Cressida Jamison, supreme ruler of the school mums. Most mothers longed to be initiated into Cressida's inner circle. Personally, I couldn't see the appeal. No amount of hair dye, makeup, or plastic surgery could hide the cold eyes and horseiness of her face. And however chocolatey she made her voice, it didn't blunt the barbs that poured from her tongue.

'Morning, Cressida. Is everything all right?'

'Yes,' drawled Horse Face. 'I just thought you'd like to know, it seems you've had a little accident.' Around her, her minions sniggered.

'Yes, I'm aware. That's having children for you. No bladder control. Now, if you'll excuse me, I'd best get home, change my trousers, and put a nappy on.' I smiled my sweetest smile and walked as calmly as I could to my car.

The drive home took the best part of an hour. If only Bertie went to the local school, I'd have far more time in my day, and even the possibility of making friends.

The day passed in a blur of chores. The only light relief came at lunchtime, when I sat down to watch the politics show I treated myself to daily. I banked several points to discuss with my sister the next time I saw her.

Before I knew it, I was back at school, waiting outside Bertie's classroom for the verdict on his achievement. It came as no surprise that there was no sign of my husband. Bertie sat beside me, fidgeting.

'Are you nervous?' I asked him, narrowing my eyes.

'No...'

'Bertie? Is there anything I should know before we go in...'

'I...'

'Mrs Simmons?'

I stood up and took Bertie's hand, my pulse rate increasing as we walked into the classroom. We sat on small chairs opposite a battle-axe of a woman, otherwise known as Mrs Bright, Bertie's teacher. She sat on a luxurious swivel chair, which gave her an over-inflated sense of power as she gazed down on us mere mortals.

'So, Mrs Simmons, I'm afraid Alberto has been getting into rather a lot of trouble lately.'

'Trouble?' I looked at Bertie, whose cheeks had turned pink.

Mrs Bright frowned, coughed, then placed a selection of drawings down on the table between us. 'Alberto has been encouraging vulgar behaviour in the other boys.'

I disguised a giggle as a cough. In front of me were a series of penises in varying colours, shapes and sizes.

'We were drawing rockets,' said Bertie, his cheeks now purple.

'Alberto Simmons, I was not born yesterday.'

'Bertie, it's important to tell the truth.' I squeezed his hand beneath the table.

'I didn't start it.'

'Then who did?' I spoke directly to Bertie, ignoring the formidable Mrs Bright as she peered down from her perch.

'It was Jack Jamison. He dared us all to draw them, then blamed me when we got caught.'

'Mrs Simmons, I'm afraid I've spoken to all the boys, and each one named Alberto as the ringleader.'

'That's 'cause Jack said he'd punch them if they grassed.'

'Jack Jamison is one of the best behaved children I've had the pleasure to teach. Behaviour like this would be so out of character, it's preposterous to pin this on him.' A muscle was twitching in the teacher's cheek, a bead of spittle squatting in the crease of her lips.

'I thought teachers weren't supposed to have favourites?' I said. Bertie gave my hand a squeeze in solidarity.

'I am merely stating the facts.'

'And the contribution the Jamison family made to the new sports hall has nothing to do with your opinion, I suppose?' I pushed my chair back and pulled Bertie up beside me. 'I'd hoped to gain an appraisal of Bertie's academic progress. But I can see my time here is being wasted. Now, if you'll excuse us.'

'There's another matter I need to discuss. Sit down.'

I stayed standing, not prepared to give another inch to the old witch. 'What is it?' I said, glancing pointedly at my watch.

'Bertie has been using foul language in class.'

'I haven't!'

'What foul language would this be?'

Mrs Bright scribbled something down on a piece of paper and handed it to me. 'I don't understand? Bertie can speak fairly good Spanish, but there's nowhere he would have learned this word.'

'I assure you he's been overheard frequently calling his friends this vulgar name. I spent several years living in Spain. Unfortunately for your son, I'm fluent in both the formal language and the slang.'

'Right, well, thank you for letting me know. I'll discuss this with Bertie when we get home.'

'Consider this a warning,' said Mrs Bright. 'Whilst we try to avoid exclusions, they are not unheard of for particularly difficult children.'

Tears flooded into my eyes as I looked down at my big-hearted, beautiful boy. *Particularly difficult*? The Bertie I knew lit up a room and brought joy to those around him. Yes, he was a free spirit, yes he enjoyed making mischief as much as the next eight-year-old, but difficult? Was I the type of parent who thinks the sun shines out of their child's backside? I shook my head. No. I knew my son, and the boy Mrs Bright was describing was not the child I'd raised.

'Goodbye, Mrs Bright.'

We'd made it as far as the door before she called out to us. 'Perhaps your husband could trouble himself to be here next time. I often find in cases like these, boys need the firm hand of their father.'

It wasn't until we were in the car that I spoke to Bertie. 'Why on earth have you been calling your friends *polla*?'

'Mum, I don't understand. It just means *cool* in Spanish. I was trying to be nice.'

'My God, Bertie. Who told you it means cool?'

'Gramps. It's what he calls Dad all the time. I asked what it meant, and he told me.'

'Right, well, I think Gramps has got muddled. Please don't use that word again.'

'OK. What does it mean, Mum?'

'That doesn't matter, you just need to know it's rude. Now, what do you want to listen to on the radio?'

As Bertie sang along to his favourite song, I pondered the fact that my father had been calling my husband a dick in Spanish for god-knows how long. I'd have to have a word the next time I visited.

Chapter Three

Sweat prickled my top lip as heat flooded my face. I pinched the credit card between damp fingers and held it out to the checkout assistant. 'Please, can you try it one more time?'

'Madam, it has already been declined twice. A third time could flag a potential fraud to your bank and then you'll be in an even worse position.'

I wasn't sure that was how these things worked and guessed the shop assistant was trying to get rid of me and clear the backlog of customers caused by my incident.

'Oh, God. I don't know what to do.'

'Do you have a different card you could try?'

'No.' I flushed an even deeper red. Rob only let me use the credit card, as it earned us air-miles for future holidays. I'd tried insisting a backup would be useful, but he'd laughed and shown me our extremely healthy bank balance. 'Do you mind if I call my husband? He may be able to sort this out?'

The shop assistant sighed. 'I can't hold your place in the queue, it's not fair to the other customers. Put the bags in the trolley and leave it here with me.'

'Thank you, I won't be long.'

It was a relief to step out into the supermarket car park, and find myself slapped in the face by an icy blast of March air. I held my face to the sky, waiting for the smattering of drizzle to calm my burning skin. After ten deep breaths, I pulled out my phone and dialled Rob's number. When he didn't pick up, I called his office, but instead of his cheery secretary answering, a robotic voice informed me I had dialled an incorrect number.

Humiliation deadened my legs, and forcing myself back into the supermarket was like walking through deep snow in a pair of stilettos. I put one foot in front of the other, aware that the shop assistant had seen me coming but was pretending she hadn't.

I waited beside the checkout, keeping my eyes on the scuffed floor to avoid any sympathetic looks heading my way. 'Excuse me...'

'Please wait a moment, madam, until I've finished serving this customer.'

I dared lift my eyes, catching the look of pity thrown my way by the middle-aged man packing up his shopping. A flash of gold caught my eye, my lids widening in horror as a dolled-up Cressida Jamison shimmered and shimmied her way towards the checkout. What was she doing here? Surely she only shopped at Waitrose?

I wiped my sweaty palms on my jeans. 'Sorry,' I said, turning on my heel and sprinting out of the shop.

'What about your shopping?' yelled the woman behind the checkout, but I was already racing towards my car, clicking the temperamental key fob and praying my escape wouldn't be hindered by a faulty fuse.

As I pulled out of the car park, I spotted Cressida wheeling her shopping towards her Porsche, sunglasses perched on her head despite the dreary day. Had she spotted me? I prayed not, but then again, what if she had? So what? Who cares? With a rush of shame, I realised I did care, and hated myself for it.

I left the salubrious suburbs and drove until I reached rows of ordinary terraced houses, children's bikes propped up in gardens with cheerful metal benches and potted plants. Rob was so scathing about this area, but I loved it. Unlike on our executive estate, here they held community workshops, pub quizzes, mother-and-toddler groups and clothes swaps. For all the luxuries afforded to us in our four-bedroom, three-bathroom detached house, we knew nothing about our neighbours, not even their names, and every scrap of grass held a sign informing children that *no ball games are allowed*.

'Liv? What are you doing here?'

My sister answered the door wearing a paint-covered apron and her usual warm smile. In complete contrast to me, she took her looks firmly from the English side of our parentage. A good few centimetres taller than me, her pale face housed a smattering of freckles, framed by silky blonde locks, her green eyes sparkling with excitement for life. She was the spitting image of our mother, so much so, sometimes it physically hurt to look at her.

'Hi, Cass. I was just passing. Actually, no, that's not true. I had an incident at the supermarket and could do with a glass of wine if there's one going spare?'

'You've come to the right place. Come in. Sorry about the mess,' she said, as we weaved our way through piles of washing and discarded toys.

'What's with the apron?'

'I'm painting the twins' room. They're going through a goth phase and want the walls black.'

'A goth phase? At ten?'

'I know,' said Cass with a laugh. 'God knows what they'll be like when they hit their teens. I suppose it's better to get this love for all things dark out of their system before then. You should hear the music they listen to. Jasper calls it death by a thousand howls.'

I smiled at the mention of my brother-in-law. Bearded, plump and full of laughter, Cass had fallen for Jasper the moment she laid eyes on him in the sixth form common room and they'd been inseparable ever since.

'Ooh, this is lovely,' I said, walking into the newly painted kitchen. 'What a gorgeous colour,' I said, stroking the bubblegum-coloured walls.

'Poor old Jasper hates it,' said Cass. 'I only painted it at the weekend. All the black was getting to me. Jasper keeps asking why I couldn't have gone for a pale blue or teal, something more manly.'

'Your husband's a saint.'

'I know,' said Cass with a grin. 'Anyway, here's your wine. Now tell me what happened in the supermarket to get you so riled up.'

I told Cass about my card being declined, but instead of the sympathy I'd been hoping for, she laughed.

'Is that all?'

'What do you mean, is that all? It was a horrifying experience.'

'God, you've become so spoiled. My card gets declined every other week. I keep a few twenty-pound notes in the car as a backup. You get used to running out of money when you live on the wages of a nurse and a police officer.'

I took a sip of my wine, and Cass reached a hand across the breakfast bar and squeezed mine.

'I'm sorry, I realise it must have been really embarrassing for you, given the circles you now move in. Didn't you have another card you could use?'

'Rob only likes me using the credit card.'

Cass choked on her wine. 'Sorry. You mean Rob restricts the money you have access to?'

'It's not like that.'

'No?'

'No. He'll give me extra if I need it.'

'How generous of him. Listen, Liv, isn't it about time you got a job, used that massive brain of yours? It must be awful relying on pocket money from your husband.'

'There's no way I can get a job and take care of Bertie.'

'Really? What do you think most females in the population do?' Cass raised an eyebrow and glugged down more wine.

'Yes, but Bertie's school is so far away, there'd be no way of getting him there if I was working.'

'I get it. Logistics can be hard. But you wouldn't need to work full-time. You could probably find a job you could do from home. You've got an amazing degree and incredible language skills. Most employers would snap you up like that.' Cass clicked her fingers. 'What are you doing for the rest of the day?'

'Housework, mainly.' My insides squirmed at the mundanity of my life compared to my warm-hearted grafter of a sister. 'I've no idea what to cook for tea given I can't buy any shopping.'

'I've got a cottage pie in the freezer you can take home with you, but it will cost you.'

'Cost me how?'

Cass reached into a drawer and slid a paintbrush across the counter to me.

'Deal.'

Chapter Four

'Perfect,' said Rob as I walked my preened self into the kitchen.

'Thank you.' I felt constricted in my figure-hugging tailored dress. My toes pinched in uncomfortable heels, and my arms ached from the hour it had taken to straighten my unruly hair.

Rob wrapped an arm around my waist and I felt an absurd rush of pleasure that my appearance pleased him. 'Did you have any luck with the bank?'

'No, bunch of incompetent fools. I was on the phone for over an hour yesterday and they still couldn't transfer me to the right department.'

'I'm not sure what to do. I need to get shopping, pay for Bertie's swimming lessons, settle the final bill for the plumber.'

'Don't stress,' said Rob, placing a series of kisses along my neck. 'I'll give you some cash to tide you over. The credit card will get sorted next week.'

I tried not to let his kisses distract me. How had I reached the point that I was screeching towards thirty with no independent means, living the life of a nineteenth century housekeeper? 'I'd better check Bertie's ready.'

Rob stopped his kissing, frowned, and picked up his phone. 'You mother that boy way too much.'

Wasn't it only a few days ago he'd told me about his own mother laying out his clothes the night before? 'I'm not fussing over him, but I know you hate being late for your parents.'

Rob ignored my explanation, his frown lines deepening as he clicked through messages on his phone. I gave up trying to talk to him and found Bertie lying on his bed watching videos on his iPad.

'We need to get going, Bertie.'

'I don't want to go.'

Neither did I. I'd rather stick pins in my eyes, or be thrown into a snake pit than spend more than five minutes with my in-laws, or grim-laws as I called them in my head. I squared my shoulders. 'Come on, it will be fun.'

'Can I go in the pool?'

I shook my head, not trusting myself to speak. Despite having an outdoor heated swimming pool among their many acres of garden, my in-laws had declared it an adult-only space, insisting the risk of snot, urine and vomit was too great to allow children into its jewel-like waters.

'Tell you what, if you're a good boy today, I'll think of a treat on the way home.'

'What kind of treat?'

'Movie night with me?'

Bertie narrowed his eyes. 'Will there be popcorn?'

'Yes.'

'Do I get to pick the film?'

'Yes.'

'OK.' Bertie jumped off the bed and shoved his iPad into his bag.

'No iPad, Bertie. You know how Grandma and Grandpa feel about devices.'

With a dramatic sigh, Bertie swapped his iPad for a comic, before hitching his bag onto his back and taking my hand.

The memory of my first visit to my in-laws' home still sent shivers down my spine. I'd been desperate to make a good first impression, but seeing their mansion (just a large house, according to Rob) in the Devonshire countryside, my insides had turned to mush and I'd lost the power of speech. The full list of disasters which occurred over that one weekend is too great to mention. But the highlights include: the heel of my cheap shoes breaking as I walked up the driveway, forgetting my in-laws' names, enthusiastically joining in a conversation about polo mints, only to realise too late they were discussing a sport. But the pièce de résistance came after an evening barbecue, when I found out I had a hitherto undiscovered allergy to seafood. I'm not sure their marble-covered bathroom has ever recovered. Oh, and Rob got drunk and announced the bombshell of my pregnancy while I was reacquainting myself with barbecued squid in the bathroom.

'Here we are,' said Rob, pulling his Range Rover to a stop outside Rigby Manor. 'Best behaviour, Bertie.'

Hugo and Marion greeted us at the door. I still expected a capped-headed servant to appear as the closest point of reference I had to how my in-laws lived was 'Downton Abbey'.

'On time for once,' bellowed Hugo, checking his pocket watch.

'Don't stand there in the doorway, come in.'

I walked past Marion, nearly choking on the excessive amount of perfume seeping from her skin. 'You look well,' I said.

'Thank you, Olivia,' said Marion, not returning the compliment. She patted her neat chignon. Her thick make-up had creased into the crevices of her face, and dabs of shimmery pink lipstick clung to her teeth. She fiddled with the string of pearls around her neck. 'Go through to the dining room. Lunch is almost ready.'

I took Bertie's hand and led him through the house, keeping him close just in case we knocked against any priceless ornaments as we went. We sat ourselves in uncomfortable high-backed chairs at the dining table. Bertie began fiddling with his napkin. I placed a hand across his to still it.

Once we were all seated, Marion brought through china dishes filled with the various items she had prepared for the Sunday roast. Rob loved his mother's cooking, but to my taste buds, it was bland and overcooked. To be fair to Marion, (something I was loath to do), nothing could compete with the patatas bravas, gazpacho, or tortillas my mother cooked in the days post-university when both my parents were finally bringing in a reasonable wage.

'So, Albert, how are you getting on at school?'

Beneath the table, I twisted a napkin between my fingers. My in-laws insisted on calling Bertie Albert, having never forgiven me for adding the 'o' to the end of his name. Perhaps if Rob had been there when I registered the birth, he could have put his Anglo-Saxon case across, but as Cass liked to say, *you snooze, you lose.*

'Um... um...'

'He's doing very well at school,' I said, coming to Bertie's rescue.

'Let the boy speak for himself, woman,' shouted Hugo. 'What's your favourite subject, Albert?'

'Spanish.'

'Of course it is,' muttered Marion, taking a delicate bite of overcooked cabbage.

Already bored with the conversation, Hugo turned his attention away from his grandson and onto his son. 'Rob, I've not had the latest quarterly figures on my investment.'

'I know,' said Rob. 'The accountancy firm we were using turned out to be a bunch of imbeciles, so there's a bit of a delay while we transfer all the figures and documentation across to a new firm.'

'Humph. Well, I'd like to have those figures across my desk soon. I've invested a hefty chunk of change and expect to see returns quickly, or I may have to rethink where I invest my money.'

'Gentlemen, please,' said Marion, her voice scolding. 'The dinner table is not the place for vulgar conversation about money. Save it for once we've eaten.'

'Of course, dear,' said Hugo.

'Speaking of work, I'm thinking about getting a job.' Goodness knows why I felt the need to share this half-baked plan. Perhaps it was that I knew no-one would ask anything about my life and I was fed up of being invisible.

'A job? Goodness me, what is the world coming to?'

'I think you'll find plenty of women work, Marion.'

'Yes, but a woman's place is at home with her family. Anyway, what do you need to work for? Isn't my son's wage enough for you?'

There it was. The old accusation, that whilst never explicitly stated, had been perched on the tip of Marion's tongue from the moment she met me. *Gold-digger.* If only she knew. Whilst being comfortably off was a luxury I didn't take for granted, I'd never been so happy as during the years of my childhood, when we'd had little in the way of money, but plenty in the way of love.

'Don't worry, mother. Olivia's having a mad-moment. It will pass.' Rob, Marion, and Hugo laughed. Beside me, Bertie shuffled in his seat.

'Mum? Can I go out and play in the garden?'

'Of course you can,' I said, knowing it would wind up my in-laws. 'Just make sure to wear your coat. It's chilly out there.'

Bertie leaned over and kissed me, then jumped off his chair and sprinted out of the room.

We were on the coffee phase of the never-ending lunch when I heard a voice calling from behind the door, 'Mum!'

'Bertie?'

'Mum, can you come here?'

'What's going on?' asked Hugo, his voice even louder than before, his cheeks mottled red from all the wine he'd drunk.

I stood up from the table. 'Bertie needs me.'

'Don't be ridiculous, woman. Get the boy to come in here.'

'Bertie, it's OK, come here and talk to me.'

The door opened an inch, a small hand beckoning me. I pushed back my chair and began walking to the door.

'Come in here this instant.' Rob's voice dripped with impatience. No movement came from behind the door. 'For God's sake,' said Rob, scrunching up his napkin and throwing it down on the table. He pointed a finger in my direction. 'See? This is what happens when you spoil a child.'

Rob stomped towards the door, stopping in his tracks as he viewed his son. 'What the hell?' His hand reached through the doorway, and he dragged a sopping wet Bertie into the room.

It was hard to tell how much of the water on Bertie's face was from an external factor and how much was from his eyes. I rushed towards him, pulling him into my arms, his sodden clothes dampening my dress.

'What happened?'

Bertie's bloodshot eyes looked from me to the other adults in the room. 'I had an accident.' His voice was a whisper, his clothes hanging from him, heavy and stretched from all the water they'd soaked up.

'Have you been in our pool?' Marion spat the words, a muscle in the corner of her eye twitching.

Bertie sniffed and wiped his nose on his sleeve. Marion bristled. Hugo tried to focus his wine-addled brain and eyes on what was happening. Rob seethed.

'I d... d... didn't mean to. I... w... w... was rescuing my pet.'

'Pet? Bertie, you don't have a pet.' I pulled a tissue from my bag and dabbed it against his eyes.

'I found a pet frog,' he whispered.

'Speak up, boy.'

I turned and glared at Hugo.

'I found a pet frog, but when I was walking past the pool, he jumped out of my hands and into the water. The chlorine could have killed him, so I had to jump in and rescue him.'

The room fell silent. Bertie's sodden hair had fallen in front of his eyes, and I brushed it away.

'Did you rescue the frog?' I asked.

'Yes, but it took ages. He's only small, so it was hard to find him, and he's a brilliant swimmer.' Bertie leaned forward and whispered in my ear. 'He's called Fred.'

Despite the anger from Rob and his parents seeping across the room and prickling my skin, I couldn't hide my smile. 'Did you put Fred back where you found him?'

Bertie shook his head.

'Bertie...' I scanned his body, my eyes resting on the pocket of his trousers. The fabric strained as something squirmed inside it. Bertie's hand reached down to unzip the pocket. 'Bertie, no!'

Before I could stop him, the pocket gaped open, and a green-brown bulbous head poked out. Bertie tried to grab it, but the frog, or toad as it turned out to be, slipped through his fingers.

'What's happening?' squealed Marion. She screamed as a pulsing, slimy body landed on the table between the carrots and swede.

'Good heavens,' said Hugo, his chair falling to the ground as he backed towards the corner of the room.

Rob leaped forward, only catching the toad on his fourth lunge. He held his hands as far from his body as he could. As he passed me and Bertie, from behind clenched teeth, he said, 'Wait in the car.'

I took hold of Bertie's arm, and heads down, we shuffled from the room.

Chapter Five

As soon as I stepped across the threshold, I knew something was wrong. Our minimalistic décor had been taken to a whole new level. The ugly grey paintings Rob claimed were an investment no longer hung from the walls. The only evidence they'd ever been there was a thin square of dust which had collected behind their frames.

In the kitchen, I found the digital radio gone, the two-hundred-pound juicer Rob used each morning no longer sitting on the worktop. The sitting room was worse: no clock, no iPad, no laptop, no sound system. The only electrical item remaining was the giant sixty-inch TV screwed to the wall.

I ran back to the kitchen, grabbing a rolling pin. The thieves could still be in the house, because the only explanation for the destruction of my home was a robbery. Phone in hand, I crept up the stairs. The only items remaining in either mine or Rob's wardrobes were the old clothes I used for housework.

It was in Bertie's room that the full horror hit me, and tears broke free. His box of dinosaurs lay on the floor beside his bed, but any toys of value, which was most of them, had been cleared out.

How had they managed to take so much in the hour and a half round trip to school? The burglars must be professionals to find the location of every valuable item we owned.

I dialled the emergency services, but before anyone answered, a text came through from Rob. *Sorry.*

Sorry for what? As a voice answered my call, I hung up the phone. Was there a rational explanation I was missing? Had Rob colluded with his mother to redesign our home while I was out on the school run? Had he discovered some deep-seated desire to give all our worldly goods to charity?

The doorbell chimed and I ran downstairs, holding the rolling pin behind my back as I opened the door.

'Good morning, madam. Can I take your name, please?'

'Um, yes, it's, um, Olivia Simmons.' Something about the uniformed man clutching a clipboard made me comply without question.

'And are you the wife of Robert Simmons?'

'Yes. What's happened to Rob?'

'I regret to inform you, we are here to repossess your property.'

I stumbled backwards. 'Is this a joke?'

'I assure you, madam, this is a serious attempt to recover the monies owed by one Robert Simmons. Two-million-three-hundred-and-fifty thousand pounds, to be exact.'

'What? I don't understand?'

'We have sent numerous communications informing you of this course of action.'

'But I haven't heard anything. What communications?'

'Letters.'

'But I haven't seen any letters!'

'I assure you, your husband is fully appraised of the situation. We require your permission to enter the property. However, you should be aware that if you refuse to comply with the court order,' the man held a piece of paper aloft, 'then we shall be forced to call in the police for support.'

My mouth opened and closed like the tropical fish Rob kept in a tank in his office. *Police?* I pictured Jasper turning up on my doorstep in a course of action which would mortify us both. 'It's fine, come in.'

'Thank you, madam. I appreciate your compliance.'

'Sorry, but could you explain what this means?'

'It means you'll need to vacate the house as soon as possible.'

'Can I take anything with me?'

'As long as it's nothing of any value.'

I pushed down an inappropriate desire to laugh. Value? It looked as though Rob had already cleared anything out of value and left me and Bertie with the dregs. 'I'll pack some bags.'

'Thank you.'

As I packed up whatever would fit in the two suitcases Rob had left, my eyes remained dry. I was on autopilot, wandering around the house as though in a dream, or having worked through a bottle of red. 'I think I'm done,' I told the bailiff, heaving my suitcases towards the door.

'Thank you. I'll need to take any house keys you have, and also those for your car.'

'My car?'

The bailiff studied his clipboard. 'Yes, I'm afraid so. The car is registered to your husband, and therefore forms part of our inventory.'

My chest filled with a cold wave of fear. What could I do without a car? How would I be able to pick Bertie up from school? My breath quickened as I handed over the keys to my life. The bailiff closed the door behind me, and I stood in our driveway, trying to unscramble the mass of thoughts swirling through my mind. Cass. I needed Cass.

'Hey, how's it going?'

The sound of my sister's voice loosened something inside me, and I choked on my words.

'Oh my God, Liv. Are you OK? What's happened?'

'I... Rob... I need to see you. Are you at work?'

'No, I'm on the night shift, so home all day.'

'Could... could... you help me out with a taxi fare if I come to yours?'

'Of course, but, Cass, you're scaring me. Please tell me what's going on. Is it Rob? Have you two split up?'

'I'll tell you when I see you,' I said, hanging up the phone. Had me and Rob split up? There was plenty of evidence to suggest we had, but as his phone had gone to voicemail during my repeated attempts to call him in the past hour, there was no way of knowing what was going on.

I pulled myself together enough to call a cab. A couple of curtains twitched in the surrounding houses. Let them stare. It would be the most excitement any of my neighbours had had in a long time if their carefully curated lives were anything to go by.

The cab arrived, and the driver helped me load my suitcases into the back. For once, the universe was on my side and my driver had both limited English and no desire to use the little he had. We wove through city centre traffic, my phone clamped to my ear as I alternated between calling Rob, his office and his parents' landline. Instead of frustration at the lack of response, my reaction was full-blown fear. Not to mention confusion. Wouldn't I have noticed if things had got so bad? I thought back to my declined credit card and the testy conversation about investments over lunch with Hugo and Marion. Perhaps the signs had been there, I'd just been too stupid to see them.

Cass must have been watching out for me, for no sooner had the driver pulled the cab to a halt than she was running from her front door, clutching her purse. After paying the driver, she helped me lift my bags from the car and carry them to her front door. Not once did she demand answers. She knew me well enough to know I'd tell her in my own sweet time.

It wasn't until I was curled on her sofa, cup of tea in hand, that the floodgates opened. Between sobs, I spilled my story out, to Cass's wide-eyed horror.

'How is that even possible? Over two million quid? What about the house, fancy cars and private school fees? He must have had access to cash to be paying for those.'

'I have a nasty feeling he's been paying with other people's cash. His dad's for starters.'

'Horrible Hugo gave him money?'

I nodded. 'A lot, I'm guessing. God knows what position his parents have been left in.'

'Do you care?'

I managed a small smile. 'Not really. I'm far more worried about Bertie. Aside from the fact I've no idea how long his school fees have been paid for, there's also the small matter of how to get him to and from school in the first place.'

'I can't believe they took your car.'

'It was in Rob's name.'

'You didn't even own a car? Liv, what do you have that's yours?'

I racked my brain but came up blank. 'Nothing. I have nothing. Zilch, nada, diddly-squat. Christ knows what I'm going to do.'

'Well, you can stay with us as long as you need. And as for the school run, borrow my car. I usually get the bus into work.'

'Are you sure?'

'Certain. You're not going through this alone. Not if I can help it.'

Later that day, I pulled up outside my son's posh school to curious glances from other parents. It could have been my tear-stained face, smart dress discarded in favour of jeans and T-shirt, or the fact I'd stepped out of a twenty-year-old Ford Escort. Either way, rather than keep my head down, I returned their stares, plastering a smile on my face and pushing back my shoulders. I'd done nothing wrong. None of this was my fault.

On my way to Bertie's classroom, a prim young woman in dark-rimmed spectacles poked her head around a door and called my name.

'Yes?'

'Mrs Simmons, the headteacher would like a quick word with you.'

'OK.' Was another teacher going to label my son a devil-child?

I followed the prim secretary through to a wood-panelled office, its enormous windows offering uninterrupted views of the extensive playing fields. Mr Kieling looked far too young to be a headteacher. He was trying to grow a beard, probably in an attempt at authority, but it had the effect of making him look like a pubescent boy.

'Mrs Simmons, thank you for meeting with me. Do sit down.'

I pulled a chair out and tried to wear an air of confidence. In contrast to the po-faced Mrs Bright, Mr Kieling's smile was warm and genuine, and I wondered if he struggled with his more abrupt staff members. I liked him and hoped whatever he was about to say wouldn't change that opinion.

'Has Bertie got into trouble again?'

'Oh no, your son is a wonderful little boy. Very bright, sporty, an asset to the school.'

'Oh. Thank you.'

'No, I'm afraid the matter I wish to discuss is of a delicate nature.'

I leaned forward in my seat, my hands twisting in my lap. 'Delicate?'

'Yes.' Mr Kieling cleared his throat. 'It's about your son's school fees.' A red smudge appeared just above Mr Keiling's

Adam's apple and began snaking its way up his neck. 'I've been trying to get in touch with your husband for some time, as the last three cheques he's given us have bounced.'

My face mirrored Mr Kieling's in colour. 'I'm so sorry. But why has no one mentioned this to me?'

'It was always Mr Simmons who dealt with fees and financial matters. We rather assumed that you...'

'Are only good for school runs and housework? Don't have a first from Oxford in PPE? Am incapable of simple arithmetic?'

Mr Keiling turned purple. I felt awful for making him so uncomfortable, but after the day I'd had, there was little capacity left for sexist bullshit, and no capacity left for beating around the bush. Perhaps if the school had contacted me sooner, I could have spoken to Rob and done some damage limitation on the mess he was wading into.

'I apologise, Mrs Simmons. I didn't mean to suggest...'

'It's fine. What's the upshot of these missed payments?'

'I'm afraid we're in a tricky spot. All our scholarship places have been filled for the year. If your outstanding bill isn't settled soon, I'm afraid we'll have to withdraw Alberto's place.'

Wow. I leaned back in the leather armchair, wondering if the day could get much worse.

Chapter Six

'Wasn't that a bit rash? You can't give up his school place just like that.' Cass leaned over and topped up my glass of wine.

'I'll grab another bottle,' said Jasper, getting up from the sofa.

'Honestly, Cass, what choice did I have? Mr Kieling said the fees would need to be paid within a week, and as we both know, there's no chance of that.'

'Couldn't Hugo and Marion help?'

'They're not answering my calls.'

'No luck with Rob either?'

'No.'

'I may be able to help with that,' said Jasper, placing two bottles, one red, one white, down on the coffee table. 'He texted me asking if I fancied a drink.'

'He what? Rob doesn't even like you!'

'Thanks,' said Jasper with a good-natured laugh.

'You're not going, I hope?' said Cass.

'It's not the worst idea. I could talk to him and find out what's going on.'

'He's such a coward,' I said. 'He doesn't dare face me, and thinks you'll be gentle with him. I agree with Jasper, Cass. At least if they meet up, Jasper can try to get to the bottom of things. Perhaps I should come too?'

'Ah,' said Jasper, looking awkward. 'He said he's not ready to see you yet and if I bring you along, he'll leave.'

'Perhaps he's forgotten I'm his wife? Mind you, if I saw him, I couldn't guarantee he'd come out of it unscathed, and I wouldn't want to put you in a tricky position, Jasper, what with you being an officer of the law.'

'When does he want to meet?' asked Cass.

Jasper looked at his watch. 'Now. He texted five minutes ago when I was in the kitchen.'

'You'd best get going then,' said Cass. 'Be sure to give him a slap from me.'

Jasper kissed Cass, grabbed his coat, and let himself out of the house.

We were two-thirds of the way through our second bottle of wine when Jasper returned. 'That was quick,' said Cass.

Jasper looked at his watch. 'An hour was more than enough. That guy's a total arsehole. Sorry,' he said, turning to me.

'No, go ahead, I agree. What did he say?'

Jasper sighed and flopped down on the sofa beside Cass. 'Where to start?'

'Start with what's happened to all our money.'

'OK. Well, it turns out Rob went into business with some guy he met while playing golf. It was meant to be this amazing opportunity to invest in a new eco housing estate. Only, it turned out the guy was a crook and the housing estate a total fantasy.'

'And Rob invested everything into it?'

'Yep, and not just your money, either. He put in a massive chunk of the money he got from Hugo, plus he staked his entire business on it. Oh, and a few more of his golfing buddies chipped in tens of thousands to boot.'

'Crap.'

'So there's no way of getting any of it back?'

'It was hard to get a clear picture, given Rob was already wasted by the time I got to the pub, but it seems not.'

'But why hasn't he told me any of this? I'm his *wife*!'

Jasper shrugged. 'Like you said, he's a coward. To be honest, I almost felt sorry for him. I got the impression he was trying to impress his parents with this latest deal. Mind you, to still be courting their approval at his age is a bit pathetic.'

'Where's he staying?'

'He wouldn't tell me, but it's not with Hugo and Marion. I don't think he dares face them.'

'Did he ask after me or Bertie?'

'Sorry, Liv. He seemed interested in nothing and no one but himself. I told him he needed to speak to you, but he said he needed time to work things out.'

'Bastard.'

'Arsehole.'

'Polla.'

I looked across at Cass and raised my eyebrow. 'You knew about Dad's pet name for Rob?'

Cass blushed. 'I may have heard him use that name once or twice...'

'You know Bertie got in massive trouble at school for calling his friends that word? Dad told him it meant cool, so he started calling all his friends polla.'

'He didn't?' Cass's own eyebrows shot up, and the muscles in her face danced beneath her skin as she tried to control her emotions.

'Cass... don't.'

Cass spluttered into her wine. 'I'm so sorry,' she said. 'I know this isn't a laughing matter and you're going through a ton of shit. But... p... p... polla. My God.'

Her laughter was infectious. Despite my entire world crashing down around my ears, it felt good to laugh. Our giggles turned hysterical, tears rolling down our cheeks until mine became confused by their origin and I bent over as sobs lurched my body back and forth.

'Oh, you poor thing,' said Cass, dropping to her knees on the floor beside me and stroking my hair.

'I wish Mum was here,' I said, once my breathing became under control.

'I think we all do, sis. I'm afraid I'll have to do.' Cass handed me a clump of tissues and a glass of water.

'Mum trained you well. As substitutes go, you'll do.'

'Thanks. Jasper, can you grab the spare duvet from upstairs?' Cass turned back to me. 'Are you sure you're all right sleeping on the sofa?'

'It's better than the streets,' I said, raising a smile. 'I can't believe Bertie settled so well after all that's happened.'

Given how little I knew myself about the situation, I'd kept my explanation to Bertie brief. I'd told him he was taking some time off school (to which he'd cheered), that he was going for a sleepover with his cousins (more cheers), and that his dad had had to go away for a while on business (a shrug of the shoulders).

'When are you going to tell him everything?' Cass asked.

'I don't know. God knows what Rob's up to, or where this all leaves us. I should probably speak to Hugo and Marion, find out what they know.' I shuddered at the thought.

'Why don't you leave Bertie here with Jasper tomorrow? He's got the next four days off and all he has planned is a bit of DIY.'

'Do you think he'd mind? I could visit Dad too.'

'You don't mind watching Bertie tomorrow, do you?' asked Cass as Jasper walked into the room. 'Liv needs to see her in-laws then pop in at Dad's.'

'No, I'd love a day with the little guy.'

'Thank you. Thank you both. I don't know what I'd have done without you.'

'That's what family's for,' said Cass. She reached down and kissed my cheek. 'Now, get some sleep. You need all your strength if you're to get through this shit-storm your husband's landed you in.'

Chapter Seven

I scrubbed my eyes with my palm and walked into a scene of chaos in the kitchen.

'Can you believe it, Mum? Emmy and Jake get coco-pops for breakfast EVERY DAY.'

'Every day? Wow. Do you guys have any teeth left?'

My nephew opened his mouth wide to show me his chocolate-milk covered teeth. I cupped his chin, peering into his mouth. 'Oooh, a few wobblers in there.'

Jake's mouth fell into a grin. 'Good. More cash from the tooth fairy.'

'How much does the tooth fairy give you?' asked Bertie.

'Pound a tooth,' said Jake, stuffing more cereal into his mouth.

'Same. Mum, have you seen Jake and Emmy's room? It's all black. It's waaaay cooler than mine.'

'I have seen it. I helped paint it.'

'Can you paint my room black? I want mine just like Jake's.'

My heart plummeted. Sooner rather than later, I'd have to admit to my son that he no longer had a bedroom of his own, or a house, for that matter. 'We'll see.'

Cass rushed into the kitchen, tying her hair up while biting on the toast Jasper held out to her. 'Emmaline May, go and wash your face.'

'I've already washed my face and cleaned my teeth,' said Emmy, her lips pouting in defiance.

'Yes, but then you went and made yourself look like a panda. You need to wash off the eyeliner.'

'Why?'

'Why? Because it's against uniform policy, but more importantly, makes you look like you've been punched in the face.'

Emmy pushed back her chair and stomped out of the room.

'And change your tights for ones with no holes,' shouted Cass to her daughter's departing back. Emmy stuck two fingers into the air and Jasper smothered a giggle.

'My God,' said Cass, toast crumbs flying from her mouth. 'I wish someone could fast forward me through the next eight years until I have a civilised woman for a daughter.'

'You love the challenge, really,' said Jasper.

'Yeah, and you were just the same at that age,' I said. 'Do you remember stealing Mum's lipstick and putting it on on the bus?'

'I remember the day she was waiting at the school gates to catch me out. She'd watched the bus leave, then raced over to the school in her car. Sneaky.'

I laughed, letting the normality of family life soothe my sleep-deprived mind. 'Bertie, you're going to stay with Uncle Jasper today while I run a few errands and visit Gramps.'

'I want to come and see Gramps too.'

'Not this time,' I said, leaning over and kissing his hair. 'How about I take you to see him at the weekend?'

'Won't we be seeing Grandma and Grandpa then?'

'Not this weekend.'

'Yes!' said Bertie, jumping from his chair, doing a dramatic air-grab, before running around the kitchen as though he'd just scored a goal.

'Don't say a word,' I warned Cass as she hid a laugh behind her hand.

With the twins dispatched to school, and Bertie settled in front of Jake's Xbox, I left the house and headed for my in-laws, my heart sinking with every mile chewed up beneath the car's tyres. When I got there, there was no car parked in the drive and part of me hoped they were out, but then I'd have to come back, which would be worse.

My shoes crunched gravel beneath them, making a jolly percussive sound at odds with how I felt. I knocked on the door and took a step back. Just as I was convincing myself there was no one home, the door squeaked open an inch.

'Marion?'

'Oh, Olivia, it's you.' Marion opened the door a little wider, and I struggled to hide my shock at her appearance. Make-up free, her face looked a good ten years older than her seventy-five years. Loose around her face, her hair fell in tangled wisps. And were those jogging bottoms? Surely not.

'Hi, Marion. How are you?'

'We've been better. I suppose you've heard the news?'

'What, that Rob's lost everything? The bailiffs turning up to repossess our home was a bit of a clue.'

'Yes, I suppose it was.' Marion sniffed, and I kicked myself for being harsh. She may come close to a pantomime villain, but in this scenario, she was a victim, too.

'How is Hugo?'

'Angry, upset... I'm worried about his heart.'

'I'm sure. Marion, do you have any idea how this happened? I wondered whether Rob might have confided in you?'

'No, he didn't. Do you think we'd be in this mess if he had? Anyway, you're his wife, shouldn't you have seen what was going on? Oh, I forgot, you're from different worlds, so I suppose you wouldn't have done.'

And there it was, her resting bitch face and sharp tongue. In some ways, it came as a relief.

'Right, well, I don't suppose you know where Rob is? There's rather a lot we need to discuss, not least the child we share.'

'I heard on the grapevine he's staying with a friend from his university days. I don't know who, and I don't know where. I tried to call him, but he wouldn't speak to me. Hugo doorstepped Rob's former secretary, but all he could squeeze out of her was that Rob had gone away. You're best waiting for the dust to settle, then he'll probably come crawling back. Not that I imagine you'll want him back, now all the money's gone.'

I didn't stoop so low as to offer a reply. Instead, I turned back to my borrowed rust-bucket of a car, and screeched away from the house in a move I hoped would leave canyons in their carefully raked gravel. Small victories, and all that.

In contrast to my arrival at my in-laws, as I pulled up outside the nursing home, a rush of warmth spread through me. I climbed out of the car and looked up to see my dad waving from his first-floor window. A rush of relief hit me that Dad wasn't reliant on Rob's money to fund his stay here. Thank goodness for small mercies.

The friendly staff at the reception desk waved me through, the pots of daffodils lining the marble entrance hall filling me with yellow-petalled optimism. My trainers squeaked across the polished floor, then sank into the deep carpet of the stairs. Dad's care home was posh, a reward for how hard he'd worked to claw himself up from jobless immigrant to professor.

I stopped outside room ten and knocked on the door.

'Si.'

'Hi, Dad.'

'Ah, hola c... c... cariño.'

I walked over and kissed his cheeks, pulling up a chair and taking his hands in mine. 'How've you been, Dad?'

'S...s... so so,' he said, waving his good arm in the air to bat away my question.

The stroke may have stolen much of his movement and slurred his speech, but Dad insisted on pretending everything was normal. I could almost believe it if I focused solely on his eyes. Warm, deep brown eyes that oozed kindness and mirrored my own in appearance. If I ended my days with as much love in my eyes as Dad's, I'd be satisfied.

'B... bring her, cariño.'

I walked to the dresser and picked up the photograph of Mum, taken the year before sickness came, ravaging her body before stealing her away from us. Only once Mum was propped up on a chair beside us was Dad content to continue our conversation.

Dad twisted the muscles in his face, willing them to express the words taunting him on the tip of his tongue. It took several attempts, but then he forced out the words in a rush. 'Have you seen the snowdrops?'

I shook my head.

Dad's muscles twitched. 'You... you...' he slapped his leg in frustration.

'It's OK, Dad, take your time.'

'Y... y... you must see them. Beautiful.'

'I'm sure they are. Have you been taken out to see them?'

Dad nodded. 'N... n... Nature walk. N... n... nature push.' He chuckled, looking across the room to where his hated wheelchair sat idle.

'That sounds wonderful.'

Dad lifted a hand and pointed a finger at my chest. Part of a code we'd developed since the stroke, I knew it meant he wanted to hear about me. If there was a chance of sparing him the worry, I would. But, behind his laboured speech and limited movement, his brain was as sharp as ever. If I lied, he'd know something was wrong and trying to guess what would worry him even more.

I leaned back in my chair and took a deep breath. 'Things with me aren't so good, Dad. I still don't really know what's going on, but it appears Rob has lost all our money. The house has been repossessed.'

Dad's wide forehead creased into a frown. 'S... staying?'

'Don't worry, Dad. I'm staying with Cassie. Bertie's loving being there with his cousins, although he doesn't know why we're there yet.'

The mention of his grandson caused Dad's eyes to twinkle and twitch. Perhaps it was that I'd named Bertie after my father, or perhaps it was that they were two peas in a pod. Either way, Dad had carved a special place in his heart for his youngest grandson, and Bertie could do no wrong in his eyes.

'Don't ask me what I'm going to do,' I said, 'because I have no idea. I suppose I'll have to start by getting a job...'

Dad nodded and smiled. My lack of work was an enigma to him, and I knew he mourned the fact my brain cells were slowly fading away beneath a mountain of washing and wifely duties. Well, not anymore.

'R... Rob... p... p... polla.' His eyes twinkled, the one side of his face which still worked pulling itself into a lopsided grin.

'Dad, you really need to stop calling my husband that, at least around Bertie. You know he started calling his friends that at school?'

A muscle in his cheek twitched, and I'm sure if it weren't so hard to push out the sound, I'd hear the laugh I loved so much.

'Sorry,' he said, but the creases around his eyes told me he wasn't sorry at all. With his good hand, he squeezed mine. His forehead folded and the muscles around his mouth worked hard to form the words he needed. 'You will... be... OK, Liv. Th... this could... be... the making... of... you.' He flopped back in his chair, exhausted by the effort of communication.

'We'll see, Dad. But let's hope you're right.'

Chapter Eight

'How was your day?'

Cass flopped down on the sofa and put her feet up on the coffee table. 'Long.'

'You're amazing, you know?'

'Yes, but I enjoy hearing you tell me.'

I threw a cushion at Cass, who caught it and threw it back. 'I mean it. The work you do, all those people you help. You really are a miracle worker.'

Cass let out her throaty laugh and pulled her knees up to her chin. She yawned loudly. 'I think you have a romanticised view of what I do on the ward. Today, a lot of my work involved bottoms and everything they produce.'

I grimaced. 'Let me fetch you a glass of wine.'

'Thanks,' said Cass, as I handed her a glass. 'How was your day? How's Dad?'

'Dad seemed fine. Frustrated by his speech, but that's nothing new.'

'Get anywhere with the grim-laws?'

'No. Can you believe I almost felt sorry for Marion?'

Cass leaned over and placed the back of her hand against my forehead. 'Just checking you're not running a fever. For a second, I thought you said you felt sorry for Marion.'

'I said I *almost* felt sorry for her. But then she ruined it by being a mean old cow and my generous feelings evaporated.'

'How much have they lost?'

'Not as much as me. They haven't had their house taken from under them, not yet, anyway. There was no car in the drive, so I wonder if they've had to sell it, but Marion wasn't about to divulge that kind of information. I asked if she knew where Rob was, but she said she didn't.'

'You believe her?'

'Yeah.' I took a sip of my wine. 'I think she's as clueless as I am. No doubt she'll rewrite history and this whole mess will be anyone's fault but Rob's by the time she tells the sorry saga to her friends at bridge club.'

'I know this is risky, seeing as you've not technically separated, but I've been dying to say it for years.'

'Go on...'

'Rob's a total arsehole, and in no way, shape or form good enough for you. What the hell did you ever see in him?'

I shrugged, swilling the wine around in my glass, thinking back over our marriage. Rob had seemed so exotic when we met in our final year of uni. He was from the kind of world I'd only ever read about in books. I'd fought hard to be an academic match for my Oxford peers, but I'd had no way of building the self-confidence which came from a life of privilege. Those kinds of lessons had been distinctly lacking at my state comprehensive.

Rob had found me looking lost and confused during a formal dinner and dance. He'd swept in like a romantic hero, guiding me through the social norms and conventions he'd absorbed since birth. All the hours spent rowing for the university team had honed his body to perfection, and when he removed his jacket, the straining of his shirt across his biceps had sent heat surging through my body.

We had drunk too much, danced all night, and when he invited me back to his room, of course, I'd agreed. During freshers' week, I'd set myself the rule of no one-night stands. Virginity seemed too precious a commodity to squander on a fling.

But oh, Rob was good. He knew exactly how to play it, to play me. He'd insisted he wanted nothing more than a nightcap and conversation and for the first hour I was in his room, he'd kept to that promise. Then he'd told me he was tired, and laid his head on my shoulder. His floppy blonde hair tickled my skin and an unfamiliar warmth filled my stomach. The next thing I knew, he'd lifted an arm and was gently scratching the bare skin of my back with his fingernails. Rather than thinking this odd, it sent a flood of tingly feelings through me I'd never experienced before. I imagined them like colourful shapes, jostling around, scratching my insides in a spine-tingling way, or sherbet, fizzing inside me. From that moment, I'd been putty in his hands.

I had put up no resistance when he suggested we move to the bed. I said nothing when he began unzipping my dress. When he put a hand in my bra I let out a whimper, but nothing that could be construed as a *no*. He'd pulled off my knickers, but I'd been too shocked by the salute from his trousers to notice.

Afterwards, even the ache in the pit of my stomach buried itself beneath a kaleidoscope of pleasure. Rob had suggested I go back to my dorm, as his scout disapproved of overnight guests. At the time, it seemed like a genuine suggestion, a good man doing the right thing. When he still hadn't called me after three days, I consoled myself that he was busy with finals.

By the time I found out I was pregnant, Robert Simmons had become nothing more than a smudge of humiliation on my soul, a man who had taken the one thing I'd kept sacred, then abandoned me once he'd had his fill.

'Earth to Liv?'

'Oh, sorry,' I said, shaking my head free of the eight-year-old humiliation. 'What were you saying?'

'I was asking what you saw in Rob?'

'Nothing.'

'Nothing? Liv, I'm a medical professional. I know babies aren't conceived out of thin air. Oh God, he didn't...'

'No, nothing like that. It was a one-night stand, OK?'

'But you told us he was your boyfriend!'

'I didn't want Dad to worry or think badly of me, not so soon after losing Mum.'

'But you got married!'

I managed a small smile as shock lengthened Cass's face. 'Yeah, I know. Weird.'

'Liv, why the hell did you marry a man you weren't even dating?'

'I decided I needed to tell him about the baby. It was the right thing to do. At best, I thought he'd tell me to get on with it by myself. At worst, I thought he'd call me a liar.'

'But?'

'I've never really known why he reacted like he did. Part of me has always wondered whether he married me to piss off his parents. I was nothing like girls he'd taken home before. He knew before I did his parents would hate me.'

'What happened when you told him you were pregnant? Did he get down on one knee straight away?'

'No, not quite. I found him doing some last-minute cramming in the library. I'm not sure he even recognised me when I walked up to him. Anyway, I told him outright why I'd come to see him.'

'How did he react?'

'He shouted "shit" at the top of his voice and we both got kicked out by a terrifying librarian. Then we went to the pub. He was kinder than I'd been expecting and honest, too. He admitted he'd never thought of me as more than a one-night-stand and had had no intention of calling me.'

'What a romantic.'

'I told him I didn't expect anything from him, but he would be welcome to be a part of his child's life if he wanted to. He said he'd think about it. He came to me the next day with a proposal. No,' I said, Cass's mouth hanging open even wider. 'Not that kind of proposal. He said he'd always believed a child should have two parents. He suggested we spend a month getting to know each other and see how things developed. So that's what we did. At the end of the month, we'd grown to like each other. He's not all bad. There's a decent guy in there somewhere. That's when he suggested marriage.'

'Marriage still seems quite the leap.'

'Remember, Cass, I was twenty-one. I'd just lost my mum and was facing a future as a single parent. This good-looking, intelligent, half-decent man came along and suggested we team up and get married. As options went, it wasn't the worst.'

'True. I just can't believe you lied to us. I was so jealous of you!'

'Jealous of me?'

'Yeah, you inherited the Latina looks, the big brain, found yourself a rich man. I thought you were up in Oxford enjoying some whirlwind romance that was the cherry on the top of an already perfect life.'

I stared at my sister in shock, then burst out laughing. 'My God, Cass, you have no idea. I hated most of my time at Oxford. I never knew how to act around the posh kids and plenty of them openly expressed their belief I didn't deserve to be there. I spent most of my time alone in the library. I was so jealous of you, my big brave sister living in a house with her friends, training for one of the most important jobs in the world.'

'Come here,' said Cass, pulling me towards her on the sofa. 'One day I'll tell you all the jobs they palm off on trainee nurses, but I think you've had enough shocks for one week.'

'I love you, sis. Thanks for looking after me.'

'I'd be a crap big sister if I didn't.'

'True, but thank you anyway. I promise we'll get out of your hair as soon as possible.'

I meant what I said, the only stumbling block was that I had no idea how to do it.

Chapter Nine

My alarm went off at five. During the week I'd been staying with my sister, I'd calculated not only what waking time would get me into the bathroom before the queue began, but also the time it took for my puffy, tear-stained eyes to return to normal.

All week Cass and Jasper had been complimenting my inner strength, how well I was coping. What they didn't see were the tear-mangled tissues I flushed down the toilet before they woke up, or how I packed my pillow away before anyone noticed how damp it was.

The truth was, I wasn't coping. I felt like a small boat lost in a vast ocean, caught in fog, with a storm brewing on the horizon, and a shark circling. The worst thing was being stuck in limbo. With no official separation from Rob, I wasn't entitled to any single-parent allowance, and my application for Universal Credit looked like it would take weeks to process.

As for moving forward with housing, my visit to the council offices had been as depressing as watching *Angela's*

Ashes. I'd been put on a waiting list, but informed I could be on it for years, and even then, I was unlikely to get anything bigger than a one-bedroom flat. Not that I was fussy, I'd have taken a shoebox if offered it, but I had a son growing bigger by the day, and whilst I'd lay my head in a hovel, I wanted better for him.

Bertie's questions had been mounting over the past week and needed to be addressed. I'd been waiting for word from Rob, but as he was still MIA, there was little I could do but tell Bertie the truth.

The sound of shouting reached me from upstairs, and I checked my watch. It wasn't yet six, and I'd expected longer to myself.

'Mum!'

Bertie stood at the top of the stairs, hopping from foot to foot. 'What's wrong?'

'I'm desperate for a wee, but Emmy's been in the bathroom for ages and won't come out. I'm going to pee my pants in a minute.'

'Come down here,' I said. Bertie ran down the stairs, his hand gripping his crotch.

'Mum, I don't think I can hold it in much longer.'

'Quick, follow me.' I opened the back door and pulled Bertie through. 'There you go, pee in that flowerpot.'

'I can't wee in there!'

'Why not?'

'It will kill the plant.'

'Fine, pee beside it. I'll fill a bowl with water and wash it away when you're done.' Bertie insisted I turn my back on him while he went about his business. 'Better?' I asked when I heard the pop of his waistband.

'Much.'

'What's up with Emmy? Is she ill?'

'I don't think so. She won't come out, and I heard her crying behind the door.'

'Right, you go through to the lounge and watch a bit of TV. I'll see what's wrong with Emmy.'

Once Bertie was snuggled up beneath my duvet, I climbed the stairs and gave a tentative knock on the door. 'Emmy? Emmy, it's Aunt Liv.'

'Go away.'

'I'm afraid I can't do that, darling. I'm worried about you.'

'I want Mum.'

'Sorry, Em, your mum's on night shifts and still isn't home. Shall I get your dad for you?'

'No!'

'OK, well either you're going to have to open this door so I can come in, or I'll have to fetch your dad.'

After a moment's indecision, the door opened. My hand flew to my mouth at the sight of my niece.

'Don't laugh,' said Emmy, bursting into loud, messy tears.

'Shh,' I said, stepping into the bathroom and closing the door behind me. 'Em, what happened?'

Emmy handed me a bottle of hair dye. 'It said it was black, but it's turned my hair green.'

'Isn't green cool?'

'No, green's totally not cool. I look like a troll.' More sobs racked her small body, and I put an arm around her.

'It's OK, we've all been there with hair disasters.'

'I bet you haven't. Your hair's amazing. I wanted mine to be black, like yours.'

'Oh, Em, you're beautiful as you are. Trust me, my hair's a pain in the bum. It takes me hours to straighten it each morning.'

'You shouldn't straighten it, it looks better curly.'

'I'll take your advice on board.' It was only after marrying Rob I'd started straightening out my natural curls. I couldn't remember if it was something he'd said, or pressure from other mums, but somewhere along the way I'd lost myself beneath steam and the smell of burning follicles. 'Em, I don't want to add to your woes, but has something happened to your eyebrow?'

A flush spread across Emmy's freckled face. 'I saw it in a magazine. It looked cool.'

'Only having one eyebrow?'

'No.' Emmy folded her arms and looked at me like I had the intelligence of a goldfish. 'It was supposed to be one small line shaved out, but the razor slipped.'

'What razor did you use?'

'Dad's.'

'That could have been the problem. Listen, I can go to a pharmacy today and buy some hair dye to get your hair back to its natural colour.'

'I can't go to school.'

'That's up to your dad.'

'But he'll make me. Please, Aunt Liv, can you talk to him?'

'I can try, but I'm not making any promises.'

'What about my eyebrow?'

'Your eyebrow will grow back quickly, and in the meantime, we can fix it with a little make-up.'

'You know how to do that?'

'Trust me, Em, I've attended enough of Rob's work parties over the years to know how to apply a bit of slap. Now come on, let's get you out of here. Any minute now the entire house will wake up needing a wee, and Bertie's already watered the garden enough for one day.'

I'd shepherded my niece out of the bathroom and downstairs for her breakfast when Jasper appeared and all hell broke loose.

'What the f...'

'Flip. That's it, isn't it Jasper, what the flip?'

Jasper stood in the doorway, his usually calm face pink. I was certain that if I looked closely, I'd see steam coming out of his ears.

'Emmy had a minor accident with some hair dye.'

Emmy stared into her cereal, refusing to look her dad in the eye.

'We were wondering if she could take the day off school? I can nip out this morning and try to find some dye to correct it.'

Emmy looked up from under her green fringe. 'Please, Dad.'

'Oh my God,' said Jasper, walking up to his daughter and cupping her chin. 'What the fu... flip happened to your eyebrow?'

'Don't worry, Aunt Liv said she can sort it with makeup.'

'Makeup? Well, you can forget a day off school. If you're old enough to go behind our back, go expressly against our wishes, and dye your hair, then you're old enough to face the consequences.'

Emmy whimpered. From the lounge, the noise of shouting filtered through the door.

'I'll see what's going on,' I said, keen to remove myself from the father-daughter stand-off. In the lounge, I found two small boys tearing chunks out of one another as they wrestled on the carpet. 'Bertie, stop that at once.'

Both boys ignored me, pushing me off as I tried to pull them apart. In the end, the only thing I could do was fling myself on the floor between them like a second-rate wrestling referee.

I managed to get both boys sitting down on the sofa, although they sat at either end, refusing to look at each other.

'Boys,' I said, hands on hips, trying to look as stern as possible. 'What on earth's going on with you?'

'Big arse Bertie lost all the points on my game.'

'I didn't,' yelled Bertie, 'there was a glitch on the machine.'

'Liar!'

'No, you're the liar!'

'Get out of my house. None of us want you here, you little loser.'

'Hey,' I said. 'Jake, that's a horrible thing to say.'

'Yeah, well, it's true. I can't sleep with him nattering away in my ear, and I can't even watch TV in the morning with you sleeping in here.'

'Don't speak to my mum like that, you little...'

The door opened just as Bertie and Jake flung themselves at each other for round two.

'What the...'

'It's OK,' I told Cass, holding each boy at arm's length. 'Just a misunderstanding.'

'It looks more than a misunderstanding.'

'Bertie, go and cool off in the garden. Jake, get ready for school. Your mum's just got back from work and this is the last thing she needs.'

Both boys skulked off, and Cass was about to sit down when a furious-looking Jasper marched into the room, dragging a sobbing Emmy by the arm.

'What the...'

'An accident with some hair dye,' I explained as Jasper opened the door, pushed Emmy out of it, and locked it behind her.

'What are you doing? You can't lock our daughter out of the house!'

'She needs to go to school,' said Jasper. 'If she never has to face the consequences of her actions, she'll never take responsibility for anything.'

'Don't you think that's a decision we should have made together?'

'You weren't here. I was. You can't undermine me now.'

As the argument between Cass and Jasper escalated into a full-blown row, I slipped out of the room and went to find Bertie in the garden.

'Can I go back in now?'

'No, not yet. Aunt Cass and Uncle Jasper are having a discussion.'

'You mean an argument, like the ones you and Dad have?'

I sighed. 'Yes, Bertie. They're having an argument, so we should stay out of their way.'

Bertie kicked the toe of his trainer against the fence. 'When can we go home, Mum? I don't want to stay here anymore. I miss my room, I miss Dad, I even miss school, though only a little bit.'

My heart broke for my son, and I could think of nothing to say that would offer any comfort. 'I'll tell you what, why don't we go for a walk? Your aunt and uncle could do with some space, and there are things we need to talk about.'

I took the hand of my beautiful boy and prepared to shatter his world.

Chapter Ten

'You didn't need to do that.'

'It's the least I could do.' I swiped a rubber-gloved arm across my forehead to remove some of the scrubbing-induced sweat. 'Did you manage to get some sleep?'

Cass leaned against the doorframe and yawned. 'A little. It took me ages to calm down after rowing with Jasper. I hate it when we argue. You've done an amazing job in here.'

We both looked around at the sparkling bathroom tiles. The hair dye had come off easier than I'd expected, so I'd set my sights on the grey-black grout, scrubbing hard with an old toothbrush. 'Thanks, I've had plenty of practice. Actually, the job centre rang me up this morning about a cleaning job that's come in.'

'What kind of cleaning job?'

'Cleaning the football stadium after matches.'

Cass shuddered. 'You can't do that.'

'Someone has to.'

'But not you. Finish up here, Liv, there'll be no grout left if you scrub any more. There's something I need to talk to you about.'

I smiled until Cass had left the room, then sank back against the bath, trying to stop the tears which were itching my eyes. She was going to kick us out. That was why she wanted to talk. I knew no one as kind or generous as Cass and Jasper, but even they had their limits. It was plain as day the house was too small for all of us, and Jake had made his feelings on the subject plain.

With rubber gloves removed, and cold water splashed on my face, I went to find Cass in the kitchen. She had the radio playing and danced her way between the kitchen cabinets as she made a pot of coffee. From nowhere, a memory of dancing around the kitchen with Mum entered my head, stealing my breath as my chest tightened. How could it still hurt so much?

'Oh, there you are,' said Cass, spinning around and stopping mid pirouette. 'Sit down, coffee's almost ready.'

I waited until I had a cup of coffee in front of me before I dared speak. 'Look, Cass, I know us being here is tough, and you'll be wanting us out from under your feet...'

'I love having you here,' said Cass, covering my hand with hers.

'And I love being here, but I know it's not easy for you all. Jake made that clear to us this morning.'

'Oh, ignore him.'

'But he had a point. Maybe if I take the cleaning job, I'll be able to find a small flat somewhere.'

'On a cleaner's wage?' Cass laughed. 'Liv, have you even checked the price of rentals these days?'

Hopelessness smothered me, and I felt as though I might choke.

'Listen, when I said I wanted to talk to you, it is about you moving out, but not in the way you think.'

'How do you mean?'

Cass took a sip of her coffee. 'OK, before I tell you this, I need you to promise you won't jump to any conclusions and you'll let me finish before writing the idea off.'

'Well now I feel reassured.'

Cass grinned. 'It's nothing terrible, I promise.'

'Go on then.'

'OK. There's a girl I work with, Gemma. I was telling her how you've come to live with us...'

My ears started ringing. Had my sister been broadcasting my bonfire of a life around the whole hospital?

'Don't worry, I kept details to a minimum,' said Cass, noticing my frown. 'Anyway, she told me about this place she lived at for a while. It's somewhere people can go when they've run out of road.'

'A homeless shelter?'

'No. More like community living.'

'A cult?'

'No. Come on,' said Cass, shaking her head, 'you said you'd let me finish. It's not a homeless shelter, it's not a cult either. Like I said, it's community living. Gemma explained it better than I am. She said it feels like an extended family. They take people in who need a bit of time and space to figure things out. Some stay for a few days, some have been there for years.'

'How much does it cost?'

'Whatever you can afford. If you can't afford to pay anything, you contribute in other ways: gardening, maintenance, cooking, cleaning. Gemma says everyone mucks in in whatever way they can.'

'Where is it?'

'Mid Cornwall, so only an hour away.'

'What about Bertie?'

'If everything Gemma said is true, he'd love it.'

'I need to get him into a school.'

'I know, but he's young and intelligent. A few more weeks of missed education won't harm him in the long run.'

'Won't it just delay the mounting decisions I need to make?'

'Another way of looking at it is it will give you the time and space you need to figure things out.'

'What if it's awful?'

'I thought we could have a look at it this afternoon, if you're keen?'

'I'm not sure keen's the right word...'

'Great. I'll finish my coffee, have a shower, then we'll set off.'

Cass carried her coffee upstairs and left me at the kitchen table. Bertie wandered in from the garden where he'd spent the past hour kicking a football against a wall. He hadn't spoken a word to me since I told him the truth, and the distance between us, however temporary, hurt my heart.

Bertie put his football in the basket beside the door and crossed the room. I thought he'd walk right past, but he stopped in front of me, climbed onto my lap and began sobbing into my hair.

'Oh my darling boy,' I said, unable to stop my own tears from breaking free. 'Everything will be all right.'

'I... I... hate Dad,' sniffed Bertie, gulping down the sadness that rocked his body. 'I hate him.'

'Don't say that,' I said. 'Dad's got himself into a horrible muddle, but I'm sure wherever he is, he's trying to fix things.'

'But he ran away.'

I had no idea how to respond, for Bertie was right. Rob had run away. He'd run away and left his wife and child to pick up the pieces, the shattered remains of the life we'd once lived. 'He'll come back,' I said, not knowing if it was true, or even if I wanted it to be.

Bertie's gulping sobs had reduced to snotty sniffles. He even managed a giggle after I protested against him wiping his nose on my shirt.

'Jake doesn't want me sharing a room with him,' said Bertie, his voice tiny and broken.

'He'll come around. He probably just needs his own space back for a while.'

'Does that mean I'll have to sleep on the sofa with you?'

'Well, Aunt Liv has found a place we could stay for a little while.'

'We're moving?'

'More like a holiday,' I said, not even knowing if this was true or not.

'If we go on holiday, when we come back, Jake might like me again.'

'I'm sure he will. Aunt Liv's going to take us to see the holiday place today so we can decide if we like it. But Bertie?'

'Hmm?'

'If you don't like it, we won't go there. OK?'

'OK.'

I pulled Bertie closer to me, breathing him in, knowing whatever happened, I'd do everything in my power to give him the life he deserved. Except for joining a cult. That was a firm no, and if I got even a whiff of that while visiting this place, I'd be out of there before they had time to light a stick of incense.

Chapter Eleven

Cass was right that the community was only an hour away. At least it would have been, if we hadn't got terribly lost.

'We've been past this pub already,' said Bertie, his nose pressed to the window.

'We've passed it more than once,' I said.

Cass reached across and slapped my knee. 'I think you'll find it's your job to navigate, not mine.'

'True,' I said, 'but these directions are hopeless.'

'Read them out to me again.'

'Go past the pub, then turn left down a narrow track.'

'But there is no track,' said Cass, bashing the steering wheel with her fist.

'There is,' said Bertie. 'I just saw it.'

'Where?' said Cass, turning her head to Bertie.

'Cass, look out.'

Cass turned her eyes back to the road just in time to avoid hitting a flock of sheep being moved from one field to another.

'It's back there,' said Bertie. 'Past the pub, just like the directions said.'

Cass reversed the car at a snail's pace, freaked out after her near-miss.

'There,' said Bertie, pointing out of the window to a tiny opening between the pub and its neighbouring house.

'Young eyes,' I said, earning myself another slap from Cass.

It took Cass three attempts to turn the car into the opening. Hedges enclosed us, the middle of the track sporting a grass mohican. Cass flinched at every turn, paranoid we'd meet another vehicle on a track barely big enough for one car. If the state of the track was anything to go by, there wouldn't be much other traffic around.

Cass's shoulders softened as we finally reached a wooden gate, a sign announcing we had reached Lowen Farm. Beside the gate stood a postbox and a structure resembling a doll's house containing fresh eggs.

'Do you want to open the gate?' I asked Bertie.

Bertie jumped out of the car in response, pulling the gate open for us to pass through. He closed it behind us and we drove on, the track widening out, ancient native trees flanking us like sentries.

Cass pulled the car to a stop at the point the track forked. A signpost informed us that to our right was Lowen farm, and to our left was the lake.

'I think we want the farm,' said Cass, inching forward along the bumpy track.

'Lake sounds nice. I wonder if there's a lake house beside it?' I said, picturing a spa. Didn't Pamela Anderson live in a lake house? A whole new set of images came to mind.

The surrounding trees thinned out, livestock grazing among open clearings.

'Wow,' said Bertie, peering through the windscreen as a large, whitewashed building came into view.

Thick vines trailed up the outside of the house, reminding me of my dad's knobbly fingers. Two large pots containing bare-branched trees framed a red front door. Beyond the main frontage, other buildings seemed to have been tacked on as an after-thought. A crooked lean-to clung to one side, and a hotchpotch of white-washed extensions made the house look like a big-bellied giant stretching out its legs.

'Gemma told us to ask for Harry,' said Cass, turning off the engine and climbing out of the car.

Bertie hung back as Cass marched towards the front door. I took his hand and gave him what I hoped to be a reassuring smile. 'It's OK,' I said. 'Remember, if you don't like it here, we won't come and stay.'

Bertie nodded, and we walked up to Cass who was already pulling on a wrought iron doorbell. We waited a good five minutes before Cass leaned forward and tried the door handle. 'Open,' she said, pushing open the door and stepping inside.

'Cass,' I hissed. 'You can't just walk into someone else's house.'

'Watch me.' She grinned and walked further into the entrance hall.

Bertie and I followed. Faded Victorian tiles in varying shades of blue covered the wide hallway floor. Several were chipped, the coat stand leaning drunkenly due to a missing tile beneath one of its legs. Any stain that once covered the banister had been worn off by years of hands, and a bucket stood at the bottom of the stairs, presumably to catch rainwater from a leak.

The sound of humming floated from a nearby room. 'This way,' said Cass.

We walked through a large, wood-panelled room, the longest dining table I'd ever seen filling its length. A mirror hung on one wall, an upright piano stood tucked into an alcove, and the scuffed floorboards shone with water from a mop and bucket leaning against a Welsh dresser.

'Excuse me? Can I help you?'

We turned to see a rotund woman with rosy cheeks clutching a duster in one hand and a brush and dustpan in the other. She reminded me of all the farmer's wives I'd read about in Enid Blyton books.

'Hello,' said Cass. 'We're looking for Harry.'

'In the kitchen,' said the woman with a smile. 'I'm Maggie, by the way.'

'Cass, Liv and Bertie. Pleased to meet you. I don't suppose you could tell us how to get to the kitchen?'

Maggie laughed. 'It's not hard to find. Go through that door and you're there.'

'Thanks,' I said. I wondered if Maggie was a paid employee or resident at Lowen Farm.

We walked through a door to the sight of a woman's bottom. For a moment I wondered if she was practising the downward-dog right there in the kitchen, but then I realised she was reaching for something beneath a cupboard.

'Come here, you little pest.'

Bertie giggled, and the woman turned her head. 'Oh, God, I'm sorry, I didn't realise we had visitors. Give me one sec.' She continued ferreting around beneath the cupboard, her entire arm disappearing as far as the shoulder.

'Got you.' The woman straightened. Both me and Cass took a step back at the sight of a rodent, swinging in the air as the woman gripped tight to its tail. 'Sorry, not the best of introductions, but I've been trying to catch this little thing for ages.'

The woman walked towards us, and Cass gripped onto my arm.

'That's so cool,' said Bertie. He stepped forward and squinted at the wriggling rodent.

'Bertie, don't get too close to the rat,' I squealed, picturing all the diseases my son could catch.

Bertie sighed and looked up at the woman. 'Don't mind my mum, she doesn't understand animals.' He turned back to me. 'It's a mouse, Mum, and a field mouse at that. A rat would be five times the size.'

I shuddered at the thought.

'Let me dispatch this little one outside, then I'll be right with you.'

'No!' said Bertie. 'Please don't kill it!'

The woman laughed, a deep, throaty laugh that felt like being spoon-fed treacle. 'Sorry, dispatch was the wrong choice of word. I've got a cage ready and waiting in the yard. I'll put him in there for now, then release him back into the wild later on. Do you want to help me get him into his cage?'

Bertie nodded. He followed the woman out into the yard, and I looked across at Cass. I'd forgotten about her fear of rodents, but it was plastered all over her pale, clammy face.

'Where the hell have you brought me?' I asked, shaking my head. 'We've been here less than five minutes and a woman has abducted my child using very similar methods to the child catcher in *Chitty Chitty Bang Bang*, only with mice, rather than sweets.'

Cass laughed, then her face dropped into a frown. 'You don't think there's more where that one came from, do you?'

'No, I'm sure it was one lone mouse who'd lost his way and was trying to find his family. His wife's probably waiting at home, wondering what was taking him so long when she only sent him out for a pint of milk.' I grinned, and Cass punched my arm.

'All done,' said the woman, striding back into the kitchen with Bertie by her side. 'Those mice are the bane of my life. No sooner do I catch one, than another appears.'

'So much for one lone mouse,' muttered Cass under her breath. I hid a giggle behind my hand.

'Your son said you were looking for me?'

'No,' I said. 'We're looking for a man named Harry.'

'Harriet Bowman. Pleased to meet you, but use my full name and I shall never speak to you again. Everyone here calls me Harry, and the kids call me Haribo, which I'm rather fond of.'

I tried to get the measure of Harry, but struggled. She wore a band around her head to hold back a fringe. Her brown hair had been twisted into a messy topknot, which flopped down as far as her ears. If the size of her topknot was anything to go by, her hair must be at least waist-length, if not longer. Her makeup and line-free skin was flushed and chapped in a way that suggested she spent lots of her time outside in all weathers. At a guess, I'd have said she was in her early twenties, thirty at the most.

Despite the cold day, she had dressed for summer. On her top half was a faded blue tank-top, and her legs were bare from the knee down, her thighs covered by wide-legged shorts. The only concession she'd made to the weather was a rainbow-coloured cardigan whose sleeves were different lengths and whose hem was starting to unravel.

'So, why did you want to see me?'

'My sister…'

I interrupted Cass, feeling it important I speak for myself. 'Me and Bertie are going through a few challenges. We're currently staying with my sister, Cass,' I said, pointing in Cass's direction, 'but there's not really room. Someone Cass knows said you open this place to people who need a bit of a break but have nowhere else to go. It sounds ridiculous now I say it out loud. Of course, you wouldn't want a random woman and child pitching up on your doorstep.'

'Hmm,' said Harry, looking between me and Bertie. 'Come through to the dining room. We can drink tea, eat cake and see if we can't come to some sort of arrangement.'

Chapter Twelve

I hauled our suitcases out of Cass's car, wondering what the hell I was doing. Somehow, half an hour chatting to Harry over a slice of lemon drizzle cake had persuaded me that staying at Lowen Farm was the right course of action. In the intervening few days, I'd been seriously questioning that decision. I knew nothing about these people, I'd seen only two rooms of the farm, and Maggie was the only other resident I'd met.

'It will be fine,' said Cass, walking over and pulling me into a hug. 'This is only a stopgap. A short break to get your head straight and figure out what you're going to do next. I'm only an hour away, and you can come back to mine the second you feel uncomfortable.'

'I'll give it a week, and then see how I feel.'

'Good plan.'

Beside me, Bertie sniffed. His falling out with Jake had been a flash in the pan, and the cousins were distraught at their separation, even if it did only turn out to be for a week.

'Liv, Bertie!' Harry emerged from the front of the house. Still wearing shorts, at least she had a jumper on today, although the front hem hung down five inches lower than the back and something weird had happened to the neckline, causing it to droop in one corner.

'Hello, Harry. Lovely to see you again. Thank you so much for this. We really appreciate it.'

Harry batted away the compliment. 'The whole ethos of Lowen Farm is to be a resting place for weary travellers, and you, Liv, seem in need of a rest. Now, how about I show you to your room?'

'Thank you.'

'Liv, I'm really sorry, but do you mind if I head off? It's only two hours till my shift starts and I don't trust myself not to get lost on the way home.'

'Of course not,' I said, pulling Cass into a tight hug. 'Thank you for everything, and I'll see you soon.'

Bertie and I would be staying in the main house. For all Harry's laissez-faire attitude, during our first conversation it became clear there were some things she took very seriously, not least her guest's safety. The house was reserved for families and couples, single men staying in separate accommodation near the lake. Each adult resident, however temporary, had to undergo a DBS check, and every room had a lockable door to ensure residents had their own space to retreat to and felt secure in their environment. It all sounded very impressive, but I had no idea if the reality would match up to Harry's Utopian dream.

'How many people do you have staying?' I asked Harry as she led me up the wide staircase.

'Not that many. We get more in the summer, especially in school holidays. Burnt-out families often come here for a week or two's relaxation, and I work closely with the council to provide respite for families in crisis. We only take people on recommendation. In your case, the recommendation came from your sister's colleague, Gemma. That way, we don't get overrun with people on the lookout for a free holiday.'

'You don't advertise?'

'Christ, no. We're an open house, but within certain boundaries. Currently, you're the only family staying with us. Don't worry though, Bertie, you won't be bored. I've already got you pegged as an animal lover and it's all hands on deck with the farm.'

As we reached the top of the stairs, I looked around. The house was a strange mixture of a farmhouse and something grander. The low ceilings gave it a cosy feel, but the house was spread over three floors, the wide staircase and landings suggesting it had once been more than a home for tenant farmers. There was something a little institutional about the faded thin carpets and fire doors whose paint was peeling.

'What did this place used to be?'

'How far back do you want to go?' asked Harry, letting out her throaty laugh. 'Before I took it on, my grandparents had run it as both a farm and a home for children in care who couldn't find foster placements. When they died, I wanted to keep their legacy alive, but I'm not experienced enough to work with disturbed teenagers, so this seemed a good compromise.'

'Do you run the place by yourself?'

'No, I have plenty of help. You'll meet the rest of the team at dinner. What time is it now?' Harry checked her watch. 'Right, so it's three now. Dinner's at six and we usually eat together. Here's your room.'

Harry opened the door onto a long, thin room, housing two single beds, a wardrobe, writing desk and not much more. 'Arrange the furniture however you like. The last people to use this room were two siblings who stayed here with their parents for the summer. They pulled the beds as far apart as they could, but you arrange them as you see fit.'

'Thanks,' I said, my hand stroking a faded section of floral wallpaper. The furnishings were eclectic, as though they'd been sourced from charity shops or car boot sales. Everything in the room was utilitarian, although as I sat down on the bed, I felt the quality of the mattress, and the white bedding was more like something you'd find in a hotel.

'The bathroom's just down the hall. As we're low on numbers, you'll have it to yourself, but if you're still here when things get busier, you'll need to share.'

'That's fine,' I said, thinking I could only spare a couple of weeks before I'd need to face the real world again.

'If you need me, I live in the annexe. It's the ugly extension tacked onto the side of the house. You'll have seen it when you arrived. Maggie and Stephan live on the top floor. They manage the place for me, so I've rewarded them with an entire floor. Oh, yes, that's something I didn't mention before. Whilst single men live apart from the main house, Stephan is the exception.'

'Oh, I assumed he and Maggie were married.'

'No, they've been best friends since they were at school, but as far as I'm aware, it's never been a romantic relationship. Stephan stayed in separate accommodation for years, but he was up at the house all the time and as they have an office as part of their accommodation, it made sense for him to move in.'

'OK.'

'Right, I'll leave you to settle in and I'll see you at six o'clock for dinner. Bertie, do you think after dinner you could help me feed the pigs?'

Bertie, who until then had been wallowing in a shocked, sad silence, perked up. 'Yes, please!'

'Wonderful,' said Harry. 'I'll see you later.'

Chapter Thirteen

I took a deep breath before opening the door. Bertie and I had spent the afternoon quietly in our room, playing cards, reading books and trying to tune the TV hanging from the wall. I'd expected Bertie to be desperate to explore, but he was subdued and listless, as though the enormity of our situation was just beginning to sink in.

'Mum? I don't want to go downstairs. Can't we eat our dinner in our room?'

'No, Bertie. It's one of the rules here. All the guests eat together.'

'Please.'

'I'm sorry, Bertie. Come on.' I held out my hand, and Bertie allowed me to lead him away from our room. His small body was shaking, and I fought the overwhelming desire to give in to my son, and my desire to run back to our room and lock the door. What were we doing here? How would staying with a group of strangers help us figure out anything? It was only delaying the inevitable.

'Ah, good, you're here.' The door to the dining room flung open and Harry smiled at us. The only concession to her usual attire was a shirt instead of a tank top. 'You've come on the right night, Bertie. It's Patrick's turn to cook, and he's made pizza.'

Feeling returned to my fingers as Bertie's tight grip loosened. 'Pizza?'

'Yes, and if you get in quick, you can choose your own topping.'

Bertie looked at me and I nodded to show him it was OK. 'Who's Patrick?' I asked, as I followed Harry into the room.

'The loveliest man you'll ever meet,' said Harry.

'Did I hear my name mentioned?' A pink-cheeked man with a shock of white hair and a wide smile filled the doorway between the dining room and kitchen. The floral apron he wore made him look simultaneously ridiculous and non-threatening. 'Pat,' he said, stepping forward. 'Very pleased to meet you.'

'Liv,' I said, taking his offered hand. 'And this is Bertie.'

Pat crouched down, his knees clicking as he did. He held out a hand to Bertie. 'Pleased to meet you, young man.'

Bertie grinned. 'I'm not a young man. I'm a boy.'

'Really? But I thought you must be at least twelve years old.'

'I'm eight. Eight and a half.'

'Oh dear, I'm losing my touch with ages. It's been too many years since I was in a classroom. Now, Mr Eight-and-a-half, would you like to help me make some pizzas?'

Bertie nodded, and the unlikely pair disappeared into the kitchen.

'Pat was headmaster at the local school for years,' Harry explained. 'His former pupils come up here to visit him all the time. Some of them are now grandparents, if you can believe it.'

'Grandparents? How old is Pat?'

'Eighty-five.'

'Eighty-five? I thought he was around sixty.'

'He's a member of the local ramblers, the bowls club, tennis club, and goes ballroom dancing every Thursday. It's all that exercise that keeps him young.'

'How long has he lived here?'

'Ever since his wife died six years ago. He started fading away, and the community rallied around and persuaded him to move in here. He's been a godsend, and not just for his cooking skills. After selling his house in the village, he used the proceeds to fund our development of cabins by the lake.'

'Wow.'

'Exactly.'

Two middle-aged ladies dressed in fleeces, Gore-Tex trousers and hiking boots walked in and sat down at the table.

'Liv, this is Christine and Elaine. They're staying with us for a month, give or take.'

'Pleased to meet you, Liv. It was Elaine who dragged me here. I lost my husband several months ago, and she forced me here to walk through my grief. You won't see much of us. Elaine forces me out onto the moor most mornings at the crack of dawn, and by the evening it's all I can do to keep my eyes open.'

'It's working though, isn't it?' asked Elaine, squeezing her friend's hand.

'Yes,' said Christine. 'Slowly but surely, those blisters take my mind off my other problems.' The two women giggled, reminding me of little girls.

'How long have you been friends?'

'Forty years, give or take. Christine saw me through when I lost my Roger, so it's only right I do the same for her.'

'What brings you here, Liv?'

'It's a long story.'

I was saved from expanding my explanation by the arrival of a couple in their forties who walked in bickering over a TV programme.

'Harry, settle this argument for us. Stephan is claiming Ray Mears is the best survival expert on TV, but I disagree.

It's got to be Bear Grylls. Poor old Ray might have the survival skills, but he can't compete with Bear in the looks department.'

'And what use is a pretty face when you're out in the jungle?' asked Stephan. 'Besides, Ray has a manly charm that Bear lacks. All that posh-voiced pretence at being *one of the lads*. No, I'd rather have Ray on my team any day.'

'Stephan, Maggie, this is Liv. She's come to stay with us for a couple of weeks, along with her son Bertie, who's currently in the kitchen making pizzas with Pat.'

'Lovely to meet you,' said Stephan.

'Yes, welcome to the farm. It's good to see you again. It's always a pleasure to see fresh faces around the table, no offence, Christine and Elaine.'

'None taken.'

Bertie walked into the dining room and cleared his throat. 'Ladies and gentlemen, dinner will be served in five minutes. Please take your seats at the table.'

'Who is that boy and what has he done with my son?' I asked Harry once Bertie had disappeared back into the kitchen.

'That's Pat for you. He'll have him reading Shakespeare by tomorrow evening, mark my words.'

'Is this everyone?' I asked when we were all sitting down.

'No,' said Harry. 'We're still waiting for Seb, although he always feeds the chickens before feeding himself, so we let him off if he's a few minutes late.'

Bertie and Pat came in bringing a selection of different home-made pizzas cut into slices and laid out on trays with parsley and basil for decoration.

'Wow, these look amazing.'

'I helped make them all,' said Bertie.

'Good for you,' said Stephan. 'We could do with another good cook around the place. The food here tends to be a bit variable... mentioning no names.' Stephan coughed and said 'Harry,' under his breath.

'Hey, at least I try.' Harry turned to me. 'We run a rota for cooking. The same with the cleaning, although if residents have jobs outside of the farm, we adjust their workload here accordingly.'

'I'm happy to contribute any way I can.'

Before I had the chance to ask any more questions about the inner workings of Lowen Farm, the door opened and a tall, lanky man walked in. His hair hung messily down his back, and his beard was so long it tickled his chest. He kicked off his mud-covered shoes at the door and showed no embarrassment that his feet were covered by more holes than socks.

'Ah, Seb. How were the animals?'

'Hungry.'

Seb pushed his hair off his cheek and tucked it behind his ear. The pizza in my hand dropped onto my plate and heat rushed to my face. I recognised that gesture. As I looked up, Seb's hazel eyes caught mine, and he held my gaze for a second too long. Did he recognise me? I prayed he didn't. The humiliation would be too much to bear.

'Who's this then?' Seb asked.

'This is Liv and her son, Bertie. They'll be staying with us for a couple of weeks.'

'Nice to meet you,' said Seb. 'I'd shake your hand, but I've been cleaning out the chickens and although I've given my hands a good wash, you never know.'

He threw a warm smile my way. It was an easy, friendly smile that suggested he had no recollection of our shared history. But then, why didn't he want to touch me? Was it really because his hands were dirty, or was it an excuse? He seemed quite happy to grab a piece of pizza with those very same fingers.

Given he'd pulled out a chair opposite me, it was hard not to look at Seb. But each time I glanced at him, his eyes were focussed elsewhere. I tried to keep up with Harry's enthusiastic monologue about how she wanted to welcome groups of disadvantaged children to the farm, but I couldn't focus. I was sitting around a table in deepest darkest Cornwall, but in my mind, I was under canvas, music blaring from the main stage as Seb, or Baz as I'd known him then, caressed me in ways I'd never experienced before.

'What do you think, Liv?'

'Pardon?' Heat rushed to my face, and I took a sip of water to cool myself down.

'What do you think about bringing groups of kids to the farm? Working with the animals would be brilliant for them. We could even run residentials, use the lake for some team-building activities, or water sports. Sounds good, yes?'

'I guess so,' I said, trying to pretend as though I'd been listening to anything Harry had said. 'It's hard to give an opinion when I've not explored the farm yet, I suppose.'

'Very true. We should put that right first thing tomorrow. I was thinking of giving Bertie a tour of the animals. That all right with you, Bertie?'

Bertie, unable to speak due to the amount of pizza in his mouth, gave an enthusiastic nod of the head.

'Great.' Harry lifted a hand for Bertie to high-five. 'Seb? You can give Liv a tour of the grounds, can't you? Me and Bertie will feed the animals, so that will free up a bit of your time.'

'Sure, no problem. I'll call for you at nine.'

Oh, God. Even his voice left me feeling like an invertebrate. 'Great,' I choked out.

This time away was supposed to be clearing my head, not muddling it. I'd try ringing around Rob's friends again, although I didn't hold out much hope. But I needed to do something, anything, to get my life back on track. I needed to be an adult, and swooning over a teenage crush did not come anywhere near my to-do list.

Chapter Fourteen

I sat on the bathroom floor, balancing the phone against my shoulder whilst brushing my teeth.

'Do you have to do that?' asked Cass. 'It sounds gross.'

'I thought you were supposed to be a hardened nurse,' I said through a mouthful of toothpaste.

'Yes, I suppose it's not bottom juice,' sighed Cass, causing me to spurt my toothpaste out across the floor.

'Crap. Hang on.' I grabbed my towel and wiped away the mess I'd made, then rinsed out my mouth.

'Where are you?'

'In the bathroom. Where else would I brush my teeth?'

'What's it like?'

'The bathroom?'

'No, dumbass, the whole place.'

'I've not seen much of it yet, but what I have seen I like. I'm still not sure coming here was the right thing to do, though. It's not going to solve anything, is it? All I'm doing is kicking my problems into the long grass.'

'Liv, you need this time. You've not been yourself for the past eight years. It's about time you took a step back from life and figured out what you really want.'

'What I want is my old life back.'

'Really?'

I pictured the fancy cars, executive home on an executive estate, the yummy mummies, weekend visits to the grim-laws. Maybe I didn't want *exactly* that version, but what was the alternative?

'How's Dad?'

'Don't change the subject.'

'I'm not. I really want to know.'

'Dad's fine, same as ever.'

'I thought I could visit him at the weekend.'

'No, leave it a couple of weeks. You need to embrace the opportunity that's been given to you. Coming back to the city would only confuse things. Dad will survive a couple of weeks without you.'

'OK, but send him my love when you see him.'

'So come on, what's it like there?'

'Good, I think. Everyone seems nice...'

'What are you not telling me?'

I let out a long sigh and perched myself on the toilet seat. 'You remember when you turned eighteen and took me to that festival?'

'I don't remember as much about it as I probably should... for obvious reasons.'

'Granted, but do you remember the boy I met?'

'The one you went stupidly soppy over, then cried about for weeks when we got home?'

'Yeah, him.'

'What about him?'

'He's here. Or, at least I think it's him. I could be wrong. If it is him, he's a lot hairier than I remember.'

'Why don't you just ask him?'

'Ask him? Cass, he totally ghosted me. I thought I was falling in love. He'd promised to keep in touch, then on the last day...poof... gone.'

'Liv, I know your emotions are heightened at the moment, but don't you think you're being over dramatic? After all, you knew him for what? Twenty-four hours?'

'Forty-eight.'

'Exactly. Don't let it bother you. Maybe mention it to him, make a joke out of it?'

'Yeah, maybe. I'd better go in case Bertie wakes up and I'm not there. I'll call you tomorrow.'

'No, don't. Give yourself time to settle in, give yourself some space to think. I'm always here on the end of the phone, but leave it a couple of days, yeah?'

'OK. Love you.'

'Love you too.'

I hung up the phone and sat down on the toilet. Cass was right, I'd hardly known Seb, if indeed he was the boy I remembered. And she was also right that I was a mess, and dwelling on irrelevant feelings from over a decade ago would do nothing to help my situation.

With a clump of tissues pocketed as a precaution for my nightly breakdown, I crept back along the corridor to our bedroom. Inside, I found Bertie sprawled face-down on his mattress. Taking care not to wake him, I pulled blankets up over him and crouched beside his bed, watching him sleep.

My life so far may not have amounted to much, but if I achieved nothing else, the beautiful boy in front of me would have made my time on earth worthwhile. Whatever happened with me and Rob, together we'd created Bertie, and nothing and no one could take that away. Somehow we'd have to find a way through together, for our son's sake, if not our own.

I climbed into bed and checked my phone. Nothing from Rob, not that I expected there to be. I switched off my phone and tried to sleep. After half an hour of tossing and turning, I picked up my book, grateful that Bertie had insisted on keeping the light on.

Flat on my back, I looked up at the ceiling. Brown tide marks stained the once white paint, and at one corner paint was peeling. From what I'd seen of the farmhouse so far, it could do with some money being spent on it before it fell down around their ears.

If only I could afford to give them something for my stay. I knew Cass had handed over an envelope on my behalf, but it couldn't have contained much, given her own perilous finances. My last thought before finally giving in to sleep was that I'd find Harry first thing the next morning and offer my services in any way I could.

Chapter Fifteen

'Where is everybody?' I asked Harry. Beside me Bertie spooned cornflakes into a bowl whilst I waited for my toast to pop up.

'Andrea and Christine have already left for their walk, Maggie and Stephan rarely surface before nine, Pat never eats breakfast, and Seb always sorts himself out in his cabin. You still all right for your tour of the farm today?'

'Yes, but I can stay here and help with some chores if that's more useful?' I crossed my fingers behind my back.

'No, you go and get a feel for the place. I prefer people to offer help once they've seen the full range of what needs doing.'

'OK.'

Bertie gobbled his breakfast up faster than I'd ever seen. He fiddled with his spoon, twirling it round in his fingers and tapping it against the table.

'Bertie, is it possible you're a little bit excited about helping with the animals today?'

Bertie's mouth spread into a grin. 'Just a bit.'

'You'll have to work hard. Harry is expecting an assistant, not a hanger-on.'

'I'll be the best assistant she's ever had,' said Bertie. Given the enthusiasm on display, I didn't doubt it.

'Knock knock.'

An involuntary flush crept up my neck as Seb appeared in the doorway. I tried to get my emotions under control. There was nothing about Seb that usually attracted me. The beanie he wore had several holes, his jacket was covered in stains, and that beard of his would be horribly scratchy to kiss. *Stop it*, I told myself. *You're a married woman. Sort of.*

'Sorry I'm early, but the weather's supposed to turn around midday, so I thought it might help to get an early start.'

'Sure, no problem. I'll just go up and grab Bertie's coat, then I'll be ready.'

'Great.'

When I came back downstairs with Bertie's coat, I found Seb and Harry, their heads nestled together, frowning at something on Harry's phone. Something about the way they stood, close together, at ease, made me wonder if there was more to their relationship than simply friendship. I pushed down the feelings of jealousy that threatened to erupt in my stomach. Who was I to care? It wasn't like I was a free agent myself.

'Everything OK?'

'Yeah,' said Harry, looking up from her phone. 'Just another in a never-ending list of things to sort out at the farm.'

Her tone was nothing like the easy-going woman who'd chatted over dinner. She sounded world weary, worn-down, and far older than her smooth skin suggested.

'Come on,' said Seb. 'Let's get going and beat the weather.'

'Are you sure it's all right to leave Bertie here?'

'Of course,' said Harry. 'I've got plenty to keep him busy.'

Seb and I stepped outside and were hit by the kind of cold that burrowed through your thick socks and laughed in the face of all your layers. I shivered and hugged my arms around myself.

'I thought we'd start at the furthest point and work our way back. That OK?'

'Yes. Hang on, we're not going on that, are we?' I pointed to an ancient muddy quad bike sitting in the driveway.

'Up to you. Either we go on that or walk miles in the cold. The choice is yours.'

'I've never been on a quad bike before.'

'It's easy,' said Seb, walking over and climbing on. 'Just sit behind me. You can either hold on to the rail at the back, or put your arms around me. Whatever's most comfortable.'

Comfortable? There was nothing comfortable about the idea of clinging to Seb's waist. I shivered at the thought, convincing myself it was from the cold.

Seb handed me a helmet and helped me squeeze it on my head. 'I've not needed a helmet yet,' he said, 'but it's better safe than sorry. Besides, the last thing the farm needs is a personal injury claim.'

I felt stung that he had me down as someone who'd sue over a broken arm. 'Where are we going first?'

'The lake. In some ways, that's the most exciting part of the farm. It's where all the potential lies.'

'Sounds intriguing,' I said, although Seb didn't hear me over the noise of the engine.

Seb drove around to the back of the house, then picked up speed as we bumped and skidded across a muddy field. The view stretched out in front of me, woodland leading down to a ribbon of water, glittering beneath the weak winter sun.

As we reached the woods, Seb slowed, picking his way between thick tree trunks and their gnarled roots that stuck up out of the muddy earth. The slower speed gave me more of a chance to admire the surrounding scenery. Even with their skeletal branches, the native trees maintained a barren beauty. New life was emerging from the forest floor, a carpet of snowdrops signalling spring was just around the corner.

The quad caught on a hidden root, jerking me back in my seat and sending pain searing through my shoulder. Seb pulled the quad to a stop, the engine turning over lazily as he looked back at me.

'Are you OK? That was quite a jolt.'

'I'm fine, it's just my shoulder that hurts.'

'You'd best hold on to me rather than the rail,' said Seb. 'You don't want to be twisting that shoulder any more than you have to.'

I wanted to protest, but the pain in my joint outweighed any sense of pride. As I wrapped my arms around Seb's waist, I was grateful for the helmet that hid my blush. What I needed was for him to be an arsehole, or have some disgusting habit that would put me off and stop my teenage-like thoughts. Perhaps he was a secret nose-picker? Or washed only once a week? Maybe he chewed his own toenails whilst watching TV, or didn't wash his hands after going to the toilet?

We continued deeper into the woods, and even through all the layers, I felt the tension in Seb's shoulders as he navigated past the obstacles thrown up by the forest floor. The trees thinned out and Seb's shoulders relaxed. The scrubby, snowdrop-filled ground changed to a green sea of moss, then to grass, and finally, there it was, the lake.

Seb turned off the quad's engine and climbed off. He pulled off his own helmet, then helped me with mine.

'Oh my God.' The view took my breath away. Of all the images I'd had in my head, none came close to the view in front of me. When I'd pictured a lake, I'd thought of a vast stretch of water, surrounded by a band of gravelly sand. Instead, the water in front of me was guarded on three sides by tree-covered granite cliffs. Plants had taken up root between the trees, speckling the grey rock and brown bare-branched trees with flashes of green.

Seb began walking to the nearest shore. Here, a small wooden jetty stuck out into the water. A cheerfully painted red and green rowing boat bobbed beside it, and three upturned canoes lay on a gravel beach.

I walked out onto the jetty, pulled onwards by an invisible force. Something about the water made me catch my breath. As thin clouds tripped across the sun, the colour of the water changed. One minute it was a rich emerald, the next olive before transforming into a silky teal.

For the first time in weeks, possibly months, maybe even years, a deep sense of peace flooded through me. The change was both physical and emotional. As my muscles loosened, my mind cleared, the stresses and strains of my situation floated away and for a moment, all I felt was happiness.

'Pretty special, isn't it?'

Seb's voice broke the spell and as quickly as they'd come, all my fears for the future came rushing back. Tears filled my eyes, and I coughed to clear the lump in my throat. Ever since Rob left, I'd been fighting the sense of hopelessness which threatened to engulf me. Somehow, this exquisite example of nature at its finest had cut through my resolve and all my pretence. I choked back a sob.

'Hey, are you all right?'

Keeping my face turned to the water, I listened as Seb's footsteps grew closer. Unable to speak, I waved a hand in the air to show I was fine. Another sob escaped as a hiccup.

'Do you want to talk? Or would you rather have some time alone here?'

I brushed my tears away with my sleeve, plastered a smile on my face, and turned to face Seb. 'I'm fine, honest. It's just the cold making my eyes sting. Tell me about this place.'

Seb took my lie as it was meant. *I don't want to talk or be alone.* He kept his eyes fixed on the far side of the lake, allowing me enough privacy to wipe my eyes with a tissue and silently blow my nose. 'We call it the lake, but really it's a deserted quarry. When it fell into disrepair, Harry's grandparents had the foresight to buy the land. It's our secret weapon, our key to success. See through there?' Seb turned his back on the lake and pointed diagonally from where we stood. 'That's Pat's cabin. Mine's a little behind his.'

'What an incredible place to live.'

'I know, we're very lucky.'

'Have you lived here long?'

'A while.'

Right, so that was how he was going to play it. Thank God I hadn't spilled my problems out to him when he seemed determined to share as little as possible with me. So far, Seb had shown no sign that he had any memory of me, and I was happy for it to stay that way. He seemed most comfortable talking about Lowen Farm, so I stuck to safe ground.

'So, what are these mysterious plans you have for the place, then?'

Seb laughed. 'There's nothing mysterious about them, not really. You've seen the state of the house? How much work it needs?'

I nodded as I pictured our mouldy bedroom ceiling.

'The lake could be our way of funding the repairs needed and continuing the legacy of Harry's grandparents. Our plan is to use the lake for water sports, school groups, youth groups, executive team building trips. You name it, we've thought about it.'

'Where would everyone stay?'

'Ah, this is where we get into dreams rather than reality. The last thing Harry wants to do is cause any destruction to the natural landscape. She'd like to build low-impact tree houses for guests to stay in.'

'That doesn't sound too expensive.'

'You'd be surprised. And on top of the work needed to be spent on the house? Well, let's just say any bright ideas you have would be welcome.'

'I'll have a think.'

'Come on,' said Seb, 'if you can tear yourself away from the lake, I'll continue the tour.'

'Sure.'

'Actually, before we go, there's one more thing I should tell you about the lake.'

'What?'

'It's safe for swimming, should you want to?'

I laughed and looked at him like he was crazy. 'Swimming? In March? No thanks.'

'It's something to bear in mind. Harry's got a wetsuit you could borrow to get you started. It... um... it works wonders if you're going through stuff. Cold water is better than anything you get from the doctors if you're feeling a little... well... you know.'

'Thanks, I think. Now, what are you going to show me next?'

Chapter Sixteen

Somehow, over dinner the night before, I'd been railroaded into agreeing to try wild swimming. I couldn't imagine anything worse, but in the face of everyone's kindness, it seemed churlish to refuse.

By halfpast seven, Bertie was happily munching through his cereal and I was fidgeting with my clothes. There's nothing as uncomfortable as wearing a swimsuit beneath three layers of clothing and I shuffled against my seat to dislodge my wedgie.

'Morning, campers,' said Pat, his cheeks even redder than usual thanks to the cold.

'Morning, Pat. Thanks so much for watching Bertie whilst I indulge in some early morning torture.'

'My pleasure. I'm always up with the lark so it's no bother. Besides, I want to hear more about Bertie's day helping Harry with the animals. From what I gathered over dinner last night, the lad's a natural.'

'I'm going to be a farmer when I'm older,' said Bertie. 'Or maybe a vet, but I think being a farmer would be more fun.'

I smiled at the thought of Rob hearing of his son's ambition. He'd better come out of the woodwork soon, or any hope of his son joining the family firm would be long buried beneath Wellington boots and a lingering smell of manure.

'Sorry, sorry,' said Harry, rushing into the dining room. 'It took me ages to find my cossie. I've not worn it for years and it was buried beneath my socks.'

'I thought you go swimming most days?' I asked.

'Yes, but I like the feel of water on my skin... on *all* my skin.'

'Oh, right, well, thank you for making an exception today.'

Harry laughed. 'Didn't want to scare you off so soon into your stay. But I'll bet you'll be joining me for a skinny dip before you leave.'

'No chance,' I said, shivering at the thought. 'Is that your spare wetsuit?'

'Yes. I hardly use it these days. Only on the rare occasions I go surfing.'

'Where's the nearest beach?'

'It's only about a fifteen-minute drive, but there are no waves on the south coast. It's the north coast you want for that, and I can rarely spare the time to drive up there. Anyway, today is about swimming, not surfing. Come on, let's go.'

Harry led me out to her mud-covered Land Rover. 'Will you be able to get through the forest in that?'

Harry laughed. 'Seb took you on the scenic route yesterday. We'll take the track today. It's much quicker.'

Whilst the track took about half the time, it was no more comfortable. The worn leather seats did little to cushion the bumps and potholes of the track, my bones shaking within my skin until I worried my teeth would fall out.

'Here we are,' said Harry, pulling up outside a cosy-looking cabin.

'Who lives here?'

'Seb. I'm surprised he didn't show you yesterday.'

'I guess there was too much else to see. How come we've stopped here?'

'One, the track's too overgrown to get any closer to the lake, and two, he has an outdoor hot shower we can use once we've been for our swim.'

My face must have betrayed my feelings, as Harry laughed and put an arm around my shoulder.

'Don't worry, Seb's no perv. He's out feeding the chickens, and even if he comes back, he's built a cubicle around the shower to protect the user's modesty. Right, you ready?'

I looked down at my many layers. 'Where do I get changed?'

'We'll get changed by the water. I usually get changed here, but you don't want to be walking down the track in a wetsuit.'

I followed Harry as she picked her way along an animal track carved into the undergrowth. Brambles caught my coat, and several times I had to stop to free myself. The ground was squelchy under foot, my trainers sinking into mud deeper than my ankles.

'We'll have to sort you some wellies for next time,' said Harry.

If there was one thing I'd learned already that morning, it was that there was nothing glamorous about wild swimming. Between the tears in my coat, mud-covered trainers, and crazy hair scraped up on top of my head, I was very glad there was no one to witness my escapade. And I hadn't even put my wetsuit on yet.

As we climbed up onto the wooden jetty, Harry handed me two plastic bags.

'Are these for my clothes?'

'No, they're for your feet. Trust me, they'll make getting the wetsuit on a whole lot easier.'

God knows what putting the wetsuit on would have been like without Harry's hack, for even with two bags on my feet, the damn thing was near impossible to get on. I hopped around on the jetty like an ungainly trainee ninja, and twice Harry caught me just in time before I toppled into the water.

When I was finally zipped up and barely able to move my arms and legs, Harry dug around in her bag and pulled out wetsuit boots and gloves. She handed a set to me, then put some on herself. I swallowed down a giggle, but it broke free and I spluttered into my neoprene-clad hand.

'What?'

'D... do... you... wear those... g... g... gloves and boots when you're skinny dipping?'

Harry's face creased into a grin. 'Of course I do. I'm not mad. I don't want frostbite on my extremities.'

'Now that's a sight I'd like to see.'

Harry began untying the strap of her swimming costume.

'Not today though,' I added.

'Come on. It's best to get it over with. Stay here too long and we'll talk ourselves out of this.'

As I was new to this particular form of torture, Harry guided me into the water, one small step at a time. Her words, *we don't want you getting cold shock,* doing nothing to build my confidence. Icy water shot up the leg of my wetsuit and I let out a small yelp. I'd promised myself before we arrived I wouldn't lose face by screaming, but as the punishing water made its way through my wetsuit, I gave into my natural urge and squealed like a pig.

Harry waded in, laughing and splashing like she was on the beach in a heatwave.

'You're crazy,' I yelled. 'This is horrific.'

'Give it time,' said Harry. 'Do you feel you're being stabbed by a thousand pins yet?'

'I feel like I c... c.... can't breathe.'

'OK, take it easy. Take slow, deep breaths. This stage will pass, I promise.'

I fought the urge to panic, and just as Harry had promised, my skin was soon being stabbed by a thousand invisible needles, but at least my breathing was almost back to normal.

'Try swimming a few strokes.'

I did as instructed, the wetsuit limiting my movement so much I was forced to doggy paddle to where Harry trod water a few metres away.

'Well done. Feeling better?'

I found my stride. No one watching would've described my strokes as elegant, but as I fumbled my way through the water, my body responded in unexpected ways. First, I had an overwhelming desire to laugh. So, I did. Harry joined in my giggles, spraying shards of green water into the surrounding air, whooping and hollering like a child on their first visit to a beach.

Tears swiftly followed my laughter. I trod water, my body suspended in a lake I now considered magical due to its ability to undo me every time I got near it.

'Keep swimming,' said Harry. 'I'll be back in a tick.'

Rather than panicking as Harry swum away, I felt a deep sense of peace. I let the tears flow as the surrounding water cocooned my tired heart.

'Ahoy there, me hearty!'

I turned around in the water to see Harry sitting inside a rowing boat, her body swathed in a thick coat, oars in hand. She leaned over the side of the boat and pulled me in. For a moment, I was stranded, half in, half out, but with a worrying amount of swaying, and plenty of pushing and pulling, I flopped into the bottom of the boat like a stranded seal.

'I know you probably could've stayed in longer given your wetsuit, but it's best to play it safe on your first time. Here,' said Harry, handing me a towel-like coat to match hers.

My teeth were chattering, my limbs shaking despite my second skin, but I wasn't sure I'd ever felt so alive. It was something like a baptism. I'd gone into the water one person, and come out, well, not a new woman entirely, but one with a little more perspective.

'Are you OK if we row to the other side of the lake? If you're too cold, just say and we'll go back.'

'No,' I said, 'I'm fine.'

'Great.'

Harry rowed in silence, smooth, powerful strokes cutting through the water, pulling us ever further from the jetty.

'What's in there?' I asked, pointing to a large-lidded basket sitting between us in the boat.

'I packed a few supplies. I'll show you when we reach the pontoon.'

I looked over Harry's shoulder and saw a wooden pontoon growing ever closer. It seemed rooted to the lake, only bobbing gently once the boat came close enough to create a small swell.

Harry pulled the boat alongside the pontoon and tied it securely to a wooden post. She reached down and lifted the large basket, dropping it onto the pontoon and waiting for the boat to stop rocking before jumping out herself.

'Come on,' she said, holding out a hand.

'What are we doing?'

'It's time for your reward.'

Chapter Seventeen

Once I was installed on the pontoon, Harry helped me out of my cold wetsuit and wrapped me back up in my towelling coat, before pulling two thick blankets from the basket and wrapping one around my shoulders and one around her own. Her final touch was producing two oddly shaped bobble hats. I put one on, laughing as it flopped down in front of my eyes.

'Urgh, another of my disasters.'

'You made these?'

'Tried to. I'm determined to get the hang of knitting. It was my New Year's resolution, but I've not mastered it yet. I've set myself a rule that I have to wear everything I make. I'm hoping the humiliation will spur me on to improve.'

Harry grinned at me and pulled a flask from the basket.

'When did you get all this ready?'

'Technically, it wasn't me. I gave Seb a list of everything I thought we'd need, and he brought the basket down to the boat first thing.'

'That was kind of him.'

'That's Seb for you.'

'You two seem close.'

Harry laughed. 'You don't mean?' She looked at me, shook her head, and gave another throaty laugh. 'Seb's my cousin, on my mother's side.'

So I'd misjudged that one, not that it made any difference to me. 'He owns the farm too?'

Harry shook her head. 'No, it was my paternal grandparents who left the farm to me.'

'Has it always been called Lowen Farm?'

'Yes, my granddad named it. Lowen means happy, or joyful in Cornish.'

'The name seems very appropriate for this place.'

'Not if you're running it,' said Harry with a chuckle. 'This place comes with its fair share of stress, trust me.'

'I'd like to help, if I can.'

'What did you do before you arrived here?'

My cheeks turned pink, though not with the cold. 'Nothing, really. I did housework and raised my son.'

'That's not nothing. Raising a child is the most important job in the world, and you seem an expert at it if my day spent with your son is anything to go by.'

'Thank you. He's pretty special, but I know I'm biased. I'm not demeaning my work as a mother, but when I was younger, everyone expected more from me. I expected more.'

'So why didn't you go for it?'

'When I got married, my husband didn't want me to work. I was happy to stay at home with Bertie when he was little, but now he's eight, and out at school from eight until five...'

'Eight until five?'

'Private school.'

'Ah.'

'Yes, it's a long day, but with a long commute, which makes finding a job that fits around it tricky. But it also means I have long hours filled with nothing more than a bit of laundry and dusting. My husband even employed a cleaner, so most of my days were spent twiddling my thumbs.'

'Nice life if you can get it.'

'I know. I sound really ungrateful.'

Harry laughed. 'No, you sound like an intelligent woman who fancies filling her time with more than dirty underwear. I couldn't live like that. I'd be bored out of my mind.'

'Yes, but boredom's the least of my worries now. Ironing pairs of pants won't pay the bills. By not working for the past eight years, I've left myself completely unskilled and unqualified for most jobs. I don't know what I'm going to do. Somehow, I need to find money for rent, not to mention getting Bertie enrolled in a new school.'

I lay back against the pontoon, the weight of all my worries pinning me down onto the wood. The past few days had been a welcome distraction, but I had to face reality again soon.

'Why have you only planned to stay here for two weeks?'

'Because whatever I am, I'm not a freeloader. Also, I've no idea what's going on with my husband.'

'What do you mean?'

'I've not heard from him since the day we lost the house almost a month ago.'

'What a shit.'

I laughed, enjoying the attempts of the weak sun to warm my face.

'Was it a happy marriage?'

How to answer that? In the end, it seemed easiest to be honest. 'Not really. We only got married because I was pregnant. I've grown fond of him over the years, but it was never any great romance. And I've had my suspicions there have been other women. Not that Rob ever rubbed it in my face. He was always discreet, but it still hurt that I wasn't enough.'

Harry propped herself up on one elbow, and I turned my head to look at her. 'Liv, I hope I'm not speaking out of turn here, but is there a reason you're waiting around for your husband before making any life decisions? I mean, it doesn't seem like he's reciprocated that respect.'

'He's Bertie's father. I owe it to my son to work things out, if I can.'

'And what model is that giving to Bertie? That a man can cheat on his wife, lose all their combined wealth, disappear for God knows how long, and she'll still take him back?'

'We made vows. In a church.'

'And?'

'Marriage is sacred.'

'But surely Rob's destroyed the sanctity of your marriage by his actions?'

I stared up at the cloudless sky, reluctant to be drawn into a religious debate about marriage. I wasn't even a church-goer, but even so, marriage seemed too precious to discard like a broken toy.

'Can I put an idea to you?'

'Go on.' I turned my head back to Harry. She'd moved her arms behind her head like a pillow and closed her eyes.

'You may not have any qualifications, but I can tell you're an intelligent, capable woman. At the moment, you're stuck in limbo, right?'

'Yes.'

'That can't be doing you or Bertie any good. And that kid needs to be in school. As much as I'd love him to help me on the farm all day, every day, he's too bright, too inquisitive about the world to be missing out on his education.'

'You think I should go back to Exeter?'

'No, I think you should stay here, at least until the summer holidays. I'm sure they'd have space for Bertie in the village school. It would give you both a bit of breathing space, a chance to figure out what you do next. And if your errant husband turns up in the meantime, it wouldn't hurt to make him wait a while before you rush back into his arms.'

'But Harry, I've got no money. I couldn't possibly stay here for months without contributing financially.'

'I've been thinking about that, too. I've been trying to get this lake project off the ground. Seb's been taking the lead, but we're so busy with the other farm work, it's hard to give the project the attention it deserves. What I'm thinking is that you could take it on.'

'Me? But I wouldn't know where to start.'

Harry pulled herself up and sat cross-legged, staring at me. 'Running a home and caring for a child requires superior organisational skills. I'm guessing you were a member of the school PTA?'

'For my sins.'

'Exactly. You have tons of transferable skills. And you won't be working alone. You and Seb can work on the project together.'

My stomach plummeted. The thought of working closely with Seb left me with an unsettling mix of excitement and horror.

'As the project hasn't got off the ground yet, and we're still waiting to hear about funding, I could only afford to pay you one hundred a week. But obviously food and board would be thrown in, and you'd be welcome to find a second job either in the village or Liskeard, which is only half an hour on the bus.'

'I don't know what to say.'

'Just say yes. Obviously, it's different from anything you've done before, so we could start with a month's trial. If it doesn't work out, you can still stay here until the summer. There's plenty of other work you can help with.'

I shivered but couldn't tell if it was from the cold or the excitement of finally having some sort of plan, at least for the next few months. 'Thank you.'

'You're welcome. Now, that hot shower is calling me. Come on, let's get back. We've got a project to get stuck into.'

Chapter Eighteen

The hot water ran over my skin like silk. It was possibly the best shower I'd ever had, and Rob had taken me to plenty of five-star hotels.

'You nearly done in there?'

'Sorry, Harry, I'll come out now.'

'It's heaven, isn't it?' said Harry, once I emerged fully dressed with a towel wrapped around my hair.

'It's amazing. I didn't want to ever get out.'

'You're telling me,' said Harry, giving a dramatic shiver followed by a wolfish grin. 'I'll get in now, but don't wait out here in the cold. Seb's back and has got coffee on the go. No need to knock. He's expecting you.'

'I should really get back to Bertie.'

'Why? He'll be having a great time with Pat. Stay for a coffee. You need to warm up properly after being cold for so long.'

Before I could argue, Harry jumped into the shower cubicle and the sound of the powerful rainwater shower drowned out further conversation. I walked around to the front of the cabin and took a deep breath. As I stepped inside, I was hit by the delicious combination of wood smoke and freshly brewed coffee.

'How was your swim?' asked Seb, his back to me as he stirred the coffee.

'Amazing. Amazingly cold.'

Seb laughed and turned to look at me. 'It's put some colour in your cheeks, at least.'

My cheeks burned brighter, and I walked over to the fire to hide it. 'Thanks for the blankets and hot chocolate. They made all the difference.'

'No problem. But don't let Harry's thoughtfulness fool you. Now she's got you in once, you'll get the usual no-frills experience from now on.'

I laughed and looked around the cabin. I'd expected an explosion of pine, but the walls of Seb's cabin were white-washed, free of paintings, the views from the windows negating the need for an artist's work. The whole of the ground floor was open-plan. Clustered around the fire sat a collection of mis-matched armchairs, covered in woollen throws in varying shades of blue and green. A sheepskin rug filled the space in front of the fire.

Seb walked over with a cup of coffee and saw me studying the rug. 'The rug's meant to be ironic,' he said. 'My sister bought it for me as a joke when she heard I was moving into a log cabin. It's unbelievably comfy though, not that I'd admit that to her.'

'It's a lovely space.'

'I've tried to tone it down since I moved in. It used to look like a sauna, and I'd be reading the newspaper expecting a gang of nude Scandinavians to show up at any moment. I couldn't live like that. Take a seat.' Seb pointed to an armchair, and I sat down, kicking off my shoes and curling my legs beneath me.

'Thanks for letting us use the shower.'

'No problem. Did it help to warm you up?'

'Yes, and this coffee's helping, too. Thanks.' I blew on the coffee and studied Seb across the rim of my mug. He wore a misshapen jumper, which I guessed must have been a present from Harry. His long hair was tied up with an elastic band, and a line of milky coffee clung to his moustache. I wondered whether my mind was playing tricks on me, whether this was the same man I'd met all those years before? Could Seb have a brother, or a twin?

'How many siblings do you have?' I asked.

'Just the one sister.'

'No brother, called Baz, maybe?' I blamed the cold water for making me so bold, but I had to know if I was imagining things.

'No, just a sister called Beth. Why?'

I noticed Seb wouldn't catch my eye, and even with all that facial hair, I could tell his cheeks had grown pink. 'Oh, nothing. You just remind me of someone I met a long time ago.'

'Couldn't have been me,' said Seb. But the way he got up from his chair and pretended to fuss with something in the kitchen told me all I needed to know. It was him. I was right. No wonder he was pretending. I would too, if I'd behaved the way he did all those years ago.

Harry came in, bringing with her a blast of freezing air. 'It's a beautiful day, but my God, it's freezing.'

'You're both mad, going in the water in these temperatures.'

'You're never tempted?' I asked Seb.

'Only when it's at least twenty-five degrees outside.'

'Wimp,' said Harry, punching his arm before pouring herself a coffee. 'Seb, I've found the answer to your prayers.'

'Oh?'

'Liv.'

Seb and I erupted into simultaneous blushes, although he had the advantage of covering his with facial hair. Harry carried on oblivious, climbing up onto the kitchen worktop and swinging her legs against a cupboard. 'Yeah, Liv's going to help you with the lake project. You can start by thinking of a better name for it. Lake project sounds like we're about to start dredging or something.'

'That's a kind offer, but I can manage it by myself.'

'Ha, yeah right. How much time have you been able to spend on it this week?'

Seb frowned and studied his coffee cup.

'Look, I'm not saying you're not capable of running the project by yourself. I'm just saying you don't have the time. Let Liv pick up some of the slack.'

'I wish you'd run this by me first.'

'Why? It's a great idea.'

I wanted the chair to swallow me whole. The cousins continued bickering, oblivious to my presence. I felt as though I were eavesdropping on a private conversation, even though that conversation was about me, and I was in the room.

'I'd better get back to Bertie.'

'Look what you've done,' Harry told Seb. 'You've made Liv feel uncomfortable. That's not the way to begin a new partnership.'

Seb ignored Harry and began washing out his mug.

'If you'd rather work alone, I'm sure there are other things I can help with around the farm. I wouldn't want to put you in a difficult position.'

'It's fine,' said Seb, his voice betraying his true feelings that it was anything but.

'If you're sure?'

'Of course he is,' said Harry. 'Why don't we set a time for the two of you to meet and get started? How about tomorrow morning after our swim?'

'Oh, I'm not sure...'

'About the swim, or the meeting?'

Both, but I didn't want to make a bad impression so used Bertie as an excuse.

'We'll see how Pat's got on with him this morning, but I'm sure he'll be happy to watch him again tomorrow. Why don't you go into the village today and inquire at the school? That will free up more of your time and stop Bertie getting bored.'

'I don't think he could get bored on the farm, but you're right. I'll call in today and find out if they've got any spaces.'

'Great. Right, Seb, we'll love you and leave you. See you at dinner tonight.'

'See you.'

'Thanks for the coffee.'

Seb answered me with a nod of the head and left me with the distinct impression he was looking forward to our first meeting as much as a visit to the dentist.

Chapter Nineteen

I found Bertie and Pat playing chess in the sitting room. Neither looked up when I walked in, both engrossed in their next move. I perched myself on a chaise longue that had seen better days and watched Bertie's forehead crease as he frowned at the board, moving the pawn in his hand back and forth until he picked the right move.

'You took my knight,' said Pat, throwing his head in his hands. 'I thought you said you'd never played before?'

'I haven't, have I, Mum?'

'No, he's telling the truth, Pat.' I smiled at Bertie, who grinned alternately at me and his opponent.

'Then I think I've met my match.'

It took a further twenty minutes before the game concluded with Pat declaring check mate.

'Good game, young man,' said Pat, holding out his hand.

Bertie reached across and shook it. 'Thank you for playing fairly. I hate it when people go easy on me 'cause I'm a kid.'

'Well, well, a jolly good loser too. You've raised this boy well, Liv.'

'Thank you.' I wondered where Bertie had learned to be a good sport. Certainly not from his father, who flew into a temper reminiscent of McEnroe if he lost a tennis match, or any game for that matter. Mind you, with Hugo and Marion for parents, it was clear where Rob's attitude came from.

'What are your plans for today?' Pat asked, packing away the chess set.

'Actually, I was about to talk to Bertie about an idea I've had.'

'That sounds like my cue to leave,' said Pat. 'Will you be swimming again tomorrow morning?'

'Only if it's not too much trouble for you to come up to the house again?'

'Trouble?' Pat laughed. 'The only trouble will come if your son beats me at our re-match. I'm going to make myself a cup of tea before I head home. Would you like one?'

'That would be lovely, thank you.'

Pat left the room and Bertie came to sit beside me. 'What did you want to talk to me about? Has Dad called you?'

'No, darling, I'm afraid he hasn't. I've been thinking about what we should do, and I wondered how you'd feel about staying here until the summer holidays?'

'Really? We can stay longer?'

'If that's what you'd like?'

'Yeah, I'd love it. I can help Harry with the animals and play chess with Pat. And Stephan said he'd take me fishing down at the lake.'

'That all sounds wonderful, but if we stay here for a few months, we'll have to see about you going back to school.'

Bertie's eyes darkened. 'But you said I'd never have to go back. If you make me see that polla Jack Jamison again, I'll run away. I promise, I'll do it.'

'Bertie,' I said, pulling him closer to me. 'I'm not talking about sending you back to your old school. I thought we could see if there are any spaces at the local school in the village.'

Bertie frowned. 'Or, I could not go to any school, and just learn how to do stuff on the farm.'

'I'm afraid that's not an option. You've got to go to school somewhere. It's the law.'

'You mean I'll be arrested if I don't go to school?'

'No, but I could get a fine.' I kept quiet about the option of home-schooling, knowing if I mentioned it, I'd never get Bertie to darken the door of any school ever again.

'Can I come with you to look at the school?'

'I don't see why not, but we probably won't get to see much. I'm going to call in and have a quick chat, then we can make an appointment to look round another time.'

'Can we get some sweets from the shop while we're there?'

I thought about the hundred pounds Dad had put in my account to tide me over. 'OK. As long as we don't spend too much. Until I start working, we're going to have to be very careful with our money.'

Bertie nodded. 'Can we see the school now?'

'Yes, just let me have a cup of tea, then we'll go.'

It was a mile walk along the track from the farm to the village, but Bertie chatted the whole way and we reached the village quickly. The village housed a post office and shop, a pub, a church and the school. Most of the houses were small stone cottages. Even the newer estate built on the outskirts of the village had houses clad in the same local stone. It was picturesque, with views out to moorland in one direction, and views to the river and valley in the other.

At the school gates, Bertie hesitated.

'It's OK, there's nothing to worry about. We're only finding out about spaces. I'm not signing you up for anything yet.'

Bertie took my hand, and we walked across a tarmacked playground to a Victorian building with large windows and a bright blue front door. I rang the doorbell, and a buzzer signalled we could enter.

The reception area was about as far from Bertie's previous school as it was possible to get. The blue carpet was faded and worn through in places, and the walls looked in need of a lick of paint. Boards housed children's drawings and photographs of the staff, who only numbered six.

'Hello, can I help you?'

'Hi,' I said, peering through a perspex screen to be greeted by a middle-aged woman with bright pink hair. 'I'm hoping for some information about the possibility of enrolling my son into the school. I wasn't sure if you have any spaces.'

'Have you just moved into the area?'

'Yes, we're staying at Lowen Farm.'

'Oh, I know it well. I worked with Mr Nickson, sorry, Pat, for several years before he retired.'

'He's teaching me to play chess.'

'Is he now? And who are you?' asked the lady, leaning closer to her screen.

'My name's Alberto Simmons, but everyone I like calls me Bertie.'

'What about those you don't like?'

'You don't want to know.'

The pink-haired lady laughed. 'Well, I hope you'll let me call you Bertie?'

'Yes. I like your hair.'

The lady laughed again. She turned to me. 'Tell you what, I'll fetch the head for you. If she has time, I'm sure she'll be happy to give you a quick tour.'

'Thank you.'

We'd only been waiting a couple of minutes when the pink-haired woman returned with a large lady who wore a suit, bow tie and a wide smile.

'Good morning. I hear we may have a new recruit. I'm Mrs Grange, very pleased to meet you.'

'Mrs Simmons,' I said, shaking her hand. 'But call me Liv.'

'Nice to meet you, Liv. You can call me Mel.'

'My name's Alberto, but you can call me Bertie.'

'Good,' said Mel, clapping her hands together. 'Now we've got names under our belts, would you like to have a look around?'

'Yes, please.'

Mel led us through to a small hall, gym equipment packed to one side, and a stage set up in another corner. 'We're only a small school, as you can probably tell,' said Mel, 'but we like to punch above our weight.'

'How many classes are there?'

'Three, all mixed age-groups. They're more of a challenge to teach, but we find it works well for our pupils. We run several after-school clubs, and of course we have my pride and joy, the brass band.' Mel stopped beside a framed photograph on the wall. In it were about thirty children holding a variety of instruments. Mel sat in pride of place at the front, a French horn balanced on her knee. 'My father was a brass teacher. When he died, instead of leaving me money in his will, he left it to the school on the condition we buy enough instruments for every pupil.'

I smiled, but wondered how I'd feel if my father made such an unusual bequest in his will.

'I'd like to learn the trumpet,' said Bertie.

'Since when?' I asked, trying to remember if he'd ever expressed an interest in music before.

'For ages,' he said, crossing his arms.

'Hmm, you don't find many trumpets in a brass band. How about a cornet? It's just like a trumpet but produces a warmer sound. Does that sound OK?'

'Yes,' said Bertie with a grin.

'Then cornet you shall learn, if you enrol in the school, of course.'

'Do you have spaces?' I asked, feeling the conversation was heading off in a brass band-themed tangent.

'Oh yes. If you and Bertie decide this school is a good fit, we can fill out all the forms before you leave.'

I tried to focus as Mel showed us around each of the classrooms, but I was struggling to wrap my head around this recent turn of events. Last week I thought we were coming to Cornwall for a couple of weeks' holiday, and now here we were, signing Bertie up to school, me taking on a new job, and with the prospect of sharing a bedroom with a beginner brass player.

Chapter Twenty

I held the phone away from my ear as Cass shrieked down the line.

'I know,' I said. 'I'm just as surprised as you.'

'I knew that place would be good for you,' said Cass. 'I felt it in my bones. But to have got a job, a six-month plan, and a school place for Bertie, all within a few days. That's blown my mind.'

'Mine too.'

'What's the school like?'

'About as different from Bertie's last one as it's possible to be. They have a big focus on creative activities and sport. And I've not even told you about the brass band yet.'

'Hang on,' said Cass, 'I've just got home. Hold on a sec while I open the door.'

'No, don't worry, I'll call you back this evening. I need to get going or I'll be late for swimming. And I've got my first meeting about the lake project straight after, so I need to go too.'

'Swimming? Wow, you must call me later, there's so much to catch up on.'

'Will do. Love you.'

'Love you too.'

'Was that Aunt Cass?' asked Bertie.

'Yes, she was on her way home from work. We should invite them to come and see us here soon. Would you like that?'

'Yes, I can show Jake and Emmy all the animals. They'll be so jealous. The animals are way cooler than a black bedroom.'

'You're right, they are. Now, come on, let's get you downstairs for breakfast. Pat will arrive soon for more chess.'

'I like playing chess with Pat, but I wish I could start school today.'

'I know, but it makes sense to start on Monday. It will give you a proper chance to settle in.'

Bertie sighed. 'I suppose. And Stephan said he'll take me fishing this afternoon. He said it will get him out of Maggie's hair, but I don't understand why he'd be in her hair in the first place.'

'It's an expression, like getting under someone's feet.'

Bertie shrugged in an *all adults are weird* kind of way.

With Bertie settled with his breakfast, Harry drove us to the lake. As Seb had predicted, this time there was no standing on ceremony, no picnic and blankets stashed away in the rowing boat. Now Harry was convinced I could survive the threat of cold-shock she became less encouraging-primary-school-teacher and more sergeant-major.

No sooner had I got my wetsuit on than we were in, sending ripples across the previously calm water. I squealed just as much as the first time, but now I knew the sensations to expect, the lack of breath and pins and needles didn't panic me. I waited for them to pass and began testing out a few different strokes. I wasn't prepared to dunk my head, and could only manage minimal leg movements thanks to the wetsuit, but I swam a good fifty metres before the cold became painful and we both got out.

I'd hoped to stay in longer to put off the meeting with Seb, but we were showered, dressed and accepting a cup of coffee in Seb's kitchen before I had a chance to gather my thoughts, or composure.

'Right,' said Harry, downing the dregs of her coffee. 'I'll leave you to it.'

'Are you sure you don't want to stay?' Seb asked, probably to avoid being alone with me.

'No, it's best I hand things over to you two from the get-go. Otherwise, I'll be tempted to micro-manage and I've already got enough on my plate. I'll see you later.'

'Bye.'

Seb turned back to the kettle and re-filled it. I pulled a notepad and pen from my bag. 'We'll need more coffee if I'm going to give you a crash course on the project.'

I sighed. Whilst on the surface, offering me more coffee was friendly, the way Seb banged about in the kitchen suggested he'd rather be anywhere but with me.

'Look, I know you don't want me working with you on this, but Harry's asked me to help and...'

'It's not that.'

'OK.'

I waited for Seb to elaborate, but he carried on fussing with mugs, milk, and coffee grounds.

'Seb, would you rather we do this another day?'

I jumped as he flung a spoon into the sink. He leaned over it, pressing down and taking deep breaths.

'I think it's best if I go,' I said.

'No. We need to talk.'

Unsure what was going on, I sat rigid in my seat, waiting for whatever he clearly needed to get off his chest. Seb laid the pot of coffee and two mugs down on the table and pulled out a chair. He sat down, his head in his hands, his fingers tugging at his long mane.

'What's this about?'

'You asked if I had a brother called Baz.'

'And you said no.'

'I lied. Well, not about the brother part. Baz was me, I was Baz.' He ran his hands through his hair and sighed. 'My friends called me Bas, short for Sebastian, then somewhere along the way, it became Baz. You were right about us having met before. I shouldn't have lied.' He looked up at me, his face taut, jaw clenched.

'Why did you?'

'Things happened that weekend that I'd rather forget.'

'Thanks.'

'No, not with you. Our time together was amazing. I... we...' he turned his head away as his cheeks turned pink. 'We were supposed to meet up on that last day.'

'I know. I waited for you for two hours. I missed watching my favourite band, convincing myself you'd be along any moment. Do you have any idea how humiliating it was having to go back to my friends alone, after all I'd said about you?' Now it was my turn to blush.

'I'd fully intended to meet you. I was on my way when I got a phone call from home.'

'What kind of phone call?'

'The kind you never want to get. My dad had been in a motorbike accident.'

'Oh my God. Did he... is he?'

'He survived, but only just. It was touch and go, and he was in a coma for weeks. I could hardly tell my mum I'd be there in a few hours once I'd hooked up with a girl

I'd just met. All I could think about was Dad. I dropped everything, left my tent, all my stuff behind. I had to get to the hospital. I had to be with him.'

'And you couldn't have messaged?'

'I'll be honest. I didn't think about it until later that day. Then I didn't know what to say. We didn't think Dad would make it, and everything was such a mess. Then the longer I left it, the harder it became to contact you. I convinced myself I'd imagined the connection between us, that it was the festival atmosphere that had gone to my head.'

So, he'd felt it too. It hadn't just been me. But had it just been youthful excitement, too many hormones? That weekend had played out like a romance novel, eyes meeting across a crowded tent, each other's first kiss, the promise of so much more... I shook the thoughts out of my head. We'd been sixteen. Now we were adults, completely different people.

'I'm sorry that happened to you, and I totally understand. But I wish you'd got in touch to let me know. I spent months thinking I'd done something wrong.'

Seb reached across the table and took my hand in a gesture that shocked us both. He snatched his hand back, beads of sweat appearing on his forehead.

'It was the beginning of a very dark time in my life. The accident left Dad paralysed, and it knocked the whole family for six. Anyway, you don't want to hear about my depressing past. We've got more important matters to discuss.'

Seb smiled at me, a smile that took me back to a muddy field laced with fairy lights, and a night of literally dancing till we dropped. His appearance may have changed drastically since then, but his smile was the same. His eyes met mine, sending a jolt of electricity through me. I should have looked away, but his eyes were like two magnets, holding me in place, trying to convey a message I couldn't quite grasp.

Seb coughed and broke the spell. My eyes fell to the notebook in front of me and I fiddled with my pen, clicking the lid on and off.

'Right, where were we?' said Seb, clearing his throat. 'Let's start with the vision for the lake project and why I'm going to need all the help I can get to make it work. Welcome to the team, Liv.'

Chapter Twenty-One

'Good morning!' Mrs Grange greeted us at the school gate with a flourish of arms and a wide smile. She wore the same suit I'd seen her in the first day we met, but on this occasion had added a bow tie covered in brightly coloured butterflies. 'How are you feeling about your first day, Alberto?'

'Good,' said Bertie. 'And you can call me Bertie.'

'Ah, yes, I forgot.' Mrs Grange turned and yelled out a child's name. The boy came running over, clearly worried he was in trouble. 'Bertie, this is Zach. Zach, I'd like you to take Bertie under your wing, as it's his first day. Do you think you can manage that?'

'Yes, Mrs Grange.'

'Zach here is in Bertie's year and is an all-round superstar. Not to mention a fine trombone player.'

'Do you like playing football?' asked Zach.

'Love it,' said Bertie. Before I could kiss him goodbye, he'd gone running off with Zach, in hot pursuit of a football.

'And how is Mum feeling about Bertie's first day?' asked Mrs Grange.

'I'm far more nervous than he is.'

'It's always the way. Bertie will be absolutely fine. There's nothing to worry about.'

'I don't doubt it, but isn't worrying a mother's job?'

Mrs Grange reached over and tapped my arm. 'You can worry all you want when Bertie's in your care, but here, all that worrying is our job.'

'Thank you. I'd better get going before I cry and embarrass Bertie on his first day.'

'Yes, you get going. If for any reason Bertie struggles, we'll call you. But assume no news is good news, and by the looks of him, I don't think you'll be hearing from us today.'

I thanked Mrs Grange and walked away from the school, noticing how many friendly smiles were thrown my way from other parents. Of all the recent decisions I'd made, deep down I was convinced enrolling Bertie into this school was one of the best. Not only had he already made a friend, if the smiles from parents were anything to go by, I might too.

Harry had asked me to pick up some milk, so I walked through the village until I reached the shop. As I pushed open the door, I noticed a handwritten sign taped to the glass. *Part-time staff wanted. Apply within.*

Whilst the hundred pounds a week Harry was paying me wasn't to be sniffed at, it wouldn't stretch very far, and anything I could do to supplement my income was to be welcomed. I grabbed a bottle of milk and carried it to the counter.

'Hello, just the milk, please. Also, I saw you're advertising for staff?'

'Yes, we are. New to the area, are you? I don't think I've seen you in here before?'

'Yes, we moved into Lowen Farm a couple of weeks ago.'

'Ah, lovely place that. I'm Beryl, I've been postmistress here for the past fifty years. I've lost count of how many times they've tried to shut us down, but the only way they'll get me out of here is in a wooden box.'

I guessed the *they* Beryl referred to was the Royal Mail, and I suspected they'd be no match for her. 'Good for you. So, about the job?'

'Ah, yes. It would be three mornings a week. My joints are bleddy stiff these days and I take a while to get going in the mornings. I've a lovely girl Flora who works Tuesdays, Thursdays and Saturdays, but she cares for her elderly mother on the other days.'

'What would the job involve?'

Beryl barked out a laugh. 'Not much more than what we're doing now. Chatting to customers mainly.' She laughed again, then leaned over the counter and lowered her voice. 'The crucial skill you need is discretion. You hear more secrets in here than in a therapist's office. I'm always the first to know who's sleeping with who, what kids are in trouble with the law, crikey, I could even tell you who's got bunions and who has piles. But whatever I hear, my lips are sealed.'

Beryl pretended to zip her lips. Something about the glint in her eye made me doubt her claims of discretion. She seemed bursting to tell me about the owner of the piles, for starters.

'So, I wouldn't need to do anything with the post office?'

'Nah, it would take too long to train you up, or whoever I give the job to. I'll reduce the hours the post office is open and the customers will have to lump it. Most of my money's made from the shop anyway these days. People don't send so many letters now they have those new-fangled easy-mails.'

Either Beryl was talking about email, or I'd missed out on the latest development in the tech world. 'So, would you like me to fill out an application form?'

'Good lord, no, I don't go in for all that. Come behind the counter and I'll see how you get on. If I like you, you get Miss Harry from up at the farm to give me a bell. Just so I know you're all right and not one of those peevs you hear about in the news.'

'Peevs?'

'You know, the brown mac brigade.'

My best guess was that she meant to say pervs, but whether peevs or pervs, I moved the conversation onto safer ground. 'What would you like me to start with?'

'Come here and I'll show you how the till works. I know exactly how much is in there, mind. You don't look like a thief, but it takes all sorts. This one time…'

Beryl didn't stop to draw breath for the next two hours. In that time, I'd met at least a dozen villagers, and knew more about their lives than I or they would like. Beryl had an uncanny way of drawing information out of people. We heard from Nicola, whose daughter was being bullied at the local high school, Frank, who was facing the desperate decision whether to put his wife in a care home, Mick, who couldn't get a doctor's appointment for his bad back and Mavis, who'd called the police on her neighbours after they got frisky with the curtains open ('it was like they wanted to put on a show for the entire cul-de-sac').

The till was old-fashioned and easy to work. The card machine took a little longer to master, but it wasn't rocket science and I'd soon got the hang of it. In a rare five minutes when the shop was quiet, Beryl showed me the stockroom, how to check the inventory, how to replenish the shelves and what to do with out-of-date stock, (put it by the door of Beryl's flat for her to eat later.)

'Right, maid,' said Beryl when the clock reached midday. 'I think that's you done.'

'OK. How did I do?'

'Not so bad, no, we'll make a shop assistant out of you yet.'

'Thank you,' I said, with no idea whether I'd passed Beryl's test.

'You get Miss Harry to give me a bell. So long as you don't turn out to be a peev or axe murderer, you can come back on Wednesday morning. Nine o'clock start suit you?'

'Yes, that would be perfect. I can drop my son off at school on the way.'

'Ah yes, little Bertie. You bring him in after school tomorrow. I'd like to meet him.'

As much as I'd tried to resist Beryl's sly interrogation technique, she'd got more information from me than I'd like, and knew a vast chunk of my life story.

'Right, well, I'll pop in with Bertie and look forward to starting on Wednesday.'

'And don't forget about Miss Harry. There'll be no job without her say so.'

'I won't forget.'

I left the shop calculating how much I'd be earning each week. Beryl had been cagey on the question of wages, so I was assuming she only paid minimum wage, but even so, it would be enough to tide us over, and like the supermarket slogan said, *every little helps.*

Chapter Twenty-Two

I sat cross-legged, leaning against a wide-trunked oak. 'What time did Maggie say she'd get here?'

Seb checked his watch. 'She should be here any minute.'

He dropped to the ground and sat beside me, not quite touching, but close enough for me to feel his warmth. My body tingled. He tugged on his beard, twisting it this way and that around his fingers. I laughed.

'What?'

'It's just that thing you do with your beard. It reminds me of when I used to style my sister's hair.'

'Oh, really? It's a habit I've fallen into. I fiddle with my beard when I'm thinking.'

'Well, I think you'd look very fetching with a braided beard.'

'Oh, you do, do you?' asked Seb, his eyes twinkling. 'Go on then, give it a try.'

I shuffled forward onto my knees in front of him. 'Are you sure?' Seb nodded, and I divided his beard into three sections. We were so close I could feel his breath on my hands. My heart pounded as my fingers began knotting the wiry hair. I wasn't attracted to facial hair, but the sixteen-year-old in me was enjoying an excuse to touch him, even if it was more wire brush than smooth skin.

'Does that hurt?'

'No,' he muttered. I couldn't risk getting caught by his magnetic eyes, so focused on his lips, chapped from spending so long outside in the cold.

'When did you grow a beard?'

Seb took a while to answer. 'I've had it a while.'

'Right.'

'You don't like it?'

'It's not that. It still surprises me. When I picture you, it's as a clean-shaven sixteen-year-old, so each time I see you it's a shock. And it seems a bit of a shame to hide your entire face under hair.'

Seb grinned. 'I'm pleased you like my face, even if you don't like my beard.'

I risked letting my gaze travel up to his face and found he was staring at me. 'I think you're done,' I said, resuming my position at his side so he wouldn't notice my blush.

Seb pulled his phone out of his pocket and turned the camera on himself. He barked out a laugh. 'I look completely ridiculous.'

'Yes, you do.'

The sound of an engine reached us. 'Crap, I need to undo this before Maggie gets here or she'll never let me live it down.' Seb yanked at the braid. His beard tangled, resulting in something resembling one giant dreadlock.

I tried and failed not to laugh.

'It's not funny. I've got a meeting with the council later. Help me, Liv.'

I tried to untangle the bird's nest hanging from his chin, but my attempts only knotted it further. 'I'm sorry, I think you may need to cut it off.'

'Is this all a ruse to make me get rid of my beard?'

'No, not at all,' I said, arranging my face to look as innocent as I could.

The noise of the car grew louder and soon Harry's Land Rover came into view, Maggie behind the wheel. Of all the residents at Lowen Farm, Maggie was the one I'd spent the least time with, but I'd immediately warmed to her and was looking forward to getting to know her better.

She jumped down from the Land Rover, her sturdy legs clad in pillar-box red Wellington boots. 'What in God's name have you done to yourself?' she asked, bending down and peering at Seb.

'Don't ask.'

'You're going to have to get that sorted before the meeting later.'

'I know.' Seb groaned and threw his head in his hands.

'It's about time you got rid of that thing. It's like a mangy flea-ridden fox hanging from your chin.'

'Wow, Maggie, you have such a way with words.'

'Don't worry, I can sort it.' Maggie turned to me. 'In a former life I was a hairdresser. I've been wanting to get my mitts on Seb's mop for years.'

'Hey, you're going nowhere near my hair. My beard could do with a trim, but don't touch the locks.'

Maggie sighed and put her hands on her ample hips. 'So, let's get started, shall we?' She pulled a can of spray chalk from her bag. 'I thought we could mark out all the areas where treehouses would go. That way, when the chap from the planning department comes round, he'll see what we're talking about.'

'As long as he understands the structures will be in the trees.'

'Of course, as they're called treehouses on the planning application, I think that's a clue. They might be tricky customers over at the council, but they're not stupid. Not all of them, anyway.'

I longed to ask how a former hairdresser had come to be an admin assistant slash general dogsbody on a co-living farm, but Maggie was already shaking her can of chalk and it didn't seem the time to pry into her past.

'Have you thought about facilities?' asked Maggie.

'Yeah, I was thinking we could build a shed to store the kayaks near the jetty.'

Maggie shook her head and tutted. 'Men. I'm talking about *facilities*, Seb. You know, washing, toileting, et cetera.'

'Oh, right. Yes, we thought we could build a block of composting toilets and have cold-water sinks for washing. If people are too soft for that, they could use my outdoor shower, but I wouldn't be encouraging it. Roughing it would be part of the experience.'

'Good, I'm pleased you've thought it through, as these are the questions the planning officer is likely to ask.'

'It's all in here,' I said, pulling a folder from my bag. 'We typed everything up as a business plan last night, and there's a FAQ section at the back.'

'A woman after my own heart,' said Maggie, taking the folder and flicking through. 'I can see you two are going to make a good team.'

After marking out the areas where the treehouses would go, we stopped for a coffee break, carrying our mugs down to the jetty. An idea had been forming in my mind ever since I first heard about the lake project, but it was only after Maggie's enthusiastic response to my business plan that I had the confidence to speak up.

I waited until we were settled on the jetty, legs swinging above the water, before raising the topic. 'I've been wondering about a fundraiser.'

'A fundraiser?'

'Yes. I know we'll be running this as a business, but there's a strong community element. We'll be using part of the profits to fund work with disadvantaged groups, so there's a charitable angle I think people would be keen to support. We could invite the local press along, and the publicity may catch the eye of potential investors.'

'It's not a bad idea,' said Seb. 'What kind of fundraiser are you thinking?'

'I wondered about an event here by the lake. We could have village fete-style stalls, a barbecue, and give people the chance to try out some of the water sports you're hoping to offer.'

'Not just a pretty face,' said Maggie. 'I'm sure the entire village would be keen to get involved, and Mel down at the school would bring her brass band along whether or not you want her to.'

'I'll speak to her about it when I take Bertie to school next week. How about we coincide with the end of term? That should give enough time for planning permission to be approved.'

'*If* planning permission is approved,' said Seb, twisting his tangled beard between his fingers.

'Don't be such a pessimist,' I said, giving him a nudge. 'It's a brilliant project with very honourable aims. It will also bring job opportunities to the village and open up the lake as a resource for locals. What's not to like?'

'Those planning officers can be tricky customers.'

'Then it's just as well we've got Liv here to charm them, isn't it?' said Maggie. She heaved herself to standing and looked down at Seb. 'Now, let's make a detour to your cabin and you can find me a pair of sharp scissors. I can't stand looking at that flea-ridden carcass on your chin for a moment longer.'

Chapter Twenty-Three

I'd grown used to spending Friday evenings alone, while Rob toured the local boozers with his mates, so it came as a pleasant surprise when three weeks into our stay, Harry suggested a movie night and all residents agreed to participate.

It turned out movie night was a regular event at Lowen Farm, the residents taking turns to pick what film to watch. Our visit coincided with Pat's turn to choose. Given its twelve rating, I wasn't sure *Forrest Gump* was suitable for Bertie, but Pat convinced me it would be fine and I capitulated. I could always take Bertie up to bed if the film became unsuitable.

Pat was already setting up the DVD player when we arrived in the lounge. It was a cosy room, with an entire wall taken up with a long, squishy sofa. A selection of faded beanbags allowed for extra seating, Bertie jumping into one to claim it as soon as we entered the room.

Maggie and Stephan were the next to arrive. 'Ta da,' said Maggie, holding a bottle of Prosecco aloft. 'I thought we should celebrate how well the meeting went today.'

'Oh, yes,' said Pat, 'I'd forgotten to ask how it went.'

'Let's just say I'll eat my wellies if we don't get planning permission. You'd think Liv had spent years as a project manager the way she answered all the bloke's questions.'

'It was a team effort,' I said, experiencing a flush of pride at Maggie's compliment. Facing the planning officer's questions head-on had been exhilarating, a chance to exercise a mind that had lain dormant for years. For the first time in a very long time, I had felt useful, like Liv, rather than Olivia wife of Robert, a piece of arm candy good for parading around at parties and little more.

Harry carried a tray into the room, laden with glasses and bowls of crisps and nuts. 'There are beers in the fridge, Stephan, if you want to fetch them?'

'Sure thing.'

'I've brought some too,' said Seb, walking into the room and handing a bottle of bitter to Pat. Seb flopped down on the sofa beside me and held up his bottle of beer. 'Cheers,' he said, clinking it against my glass. 'Here's to getting the project off to a flying start.'

I looked up at him, and he smiled, holding my gaze. 'I think celebrations may be premature,' I said, taking a sip of my wine.

'Who's the pessimist now? You were amazing earlier.'

'Thank you,' I said, unable to look at Seb in case he saw how happy his compliment made me.

Andrea and Christine arrived, sitting down beside Seb. Andrea reached into her handbag and pulled out a box of chocolates. 'It would have felt wrong to bring anything else, given the film we're watching.'

'Life is like a box of chocolates...'

'Yes, all right, Pat,' said Harry, sitting beside me on the sofa. 'Give it a rest. You've been saying that all day.'

'Well, I think we're ready to hear it from the man himself,' said Pat, pressing play on the DVD player. 'Budge up everyone.'

Everyone on the sofa squashed together, leaving Seb's leg pressing against mine, the smooth skin of his arm sending electric shocks through my own. Bertie shuffled his bean bag back until he was leaning against my legs. He had his own bowl of popcorn and had waded through half before the film had even started.

When it became clear, as much to Pat's embarrassment as my own, that the film was not suitable for Bertie, he ran upstairs to fetch his iPad, then repositioned his bean bag so his back was to the TV, headphones on.

An hour into the film, I lost my battle against tears. I let them stream down my cheeks, hoping that in the darkness no one would notice. A hand reached up and I held my breath as Seb caught a tear with his finger, gently brushing it away from my cheek. I looked at him, the glare from the TV exposing the dampness in his own eyes. Without thinking, I reached for his hand, his fingers interlocking with mine. It felt so natural, I only let go when Bertie looked around to ask how much longer was left of the film.

By the time the end credits rolled onto the screen, the air was full of the sound of sniffing. No one moved to switch on the light, each needing a minute to hold a tissue to their eyes or blow their noses.

'I'm sorry you had to sit out the film,' I told Bertie.

'It's all right,' he said with a shrug. 'I didn't like the kissing. That part was gross. Playing Minecraft was much more fun.'

'Yeah, girls are gross, aren't they?' said Seb, winking at me.

'Top up anyone?' asked Pat, offering out a bottle of wine.

'I'd better get Bertie into bed,' I said, 'but if there's still some left by the time I come back down, I'll join you in a nightcap.'

Bertie let out a dramatic yawn, stretching out his arms above his head. 'I'm too tired to walk upstairs.'

'You're too big for me to carry, so you'll have to. Come on.' I held out a hand, but Bertie curled up into a ball, his fake snoring causing laughter among the assembled adults.

'How about I help you up there?' said Seb. 'Has anyone ever given you a fireman's carry?'

Bertie uncurled himself and frowned at Seb. 'What's a fireman's carry?'

'Stand up and I'll show you. That is, if you're not too tired to stand.'

Bertie climbed off his bean bag and stood in front of Seb. In one swift movement, Seb had a giggling Bertie thrown over his shoulder. Rather than despairing that I'd never get Bertie settled after the excitement, I relished the sound of his giggle. It was wonderful to see the recent change in him, from a quiet, brooding young boy, to one whose eyes sparkled, and who jumped out of bed each morning, desperate to see what the new day would hold.

I wasn't stupid, I knew we were in a honeymoon phase at Lowen Farm and soon the realities of life would encroach on our state of happiness, but I intended to embrace every second while it lasted. It was the least we deserved after our recent stress.

Once in our bedroom, Seb leaned forward and lowered Bertie down. He pulled off his shoes and brought the duvet up to his chin.

'Can I have a story?'

Seb looked at me. 'No,' I said, 'it's way past your bedtime. You'll be in a terrible grump tomorrow if you don't get to sleep now.'

'What are we doing tomorrow?'

'I don't know yet.'

'Actually,' said Seb, 'I need to go into town in the morning to run some errands. There's a train from town straight to the beach. I wondered if you and Bertie would like to come with me? It seems a shame you've not seen any of the local area yet.'

'Ooh yes please,' said Bertie, answering for both of us.

I laughed. 'It doesn't look like I've got much choice.'

'Goodnight, Bertie,' said Seb, ruffling his hair. 'I'll see you in the morning.'

'Good night,' said Bertie, his words caught in a loud yawn.

I walked over and kissed Bertie's cheek. 'Will you be OK here if I go downstairs for a little while?'

'Mmm,' said Bertie, already drifting towards sleep.

'Are you sure you want us tagging along with you tomorrow?' I asked Seb once we were back downstairs.

'I wouldn't have offered if I didn't. Bertie's a great kid, which must make you a great mum, by the way.'

'Thank you. Are you staying for another drink?'

'No, I'd best get home.'

I hid my disappointment behind a smile. 'OK, I'll see you in the morning.'

I joined the others and topped up my glass. Whilst I enjoyed being in their company, I struggled to concentrate on the conversation, my mind straying to the feeling of Seb's hand in mine. I told myself it was the gesture of a friend, and nothing more. But every time my thoughts returned to that moment, a frisson of excitement caught me off guard.

'I'm going to head to bed,' I told my friends. They wished me goodnight, and I made my way upstairs, hoping that a good night's sleep would clear my head of all the foolishness currently filling it.

Chapter Twenty-Four

'Ready for an adventure?' asked Seb. He was leaning against Harry's Land Rover, looking smarter than usual with his newly trimmed beard and thick winter coat.

'Yes,' said Bertie, running up to him. 'Can I sit in the front?'

'As long as your mum doesn't mind?'

'No, that's fine.'

Seb opened the door and lifted Bertie into the passenger seat.

'Do none of you have your own cars?' I asked, climbing up onto the back bench seats.

'No, there's no need. Between this and the quad, we're covered for any trips we need to make. We all contribute to fuel costs and any maintenance needed.'

'It's such a good system. I'm amazed how smoothly things run here.'

Seb switched on the engine, shouting over its noisy growl. 'It doesn't always. Not everyone who comes here fits in. If someone's too individualistic or has a big ego, they don't last long. Likewise, people looking for a free ride. It's why Harry introduced the recommendation system. When she first started up, she'd take in anyone who showed up at her door. That led to a few tricky situations and a couple of scary ones.'

'I can imagine.'

'Do we fit in?' asked Bertie.

'You do. That's why you're still here. All the help you give Harry with the animals and your mum gives me with the lake project, well, that shows the kind of people you are. You're happy to muck in. That's what you have to be like to live here.'

'Why did you come here?' asked Bertie.

Seb didn't reply. I looked at his reflection in the rear-view mirror. His eyes were fixed on the road, the muscles straining in his face as he held them taut. 'It shouldn't take long to reach Liskeard,' he said, ignoring Bertie's question. 'The roads are nice and quiet at this time of year.'

As the Land Rover picked up speed, the engine grew louder, making conversation impossible. We pulled out of a junction and joined the dual carriageway, smoke spewing out of the Land Rover's exhaust. Seb clicked the indicator, and we joined a smaller road, until we found ourselves in a residential area on the outskirts of town.

'I'll park at the station,' he shouted. 'Are you OK to explore for a bit while I run some errands? I need to go to the bank and pick up a few things from the hardware shop.'

'Of course,' I shouted back.

At the car park, we parted ways, agreeing to meet again in an hour. All Bertie wanted to do was go to the park and join in a game of football a group of boys were playing. I insisted on at least getting a glimpse of the town, leading him past a series of independent shops and cafes. But after fifteen minutes of exploring, his pestering became too much, and I relented and took him to the park, where the local boys welcomed an extra player.

While Bertie played football, I pulled out my phone and made the call I'd been putting off all week.

'Hello?'

'Hi, Marion, it's Liv.'

'Olivia? Is this about Rob?'

'What do you mean?'

'Oh, I assumed he'd have been in touch by now.'

'No, he hasn't, and I still don't know where he is.'

'Right, well, if you must know, he's staying with us at the minute.'

'Since when?'

'Since two weeks ago.'

'And none of you thought it might be a good idea to tell me? That, oh, I don't know, maybe he'd like to get in contact with his son?'

Marion let out a long sigh. 'There's no need to be so dramatic. Poor Robert has been through a lot.'

I tried to splutter out a reply, but couldn't squeeze the words past my anger.

'If he was here, I'm sure he'd have spoken to you, but I'm afraid he and Hugo are out playing golf.'

'I see. Well, you know what, Marion? When he gets in from his game of golf, perhaps you could pass on a message for me?'

'Go ahead, I've got a pen and paper here.'

'Good. Tell him I'll be contacting a solicitor this week to begin divorce proceedings.'

I hung up the phone, my hand shaking, my breaths ragged. If my three weeks at Lowen Farm had taught me anything, it was that I deserved more than someone who'd prioritise a game of golf over his wife and son's welfare. Rob didn't know we'd landed on our feet. For all he knew, we were still squashing into my sister's tiny terrace, or sleeping in a homeless shelter somewhere. And what did he think we were doing for money? What did he think was happening to Bertie's education?

By the time we met Seb back at the car, I'd calmed down a little, not least thanks to a call with Cass, who'd confirmed

I was making the right decision. She'd led me back over my marriage, reminding me of every time I'd cried on her shoulder about the other women, or how little Rob seemed to like, let alone love me.

'Everything OK?' asked Seb, frowning as he looked at me.

'Yes, fine, why?'

'I don't know, it's just you seem a bit... never mind. I've got our tickets. The next train arrives in ten minutes, so we'd better get a move on.'

Bertie spent the entire journey to Looe with his face pressed against the window. Despite growing up fast, he hadn't lost his wonder at the world around him, and I prayed he wouldn't change too much in the coming years. He helped me see the world through his eyes, marvelling as a river tripped and stuttered along the base of a tree-lined valley before widening out as it opened itself up to the sea.

'Wow, what a beautiful train journey,' I said as we stepped off the train and onto the platform.

'Yes it is, isn't it? I never get tired of it. Now, how about we start with the amusement arcade, then have a walk along the harbour and beach, before rewarding ourselves with fish and chips?'

'Sounds good,' I said.

'And even better if we get to have an ice cream,' added Bertie.

'Ice cream? It's freezing.' I shivered to emphasise my point.

'Mum, you have to have ice cream at the beach.' Bertie rolled his eyes then fell into step beside Seb as we began walking towards the town.

I hung back, watching them. It was easier to have fun with a child if you weren't responsible for the less interesting parts. Even so, as Seb and Bertie chatted away, I couldn't remember Rob ever being so at ease in his son's company. It always felt as though Bertie were an inconvenience to Rob, something that stopped him from living life to the full. He played the role easily enough at school cricket matches, or family barbecues, but I'd never seen him get down on the floor to play Lego, or read a bedtime story. Ever since Bertie was born, all practical duties had been left to me, but I'd hoped as Bertie grew older, Rob would connect with his son. I supposed there was still time, although not much could be achieved with zero contact.

In the end, we had to drag Bertie out of the amusement arcade, tempting him with the promise of an ice cream as soon as we reached the beach. Heads down, we tried to ignore the cold gusts of wind as we followed the path of the river toward the sea.

I screamed as something wet landed in my hair. 'What the...?' My fingers reached up, coming away caked in green and white slime. 'Oh no.'

'What's wrong, Mum?'

'I think a seagull has pooped on my head.'

'Let me see,' said Bertie. I bent my head, and he laughed. 'That's so gross.'

'A, it's not funny, and B, being pooped on by a seagull is lucky.'

'Doesn't look very lucky to me,' said Bertie. 'Don't worry, I'll get them for you.'

Bertie began chasing seagulls across the beach with gusto. Seb pulled a tissue from his pocket. 'Shall I?' he said, pointing to my hair.

'Yes, please.'

He stood beside me, picking out strands of curls and running his tissue across them.

'I love your curls.'

'Even covered in bird shit?'

'Even then. Hey, are you sure everything's all right?'

'Well, it was until five minutes ago.'

'No, I mean earlier, after you'd been to the park. You looked kind of sad.'

'If you must know, I'd just told my mother-in-law I want a divorce.'

'You're divorcing your mother-in-law?'

I turned to look at him and saw his eyes were glinting. 'No, of course not, although I would if I could. It turns out my spineless husband has moved back in with his parents but not thought to let me know.'

'You didn't speak to him?'

'No, he was out playing golf.'

Seb grimaced. 'He sounds like a real catch.'

'I'm sure he could make someone very happy, but that person will never be me. I've realised that since we came to stay at Lowen Farm. We were only together for Bertie.'

'How will Bertie take the news?'

'I've no idea. I don't even know where to start with divorce, but I'll never stop Rob seeing Bertie, whatever happens. Are you nearly done freeing my hair of poop?'

'Yeah, there's still some in there, but it will take half a bottle of shampoo to get rid of it. In the meantime, how about we get some fish and chips? And Liv?'

'Yes.'

'I'm here for you and will help you in any way I can.'

'Thank you.' I reached across and squeezed Seb's hand. His thumb stroked my palm, and it was only when a seagull dive-bombed us that we pulled away.

Chapter Twenty-Five

'How was it?'

When I walked into the kitchen, Harry was on her hands and knees laying mouse traps. 'Good, although I'm not sure Beryl trusts me. She still hasn't left me alone in the shop and I've been there for weeks now.'

Harry looked at me and laughed. 'You don't think she's going to be in her flat watching TV with her feet up, do you?'

'She said her joints were playing up and she needed a rest when she employed me.'

Harry laughed again. 'A rest from the work, maybe, not a rest from the gossip. She'll be there with you every day, mark my words. Beryl prides herself on knowing everything about everyone. She wouldn't risk missing out on any tidbits of information. She's all right, just watch what you say around her.'

'I think it's too late for that. MI5 missed a trick. She would have made an excellent spy with her cuddly old lady act. She had me spilling my life story in under five minutes. Anyway, how are the preparations going?'

'Great. Maggie's made a hundred cupcakes and Stephan is currently in the lounge blowing up balloons.'

'What would you like me to do?'

'I thought we could lay an Easter egg hunt through the woods. Seb's going to make a start after lunch. Could you help him?'

'Sure. What's the prize?'

'The winner gets to name and adopt one of the lambs. Obviously it will stay here, but their prize will include visiting rights.'

'That's a lovely idea, but what will happen when the time comes for the lamb to... you know... end up as someone's roast dinner?'

'We'll keep the winning lamb as a breeder. That way, it will avoid a sticky end.'

'I see you've thought of everything. Where's Seb?'

'Fixing a leak in my annexe. Go and find him if you like.'

As I walked through to the annexe, my newly formed business mind whirred with the possibilities the planned open day would afford us. The entire school had been invited up to the farm for the afternoon. Not only would it be an excellent test run for future events, it would give me a great piece of evidence for the funding bid I was writing.

A *proven track record* was one requirement for the lengthy form.

I paused at the door to Harry's annexe. Although not out of bounds, since arriving at Lowen Farm I'd realised how much Harry must need something of her own, so had never invaded her space. Although I knew she wasn't there, I knocked on the door anyway.

'Come in. Oh, hi, Liv.' Seb was up on a ladder, fiddling with a light fitting. 'How was work?'

'Good. I heard all about the war Carol is raging on cats in her garden and Mavis's naughty neighbours have been at it again.'

'Crikey, I don't know where they get the energy.'

'What are you doing?'

'Water's leaking through this light fitting and I don't know why. What Harry needs is a professional, but she can't afford to call one out, so I'm trying to do a bodge job with the help of my assistant Google.'

'Good luck. Harry said she wants us to lay an Easter egg hunt in the woods.'

'Yeah. Just give me a second to get this sorted and we can get started. Harry's already written out the clues and there's a chocolate egg to go with each one. All we have to do is hide them.'

'Sounds easy enough.'

'Hmm,' said Seb, frowning in concentration as his hand felt around in the ceiling cavity. As his arm reached further, his T-shirt lifted, exposing a flat stomach toned from manual labour rather than the gym. I tore my eyes away, not wanting to be mistaken for one of the *peevs* Beryl was so fond of discussing.

'This place is different from what I was expecting,' I said, looking around Harry's domain.

'What were you expecting?'

'I don't know, something a little more chaotic, maybe?'

'That's the last thing Harry needs with all she has to juggle and keep in her head.'

'True.'

Harry's living room was sparse, but in a cool Scandi way. The walls were painted white, and rather than carpet, stripped wooden boards covered the floor. A small bookshelf sat beside a wicker high-backed armchair, but other than the books, the room was free from clutter of any kind.

'Are these Harry's grandparents?' I asked, picking up the only framed photograph in the room.

'Yeah, they were an amazing couple. I didn't know them all that well, but we came to visit them a couple of times. They left big shoes to fill. It's no wonder Harry feels the pressure to work so hard. Right, I think I've done all I can here. I'm going to have to go up onto the roof, as I suspect that's where the problem lies, but not today. We've got an Easter egg hunt to lay.'

As Seb climbed down the ladder, his foot slipped. I watched in horror as in what felt like slow motion, he lost his balance, his arms flailing above him as he landed flat on his back on the wooden floor.

'Oh my God.' I rushed over to where he lay groaning. His eyes were closed, and I held his face in my hands. 'Seb? Can you hear me?'

His eyes opened, and a smile tugged at his lips. He pierced me with *that* stare, and I removed my hands from his face before they could turn clammy. 'Are you badly hurt?'

Seb winced. 'The only thing I've hurt is my pride... and my bum.'

'Ah, right, well, I'm not sure there's much I can do for bruised bottoms.' I held out a hand, and he took it, letting me pull him until he was sitting inches from me. 'At least you didn't have far to fall,' I said, trying to break through the thick air between us. The annexe felt suddenly stuffy, like all the oxygen had been sucked out.

With a cough, Seb broke eye contact and turned towards the ladder. 'I shouldn't have taken my boots off. It's a rooky error, climbing a ladder in socks, but my boots were covered in mud.'

'Don't worry about it, as long as you're all right, that's the main thing. Come on, let's get that trail laid before sixty children arrive demanding chocolate.'

Chapter Twenty-Six

The farm was in chaos. Children tore between the animals, fields and woods, high on sugar from all the chocolate eggs they'd consumed. Two children had already thrown up, and I was keeping a close eye on Bertie, who'd collected more than his fair share of chocolate. Parents seemed happy to let their children run wild, content that with teachers also present, no harm would come to their offspring. Given that Mrs Grange was completely focused on an in-depth discussion about brass bands with Stephan, I felt the need to keep an eye on the hordes of feral children, fearing potential lawsuits should they come to any harm.

There had been a near miss when a cocky seven-year-old decided the pigs were too cramped in their enclosure and left the gate open for them to run wild. I reached them just in time, the large sow grunting in protest as I shoved her and her offspring back behind their fence.

Another child had found it hilarious to torment one of our goats by pulling its tail until the offended animal turned its horns on the child and butted it a safe distance away.

Given the surrounding mayhem, I didn't notice the battered Ford Escort pull up, and only became aware of my family's arrival due to the screams from Bertie as he raced across the driveway. I chased after him, flinging myself at Cass as soon as she stepped out of the car.

'Wow, that's a greeting and a half.'

'I can't believe you came.'

'I said we would.'

'I know, but you didn't sound sure you'd be able to get the kids out of school early.'

'If anyone asks, they're at the dentist. I brought someone else along too.' Cass disentangled herself from my arms and opened the passenger side door. I looked past her and burst into tears at the sight of my dad smiling through the window.

'Hola, cariño.'

'Hola, Papa.'

'Give me a hand with the wheelchair, would you?' asked Cass, wrestling the cumbersome contraption out of the boot. Between us, we got Dad out of the car and into his much-resented chair.

'U... u... I... had to... s... s... see where....'

'Dad wanted to see where you're living,' said Cass, squeezing her father's hand. 'And he's been desperate to see Bertie.'

Bertie grinned and climbed onto his grandpa's lap. He wrapped his arms around his namesake's neck and squeezed until Dad choked.

'I think Bertie's missed you too, Dad.'

'Gramps, can I push your wheelchair?'

'I'd... be... o... honoured.'

'Great. I'm going to show you everything. Except our bedroom 'cause that's upstairs, but I'll show you everything else. There are tons of animals here and Harry lets me help look after them. The pigs are my favourite, but the goats are funny, and the lambs are really cute, so I guess I have lots of favourites. Hey Gramps, you could come and see the lake too. Seb can put you on the back of his quad bike.'

Before I could intervene in Bertie's ambitious plans, he'd wheeled Dad off around the side of the farmhouse, ready to begin his guided tour. Jake and Emmy ran after him. If they minded being passed over in favour of Dad, they weren't showing it.

'I'm worried I'll never get them home,' said Cass. 'Have you got time to show me around, or are you on duty?'

I looked at my watch. It was four o'clock, and I'd been watching other people's children like a hawk since they arrived at one. 'I think I've earned a break. How about I show you around the farmhouse first, then take you down to the lake?'

'Lead the way.' Cass linked arms with me, apologising that Jasper hadn't been able to get out of his shift.

'We're not going anywhere anytime soon, so he'll have plenty of time to come for a visit.'

The farmhouse was full of bodies, adults leaning against worktops drinking glasses of cider, children grabbing handfuls of cake from the various tins laid out in the dining room. I kept my tour of the farmhouse short and sweet, wanting my sister to myself rather than sharing her with half the village.

'Will the kids be OK if we explore the grounds?'

'Yes, they'll be fine. Bertie knows his way around and everyone from Lowen Farm will keep an eye on him.'

'I think I'm more worried about Dad. God knows what they're doing with him.'

'Good point. How about I prise Dad away from Bertie and we take him down to the lake? I was going to suggest we walk, but I'm sure Harry would let me borrow the Land Rover to drive him down there.'

'OK, you go check with Harry, I'll find Dad.'

Ten minutes later, with the help of Stephan, we had Dad in the Land Rover, his wheelchair stowed in the back and were heading down the track to the woods. I threw regular glances at Dad to check he was all right, but each time he had his eyes trained on the scenery around him, a contented smile on his face.

'It's lovely, isn't it?'

Dad nodded, turning to me with a smile. 'B.... beautiful.' He pointed a finger at me and gave a thumbs up.

'Yes, Dad, I'm very happy here. I'm not sure how long we'll be able to stay, but I'm going to enjoy every second we get to spend here.'

At the end of the track, I parked up the Land Rover and helped Cass get Dad settled in his wheelchair.

'The track is pretty hard going from here to the lake. You wait here with Dad, and I'll see if Seb's home and can help us.'

'Ooh yes, I'm looking forward to meeting your mystery man.'

'He's not my mystery man.'

'Whatever you say,' said Cass with a wink.

I left Cass and Dad admiring the primroses and daffodils and ran towards Seb's cabin. I found him out on his deck, beer in one hand, book in the other. 'Hiding?' I asked.

Seb looked up and grinned. 'You caught me.'

'Look, I know you're enjoying a bit of peace, but I wondered if you could help me with something?'

'Does it involve children? One of those feral beasts kicked me in the shin when I wouldn't give him a fifth Easter egg, and another put a handful of worms down my pants when I was bending over to feed the chickens. It's not funny,' he said as I tried not to laugh.

'I promise there's not a child in sight. My sister has brought my dad for a visit. We've got him as far as we could in the Land Rover, but he's in a wheelchair since his stroke and I know he'd love to see the lake.'

'You want a hand getting him down the track?'

'If you don't mind?'

'Not at all.'

Seb laid down his book and beer and followed me back to where Cass and Dad were waiting.

'Dad, Cass, this is Seb. Seb, this is my sister, Cass and my dad, Alberto.'

'Is that a Spanish name?'

'Si,' said Dad, holding out a shaking hand. Seb took it and began chatting to Dad in fluent Spanish.

'Hang on, since when do you speak Spanish?'

'Since I spent a year in South America,' said Seb, taking hold of the wheelchair and pushing it toward the lake.

'Well, he is indeed mysterious,' said Cass as we walked a few paces behind the men. 'And pretty hot, even with that awful beard.'

'You should have seen it before. That's the new, improved version.'

'Aside from working with a sexy man who's prepared to push your father and his heavy wheelchair along a dirt track, how is everything else going?'

'Good. Really good. Bertie loves school. He seems to get on with everyone, but has a group of five close friends. They come over to the farm most weeks either for dinner or to help with the animals. And my job's going well, both my jobs I should say. We're making great progress with the lake project and have meetings lined up with potential investors next week. The shop's good too. It doesn't require much brain power, but it makes me feel part of the village, and Beryl's lovely, in her slightly odd way.'

'I'm so pleased. It's amazing to see you growing into yourself, finding your passion.'

'Working in a corner shop?'

'No, the lake project. I can tell how passionate you are about it, and it's about time you put that brain of yours to good use. I almost don't dare ask, but how are things on the Rob front?'

'Still no news. I know he's still with his parents. I've heard nothing since dropping my bombshell in Marion's lap, but I bit the bullet and called again last week. It's important he sees Bertie, even if he won't see me.'

'How did that go?'

'He was out playing golf again, if you can believe it. Marion told me he'll be in touch soon to arrange time with Bertie, but there's still no word. I feel awful ending our marriage via my mother-in-law, but he didn't leave me with much choice. I think I did it in part to force him out of the woodwork, but clearly it didn't work.'

'I'm sure it will all work out in time, it will have to. Rob can't stay in hiding forever.'

Chapter Twenty-Seven

The gnarled fist jabbed in the direction of the lake. Seb bent down in front of Dad's wheelchair and spoke to him in quiet Spanish. He then waited patiently as Dad forced words from between his stubborn lips. Seb walked over to where Cass and I stood beside the jetty.

'Alberto would like to go out on the lake.'

I looked at Cass. 'I'm not sure that's such a good idea.'

'Is he at risk of falling ill?' asked Seb.

'Well, I suppose technically he could have another stroke, but no, it's more how we'd get him in the boat. What do you think, Cass?'

Cass shrugged. 'I'm not sure.' She peered down into the water where the small rowing boat sat bobbing on the water. 'There's no way we could get him in from here. Would it be possible to bring the boat up onto the beach and get him in that way?'

'Yes, quite possible. Liv, would that be OK with you?'

Seb had placed a hand on my arm, and I flushed as Cass saw it and smirked. 'If you think it's doable, then I don't see why not.'

'There won't be room in there for all of us,' said Cass. 'How about I help you get Dad into the boat, then you two go out on the water with him and I'll head back to the farm and check on the kids. Will you be all right helping Liv get Dad back up to the farmhouse after, Seb?'

'Yeah, sure. But if you'd rather go out in the boat, I don't mind going up and minding the kids?'

'God, I wouldn't inflict that on you,' said Cass, 'and besides, there's no way we'd be able to wheel Dad back up the track without you.'

'OK, if you're sure.'

Seb untied the boat from its moorings and pulled it up onto the beach. Although the wheelchair was heavy and ungainly, Dad himself was light, his once strong muscles wasting away since the stroke stole his movement. Seb lifted Dad easily into his arms, and placed him in the front of the boat, where he could lean against the gunwale.

'Wait here with your dad,' said Seb. 'I'll be back in a minute.' He ran off toward Pat's cabin, appearing minutes later with a selection of cushions.

'You're my guest of honour, Alberto. I thought the least you deserved was a little comfort.'

Seb arranged the cushions around Dad to make sure he was secure and not at risk of falling. We all knew the cushions were for Dad's safety rather than comfort, but the way Seb had retained Dad's dignity with his pretence brought a lump to my throat.

'Liv, you sit in the back by the tiller. I'll give us a push off, then climb in the middle with the oars.'

I took up my position in the boat and Seb pushed hard against it, the sound of gravel on wood soon replaced by the splash of water. Seb waded through the shallows, climbed into the boat and picked up the oars.

From the shore, Cass whooped and cheered. I turned to look at her and saw tears rolling down her cheeks. I was keeping my own in check, just. To see Dad out of his nursing home was one thing, to see him out on a lake, his eyes bright, a breeze teasing his hair was quite another.

Seb's muscles strained as the oars sliced through the water, peppering jewel-like droplets onto the lake's surface as the wood rotated in the air. He kept up a stream of fluent Spanish. My language skills had grown rusty from lack of use, but I could follow enough to know he was telling Dad all about the lake project, and specifically my role in it. Dad's face was creased in a wide smile, his eyes watering, although whether from the breeze or tears was impossible to tell.

At the far end of the lake, Seb paused his rowing, allowing the boat to bob lazily beneath branches which were displaying the first buds of spring leaves. Insects teased the lake's surface, performing acrobatic displays for us in the unusually warm spring sunshine.

'Did I tell you about my swimming, Dad?'

Dad shook his head.

'Harry's had me swimming in this lake every morning since I got here.'

Dad mimed an exaggerated shiver.

'Yes, it's bloody freezing. Harry's promised me it will warm up in the summer, but I'm not sure I believe her. Mum and Dad met at a lake, didn't you, Dad?'

Dad nodded, a faraway look in his eyes.

Seb turned to Dad. 'Was that in Spain?'

Dad shook his head.

'It was at Lake Garda in Italy,' I said. 'Me and Cass used to love hearing the story. Is it OK if I tell it, Dad?' Dad smiled by way of an answer. 'They were both eighteen, just finished school and they'd each travelled to Lake Garda to work in a hotel for the summer. Mum was waitressing, Dad was behind the bar. Mum couldn't speak Spanish back then, and Dad had very little English, so they communicated in the little Italian they both knew. My mum always used to say Dad wooed her by talking about pasta, as he'd only made it as far as the food module in his Italian classes. Anyway, by the end of the summer, they were engaged.'

'Engaged?' Seb turned to Dad. 'How on earth did you manage that when you couldn't speak the same language?' Dad did his best attempt at a raised eyebrow, and Seb laughed. 'Alberto, you sly old dog.'

'Ro...romantic,' said Dad.

'Anyway,' I said, keen to move the conversation on from my dad's non-verbal seduction techniques. 'Dad followed Mum back to England and the rest, as they say, is history.'

'Did you ever go back to Lake Garda as a family?'

'No, me and Cass begged and begged. But even if we'd had the money, I think Mum and Dad wanted to keep it as their special place. Is that right?'

Dad nodded, his eyes cloudy as he travelled back to a time and place when his body had worked properly, and he still had the love of his life by his side. I watched him, wondering if I'd ever get to experience a love like my parents had shared. Don't get me wrong, their marriage wasn't perfect, but at the heart of it was a deep respect and friendship that always saw them through challenging times. I swallowed a lump in my throat as I remembered the way mum and dad would dance around the house together, play Scrabble in the evening, take turns to make each other cups of tea in the morning. Simple gestures of love that were taken for granted until they were gone.

Sensing the shift in mood, Seb attempted to bring us back to the present. 'I'm afraid our lake can't compete with Lake Garda in size or grandeur, but I'm hopeful we can create some special memories of our own here.'

'Un lugar feliz. With... Liv,' said Dad.

Seb's cheeks flared red, and he almost dropped his oars. 'Oh, um, well...'

'He was talking about the project, Dad. We're going to make amazing memories with the people who come and stay here.'

'To... gether.'

'Yes,' I said. 'Together.' Unable to look at Seb, I focused my gaze over his shoulder to where my dad sat, head tilted to the sky, his skin less creased than I had seen in a long time. If I ever found even a fraction of the love my parents had shared, I'd be happy with my lot.

Chapter Twenty-Eight

Despite labelling it as a meeting, Seb had invited me to his cabin after dinner and promised wine beside an open fire. I didn't want to look as though I expected anything more than a productive evening pooling ideas for the project, so had selected a clean pair of jeans and my favourite teal jumper to wear. The temptation to apply more makeup than usual was strong, but given we'd be eating dinner with the other residents first, I was reluctant to draw attention to myself and raise any eyebrows.

Since deciding to end my marriage, I felt three stone lighter, as though the weight of waiting for Rob to hand me my fate had been dragging me down. There had been no calls from Marion's landline since my rash announcement, and I was no further forward with divorce proceedings, but at least I felt more in control.

'Can I come to Seb's house with you?' asked Bertie.

'No, we've talked about this. You've got your first band concert tomorrow. You need to get an early night.'

'What if I can't sleep?'

'Maggie and Stephan will be downstairs, so if you can't sleep, find them and they'll tuck you in again. Mind you, after cleaning out all the animals with Harry after school, I don't think you'll have any trouble sleeping. Now go and wash your hands ready for dinner.'

Bertie shuffled out of the room, and I checked the messages on my phone. Nothing.

'Ready,' said Bertie, waiting for me by the door. I'd told him Rob was back in town, but Bertie hadn't yet asked to see him. I'd need to arrange a meeting soon, but had decided to give Bertie time to settle into his new school before disrupting his life further.

It was Andrea and Christine's turn to cook dinner. Having decided to stay on an extra month, their time at Lowen Farm was now drawing to a close. The healthy vegetable casserole they served was greeted with thanks, but as Pat and Harry pushed cauliflower around their bowls, it was clear they were hankering after something more meaty.

The last thing I wanted was to offend Andrea and Christine, but with my stomach doing somersaults, it was hard to force the tasteless dish down and my bowl was still half-full by the end of the meal.

'Sorry,' I said, as Andrea cleared my bowl. 'Me and Bertie had a big lunch and are still full.'

Bertie kept his eyes on the table, happy to go along with my lie.

'It appears everyone had a big lunch today,' said Christine with a sigh. 'I'm sorry everyone, I'm trying the approach of healthy body, healthy mind, but it was rather lacking in the taste department, wasn't it?'

'No, it was lovely,' lied Harry.

'Right,' said Seb. 'We'd best get going.'

'I'll just get Bertie in his pyjamas, then I'll be with you.'

'Pyjamas? But it's nowhere near bedtime,' grumbled Bertie.

'And you're not going to bed yet. Maggie and Stephan have said you can stay up and watch TV with them, but if you're already in your jimjams, that's one less job for them.'

'Fine,' said Bertie, sighing as he followed me upstairs.

In the end, it took me a further half an hour before Bertie was in his pyjamas and I was ready to leave. 'Sorry,' I said, jumping into the Land Rover. 'Bertie's so excited about his first brass band concert tomorrow, he wouldn't stop talking.'

'Don't worry, it will have given the wine longer to chill.'

'Yum,' I said, licking my lips at the thought.

As soon as we arrived at Seb's cabin, he set about lighting a fire in the fire pit beside the porch. I settled down in a wicker chair, a blanket across my legs. Seb appeared with a bottle and two glasses and poured out the wine.

'I'm sorry to drag you all the way out here, but I wanted to talk to you about something,' said Seb, twisting the stem of his wine glass between his fingers.

'About the project? Yes, I know, that's why I'm here.'

'No. I... we...' He took my hand and laced his fingers into mine. 'Am I imagining this?'

I looked at the man I'd grown to have so much respect for. The man I now considered among my best friends. The man I simultaneously knew so little about, yet felt I knew all I needed to. 'No, you're not imagining it.'

'I don't know if it's residual feelings from when we were young, unfinished business, or something new that's worth exploring. What I know is that now isn't the right time to take things any further.' Seb unlaced his fingers, holding his hands in his lap.

'Right, I see.'

'Liv, it's not because I don't want to. That's not it at all.'

'Then why?'

'You've only been single for a couple of months and you're about to embark on what could be a messy divorce. It wouldn't be fair to drag you into some new relationship when you've got all that going on.'

'Isn't that for me to decide?'

'There are things I haven't told you about my past. I don't feel in a position to risk our friendship. You're too important to me. What if you end up patching things up with Rob?'

'Not going to happen.'

'But you've not even seen him or spoken to him. How can you be so sure?'

'I just am.'

'I think we should wait. I'm prepared to wait for you as long as you need.'

'And what if I meet up with Rob? What if I draw a line under my marriage and am a free agent?'

'Then we can revisit this conversation.'

I downed the wine left in my glass and stood up.

'Liv, there's no need to go.'

'Yes, there is. Seb, the feelings I have for you... at first, I thought I was just harking back to a teenage crush. Then I thought I was on the rebound. But now? Seb, I've never felt anything like this. I've never met anyone like you. So, yes, we will return to this conversation, but right now, there's a call I need to make.'

I leaned over and kissed Seb's cheek, then pulled back, my hand still on his neck. I turned to go, but he grabbed my wrist and pulled me back to him. His lips met mine, our teeth clashed, his beard scratched my skin, but none of it mattered. He pulled me onto his lap, hands clasping locks of my hair as my own gripped his neck. And then he pulled away, breaking the spell.

'Sorry.'

'Why?'

'I shouldn't have done that.'

I leaned forward, trying to recapture the magic of moments ago. Seb shifted back in his chair, and with the gentlest of pushes, moved me off his lap. I took his hand and pressed it to my lips. 'I'd better make that call.' Without looking back, I jumped down from his deck and set off into the woods.

It wasn't until the farmhouse came into view that my heart rate returned to normal, and I felt able to make the phone call I was dreading. I sat on a tree stump and pulled my phone from my pocket. Marion answered on the third ring.

'Marion, it's Olivia. I need to speak to Rob.'

'I'm afraid he's not available.'

'Then give me his mobile number.'

'I can't do that.'

'I'll tell you what, Marion. I'm going to ring your house every five minutes from now until Rob finally agrees to speak to me. There are things we have to discuss, and he can't keep putting it off forever. What about his son? Doesn't he want to see Bertie, even if he's cut all ties with me? Now, either he is genuinely out, in which case you can give me his mobile number, or he's hiding in your house.

If it's the latter, please fetch him for me and reassure him I won't bite.'

With a loud sigh, I heard a click as Marion rested the receiver on her telephone table, and then the faint sound of her high heels on the polished floor. Just as I was about to give up hope of ever getting hold of my husband, his voice came down the line.

'Olivia.'

'Rob, at last, the wanderer returns.' I waited for some sort of explanation for his prolonged absence in our lives, but none was forthcoming. 'We need to meet. There are things we need to discuss.'

'Tell me where and when and I'll be there.'

'Really?'

'Yes, you're right. I can't keep hiding forever.'

Chapter Twenty-Nine

I wiped my sweaty hands on my jeans and took a deep breath. Warm orange light spilled from the pub windows and the noise of lively chatter met me through the door. It was silly to be so nervous; I was meeting the man I'd shared my life with for eight years, and yet I had no idea what version of him would greet me.

But I had to do this. How could I possibly move on without ending the previous chapter?

It was easy to find Rob in the busy bar. All I had to do was follow the direction of the hungry female eyes, which kept straying towards him. I couldn't blame them, you couldn't fault Rob in appearance, but if they knew what he was like, they might not be so keen.

'Olivia,' said Rob, standing to greet me and kissing me on both cheeks.

'Rob. Are you OK for a drink?'

Rob downed the third of a pint he had left and handed me his glass. 'A pint of lager, please.'

I kicked myself for my generosity. Rob may have gone bankrupt, but I doubted he was working two jobs to make ends meet. A far more likely scenario was that he was withdrawing regular amounts from the bank of Mum and Dad. I should have made him pay for his own beer.

After disentangling myself from a conversation with the over-friendly barman, I carried our drinks back to the table. I'd opted for lemonade, the safest bet if I wanted to keep my wits about me.

'You look well,' said Rob, his eyes scanning me, a frown crossing his face as he took in my natural hair.

'So do you,' I said. He did look good. His flawless skin had turned the colour of demerara sugar, the same colour it always went after a holiday. His hair shone, flopping down from his side parting, and his crisp white shirt and chinos looked freshly pressed. The last thing he looked like was a man who had lost everything.

'So,' I said, 'where have you been for the past three months?'

Rob dismissed my question with a wave of his hand.

'I'm serious, Rob. As your wife and mother to your child, the least you owe me is an explanation.'

Rob sighed and took a long draught of his beer. 'I had to get away, you know, after all that happened. I was holed up at Dad's place in France for a couple of months, but God, it's boring there on your own.'

'That must have been hard for you.'

'It was,' he said, missing the irony of my words. 'Look, Olivia, I'm so sorry for doing a bunk and leaving you to deal with everything. I suppose I had some sort of breakdown.'

I refrained from saying that he was lucky to have had that option, and a house in southern France to do it in at that. What would have happened to Bertie if I'd lost my shit?

'I let everyone down, you, my employees, Mum and Dad. It was hard coming back, facing up to what I'd done.'

'And what was it you did, exactly? I knew nothing about our financial troubles until the bailiffs turned up at our door.'

'Well, you wouldn't have, would you? You never took any interest in the business.'

I choked on my lemonade. Never took any interest? More like he wouldn't ever let me. 'You were about to tell me what went wrong.'

'I was screwed over. I was a mug. The guys who persuaded me to go into the development were really convincing.'

'And you didn't do due diligence before going into partnership with them?'

'Due diligence?' Rob laughed. 'Where did you learn that, an episode of *Judge Judy*?' He laughed again, taking another glug of his pint.

Before I had a chance to get angry, a realisation dawned on me. For all Rob's talk, for all the showing off and expensive luxuries, sitting in front of me was a man who was crap at his job. A man who lacked the skills to run a successful company. He wasn't a bad man, just a man whose competence didn't match up to his ego. I almost felt sorry for him and wondered, if, given free rein over his life, what he actually would have wanted to do? I doubted it would be property development. He seemed to enjoy the idea of his job more than the reality.

'Rob, we need to talk about us.'

'Yes, Mum told me about your mad moment. You're not serious about getting a divorce, are you? I thought if I left you to calm down, you'd come to your senses.'

'I'm sorry, Rob, but my mind's made up.'

'But things were fine before. All this business with the money is just a blip. I'll have a new business up and running in no time.'

'Rob, things might have been fine for you, but they weren't for me.'

'But I gave you everything.'

'Did you? What about all the other women?'

'What other women?' Rob's tone was outraged, but he fiddled with his pint glass and couldn't look me in the eye.

'Rob,' I said, placing a hand on his. 'There's no need to lie anymore. I'm not upset, I'm not angry, I just want the truth.'

'You make it sound like I slept with an endless stream of women. There was only ever the odd one-night stand at a work do. Nothing serious.'

'Maybe not to you, but that's not the kind of marriage I want. You did a very honourable thing when you married me, but did you ever truly love me?'

'Did you ever truly love *me*?' His tone was accusatory. I'd demanded honesty from him. Now it was my turn.

'I loved the idea of being married to you.'

'Thanks, that's got to be the world's worst compliment.'

'Sorry, but it's important we're honest. You want a certain kind of wife, and I'm not it. I've done my best over the years to pretend to be what you want, but it just isn't me. I think we'd both be better off starting again.'

'Mum will be furious.'

'If it's money she's worried about, she needn't be. Given the state of our finances, I don't intend to ask for anything, and I certainly wouldn't dream of going after your parents' money. Anyway, it doesn't matter what Marion thinks. What do you think? Do you really want to stay married to me?'

Rob stared at his pint, then slowly shook his head.

'That's what I thought. But I'd like us to stay friends. We're going to be tied to each other for life, given we share a son. The least we can do is try to get on for his sake.'

'I'd like to see him.'

'Of course. We'll have to work out some sort of custody arrangement. Given we're now living a little way from each other, it would work best if you had him on weekends. How often is something we can decide on later. How does that sound?'

'Very reasonable. Olivia, I know I've not always been the best dad to Bertie, but I'd like to do better. I've missed him these past few months. It's surprised me just how much.'

I smiled at Rob, thinking how much nicer he seemed now I didn't have to be married to him. I could imagine a future where we stayed friends. Perhaps we could meet up for Bertie's birthday celebrations, or for Christmas. We didn't work as a couple, but there was nothing to say we couldn't co-parent successfully.

With nothing left to say for the time being, we said our goodbyes, agreeing to each instruct a solicitor and arrange a time for Rob to visit Bertie. I left the pub with a spring in my step. There was someone I needed to see. Now I was as good as a free agent, there was nothing to stand in my and Seb's way.

Chapter Thirty

After calling in to the farmhouse and confirming Bertie was asleep, I borrowed Harry's Land Rover and drove as fast as I could down to the lake. I ran to Seb's cabin, hammering on the door and peering through windows.

'He's not in,' came a voice through the twilight.

'Oh, Pat, you made me jump.'

'Sorry. I heard all the banging. Is everything all right?'

'Yes, I just need to speak to Seb. It's quite urgent. Do you know where he is?'

'Out on the lake, I think. I saw him heading down there with his fishing gear.'

Fishing? There was so much about Seb I didn't know and couldn't wait to discover. 'Thanks, Pat. I'll go and find him.'

'Good, good. I need to get back to my chess set. I'm practising again for the first time in years. Your son is coming perilously close to beating me, and we can't have that.'

I laughed, thanked Pat again, and ran down to the water's edge. Squinting through the fading light, I could make out the rowing boat bobbing in the middle of the lake. Seb had his back to me, staring out at the water, a fishing rod in his hands.

'Seb?'

He spun around, and the boat wobbled. I watched him raise his hand as though shielding his eyes from the sun which had long since set. My arms scooped through the air.

'Liv?'

'I need to talk to you.'

'What?'

I cupped my hands around my mouth and shouted as loud as I could. 'I need to talk to you!'

'OK. But I need to pack up here.'

I paced the jetty in frustration. Adrenaline coursed through me. My skin tingled like I'd fallen into stinging nettles, and I could feel the thump of my heart as it pumped blood through my veins. It was no use. As Seb took an age to carefully pack away his fishing gear, I felt like my body was on the verge of spontaneous combustion.

I kicked off my shoes and pulled my jumper up over my head. Hopping from foot to foot, I peeled off my tight jeans. When all that was left was my bra and knickers, I balanced on the edge of the jetty before plunging into the water below.

I emerged screaming and realised this was the first time I'd dunked my head. It was not an experience I'd repeat anytime soon, pain searing through my skull as my brain froze with cold. I trod water for a minute, waiting for the effects of the cold to flush through my body, then I began strong, fluid strokes, gaining ground on the boat.

Seb leaned over the edge of the boat and grabbed my hands. 'What are you doing, Liv? You're completely mad.' He was laughing and struggled to pull me out of the water. I clung onto his hands, using my feet to push against the boat and gain some traction. With one last heave, I flopped into a heap on the wooden floor, my knee catching on the bench.

'Ow,' I said, rubbing my red skin.

'You're crazy,' said Seb. 'I've got no towel, no blankets. You're going to catch your death.' He removed his jacket and wrapped it around my shoulders. With the sleeve of his hoodie, he wiped the water from my face and smoothed back my hair.

'Now you're going to get cold too.'

'I don't mind. What's happened, Liv? What couldn't wait for me to get back to shore?'

'This,' I said, climbing up onto my hands and knees and leaning towards him. My kiss took him by surprise, and he had no time to protest. He pulled me towards him, my damp underwear soaking his clothes.

His kisses travelled to my neck, sending a whole different kind of shiver through me than the cold water had caused.

'Liv, we said we wouldn't do this.'

I rocked back onto the floor of the boat, crossing my legs and taking his hands. 'No, what we said was that we'd wait until I'd sorted things out. Well, I've sorted things out.'

'What do you mean, Liv?' Seb reached forward and pushed a damp strand of hair away from my eyes.

'I met up with Rob this evening.'

'And?'

'It went really well. He's happy to go ahead with the divorce. I think it may have been the first honest conversation we've had since we got married. We still need to sort out the fine print, but I think we can make it work. I even think we can do it amicably, which will mean less suffering for Bertie.'

'Wow. That's amazing. So, you weren't tempted to go back to him?' Seb began planting kisses on my collarbone, moving up my neck, but stopping just short of my lips.

'Seb, do you think I'd have jumped in a freezing lake wearing nothing but my underwear just to kiss you, if I was tempted to go back to Rob?'

'Maybe you just fancied a swim?' His kisses moved up to my ear, then back down, circling my mouth, before travelling back down towards my chest.

My fingers sunk into his hair, and I leaned back. Seb shifted his weight, leaning against me, kissing harder. I let out a giggle.

'What?'

'Seb... this is amazing, but there's something poking into my back. Ow, God, that's really painful.'

Seb pulled me forward. 'Oh, it seems you were leaning against the rollick.'

'Is that some sort of euphemism?' I asked, looking behind me at the metal horseshoe that held the oar.

'Hmm,' said Seb, looking around the small boat. 'I'm wondering if this is the best place for...'

'For?'

'For whatever is happening here.'

We both laughed, and he wrapped his arms around me, holding me tight. 'Let's get you back to my place. I'll get a fire going, put the kettle on, and you can get warmed up.'

Seb lowered me down onto one of the bench seats, keeping his eyes fixed on mine as he picked up the oars and began rowing towards the shore.

'I didn't know you fished.'

'There's lots you don't know about me.'

'I want you to tell me everything. I want to know everything there is to know.'

Seb looked down at the bottom of the boat. 'You might not like everything about me.'

'Well, you won't know that until you try me, will you? Seb, I think I've proved I'm serious about us, don't you? I'm not in this for some fling. I'm in this for everything, good and bad.'

Seb stayed quiet, pulling on the oars. When we reached the jetty, he secured the boat to its mooring, jumped out, and held out a hand to me. I took it, noticing the callouses on his palm from holding the oars. Without a word, I gathered up the clothes strewn on the deck. I tucked them under my arm, taking his hand and letting him lead me home.

Chapter Thirty-One

'Hey,' I said, rolling onto my stomach and propping myself up on my arms. Seb lay beside me, supporting his head in the crook of his elbow. 'I think you need to send a thank you note to your sister.'

'Huh?'

'You need to thank her for this sheepskin rug. It was an excellent addition to your decor. So soft, so comfortable, so...'

Seb pulled me down on top of him, planting slow, light kisses on my bare skin. 'It's a relief that it's finally seen some action. It was getting embarrassing, all cliche, no substance. Now I feel I've stepped into a cowboy romance.'

'Or a Christmas movie. There's often some sheepskin action in those.'

I flopped onto my back with a satisfied sigh. I couldn't remember the last time I'd felt so happy or content.

'Coffee?' asked Seb, propping himself up on his elbow and looking down at me. 'You're so beautiful, Liv.'

'Thank you, but no thanks to coffee. I'll never sleep tonight if I have caffeine this late. I don't suppose you have any chamomile tea?'

'Actually, I think I have some in a cupboard somewhere.'

'I thought you would. You look the type.'

'What's that supposed to mean?' asked Seb, reaching down and tickling me.

'Stop it, it was a compliment.' I squirmed beneath him, batting his fingers away. 'You look like a hippy, but a very sexy one.'

Seb jumped up, and I couldn't help admiring his physique. All the work he did around the farm showed in his well-defined muscles, but there was nothing self-conscious or curated about his body. In many ways, there was also nothing exceptional. What made him so attractive to me was his complete ease in his own skin. His own body confidence was contagious. Only a few weeks ago, I wouldn't have dreamed of exposing the lumps and bumps I'd acquired with motherhood in such a brazen way.

'Wait there,' said Seb, throwing me a blanket. 'You think I look like a hippy? I've got something to show you which may surprise you.'

I pulled the blanket up around me. Seb disappeared into the bathroom, coming out wrapped in a fluffy navy dressing gown. He paused in the kitchen to flick on the kettle, then disappeared into his bedroom.

The roaring fire threw warmth across me and by the time Seb returned with two hot drinks and what looked like a photograph album, my eyelids were drooping and I was fighting off sleep.

'What's that?'

'My past. One year of my past, to be exact. But it will tell you all you need to know about me. I should have shown you this before we... you know, but well, I don't think it was my brain controlling my actions. If, after you've seen this, you don't want to continue things, I'll completely understand.'

I shuffled until I was leaning against the leg of an armchair. Seb sat down beside me, handing me my tea. He stared into the fire, his brow furrowed, chewing on his lip.

'You don't have to show me this now.'

Seb shook his head, as though coming out of a trance. 'I do. I should've done it sooner. It can't wait any longer.' He laid his mug on the floor and picked up the photograph album. The protective paper crackled as Seb turned a page.

The first photograph he turned to was a family portrait. A smart woman with cropped blonde hair smiled into the camera, her hand resting on the back of a wheelchair. The man in the wheelchair sat unsmiling, as though the woman were doing the work of appearing happy for both of them. His legs were bent to one side, thinner than the rest of his body, and a pair of plaid slippers covered his feet. On his body, he wore a leather jacket, and I could see a tattoo poking out from the top of his shirt.

To the left of the wheelchair stood a pretty young woman. Her blonde hair hung just below her shoulders, her makeup free face impassive. She held her hands in front of her as though creating a barrier between herself and the source of her discomfort. Her legs were crossed at the ankle, and as I looked closer, I could see she was chewing her lip in much the same way Seb did.

'Is that you?' I pointed to a tall, broad, clean-shaven man.

'Yes, if you can believe it.'

'But you look so different.'

'I know.'

Seb tried to turn the page, but I stopped him. In this photograph, he was neither the long-haired casual dresser I knew now, nor the floppy-haired emo-teen in baggy jeans and eyeliner I'd met at sixteen. The Seb staring out of the photograph wore what even to my un-trained eye looked like a designer suit. It was tight fitting; the fabric stretching across bulky arms and broad shoulders. His hair was cropped so close to his head it was almost a buzz cut.

'Tell me about this version of Seb.' I took Seb's hand and squeezed it, bringing it to my lips and kissing his rough skin.

Seb sighed. 'This version of Seb wasn't someone you would've liked.'

'How do you know?'

'Because not many people did, and I see the type of people you're drawn to. The one thing they all have in common is kindness. This man,' said Seb, jabbing a finger at the photograph, 'was not a kind man. He was selfish, arrogant, and thought he knew better than everyone around him.'

'What's the deal with the suit?'

'I worked in the city, in investment banking. After Dad had his accident, the atmosphere at home became toxic. He couldn't get over what had happened to him, refused to accept it, blamed the world and his wife for an accident which, at the end of the day, had been caused by his own carelessness.'

'While I was in sixth form, an investment banking firm came in to do a talk at school. They were running an apprenticeship scheme for kids from deprived areas like mine. Before Dad's accident, I was on course for straight A's. My grades had slipped after things at home took a nosedive, but the company agreed to give me an interview if I could turn things around.'

'What did you do?'

'Worked my arse off. I knew if I could score an apprenticeship with the company, it would be my ticket out of my shit life. So, I spent the next six months holed up in my room, studying. I lost several mates in the process, but I was so focused on my goals, I didn't have time to bother with insignificant things like friendships.'

'What happened? Did you get the grades?'

'Yes, the highest set of A level results the school had seen in years. The teachers tried to persuade me to go to uni. It would have looked good for the school, but I was set on a different path.'

'Did the company stay true to their word about the interview?'

'Yes, but not immediately. I had to badger them until they'd see me. After plenty of what could be considered stalking, I went up to London for the assessment weekend and got the apprenticeship.'

'That's amazing.'

'Yes, it was for a while. I jumped straight into the work hard, play hard lifestyle. I had a lot to prove. Most of the other apprentices had come from posh schools and backgrounds. The job was about so much more than playing with other people's money. When it came to wooing potential clients, they had certain expectations. The schmoozing came naturally to most of the guys, but I was learning all these weird expectations from scratch.'

'Like what?'

'Like the colour of your shoes, for starters. I realised on my first day I was the only one in the office wearing brown brogues. I had to extend my overdraft to buy a new black pair. But I'm a quick learner when I have to be. I was soon moving up the ranks, pulling eighteen-hour days sometimes fuelled by drugs and booze.'

'You got into drugs?'

'In that company, cocaine was seen as no worse than coffee. Everyone was doing it. The hours would have been impossible otherwise. Uppers to keep you going, downers to help you get a few hours' kip.'

'You liked the lifestyle?'

'I didn't give myself time to think about it. There was no downtime. If I wasn't at work, I was trying to transform myself into the perfect package in other ways, getting buff in the gym, being seen at all the right clubs and restaurants, driving the right car.'

'How long did you stay at the company?'

'Five years. I barely spoke to my family in that time. My entire focus was on making a success of my life. My poor sister and mum were left to deal with all my dad's shit. I didn't answer any of their calls, never went home to visit. The only reason I'm in that photo was because it was Mum's fiftieth and I couldn't get out of it. I turned up in my BMW, took them out to a fancy restaurant that made my mum uncomfortable, bought her a Tiffany necklace I knew she'd never wear. My game plan was to flash the cash and get out of there as quickly as I could. If someone had told me I'd be back living at home a month later, I'd have laughed in their face.'

'You left your job?'

'Ah, this is where things get messy. You'd better turn the page.'

Chapter Thirty-Two

I turned the page of the photograph album and had to do a double take. 'This is only a month after the last photo was taken?'

'Yeah, give or take a couple of weeks.'

A gaunt, grey Seb stood outside what looked like a hospital, his arm around his mum. He wore a loose-fitting grey tracksuit, and his hair had grown out of its buzz cut, sitting limp and greasy on his head.

'What happened?'

'I had a breakdown and was sectioned. My therapist said that the trip home probably triggered it. I'd been trying to run away from who I was and where I came from for years. Going home for Mum's birthday made me realise how futile all that had been. You're wondering why I was sectioned?'

I nodded.

'Everyone thought I'd tried to take my own life.'

'And you hadn't?'

'No, not in such absolute terms. When I got back to work after Mum's birthday, I guess I saw my life for the sham it was. I made it through one working week, then went out on a massive bender. I wanted to block everything out, not end it all. Me and a few colleagues went out drinking, then out to a club. As well as drinking my body weight in shots, I took any drugs I could get my hands on. I don't remember anything about that night. All I know is what my therapist has told me. I ended up in some random girl's house. When she couldn't wake me, she called an ambulance. Given how much drink and drugs I had in my system, it was labelled an overdose, and I was sectioned for my own safety.'

I pulled Seb towards me, kissing his hair as he rested his head on my shoulder.

'After I was discharged, I moved back home. But it never would have worked for long. Dad couldn't handle having another invalid in the house, and my being there was making things even harder for Mum. It was Harry who came to my rescue. She'd just inherited this place and offered me the chance to live and work here. I honestly think she saved my life.'

'The thing I don't understand,' I said, 'is why you haven't told me any of this before?'

'I didn't want to scare you off. Not everyone's comfortable with mental illness. The thing is, Liv, although I'm so much better than I was, I still go through dark times. And

I'm still on antidepressants, even though I'm trying to wean myself off them. Being with me will never be a walk in the park. I know how to manage my depression better than I ever have, but sometimes it creeps up on me, and I'm not much fun to be around when I get down.'

'Seb, I'm not with you because you're fun. You don't have to be happy around me all the time. God knows I won't be. I'm with you because I want to be with you. I want to know you, all of you, not just the good bits.'

Seb tilted my head toward him and kissed me. 'You're amazing, Liv. I can't believe I've got another chance with you. But I don't want you to feel pressure to stay with me if at any point it doesn't feel right. I'm terrified of losing you, but I'm not about to do anything stupid if things go wrong. I've invested too much money into my therapist to squander it now.'

'I don't feel under pressure. And as for things going wrong between us, Seb, they're only just getting started. Don't go predicting our demise so early into our relationship.'

'So, this is a relationship, then?'

'If you want it to be?'

'What about the others? What about Bertie?'

'I think we should keep this to ourselves for a while. It would be so confusing to announce a new relationship to Bertie before he even knows about the divorce.'

'I agree. He has to come first. I totally respect that.'

'Speaking of Bertie, as much as I'd like to stay here all night, I'd better be getting back. Maggie and Stephan will be in bed by now, and I don't want Bertie to wake up without me there.'

'Of course.'

Despite the cold night air whistling through gaps in the Land Rover door, as I drove back to the farmhouse I felt as though I was glowing. Would the others be able to tell what had happened by looking at my face? When I arrived home, Maggie was the only resident still awake.

'Sorry for being so long,' I said.

'No problem at all. Bertie went to bed like an angel and hasn't troubled us since. I was just making a hot chocolate to take up to bed. Do you want one?'

'No, I'm exhausted, but thanks for the offer.'

'How did it go?'

My cheeks flushed. 'How did it go?'

'Yes, with your husband,' said Maggie, frowning at me.

'Oh, that, yes, it went surprisingly well. I'm hopeful we can move forward amicably, and now he's resurfaced he's keen to see Bertie.'

'Thank goodness. A boy needs his dad. Well done for being so mature about everything. After what your husband put you through, no one would blame you for wanting revenge.'

'And I might if I didn't have Bertie to think of. Speaking of which, I'd better check on him.'

'You do that. That boy's a credit to you.'

'Thank you and thank you for babysitting.'

'Our pleasure. Goodnight.'

'Night, sleep well.'

'You too.'

Bertie was sound asleep when I crept into our bedroom. His snuffles and snores made me smile, and I pulled his covers up to his chin, running a hand across his thick hair. After all Rob and I had put him through recently, it was an enormous relief to know things were looking brighter. And with Seb by my side, I felt I could face anything. Things were on the up, and it was about time too.

Chapter Thirty-Three

'Happy birthday to you, happy birthday to you, happy birthday dear Harry, happy birthday to you.'

As Bertie walked into the dining room carrying his home-made cake, Harry burst into tears. Bertie laid the cake down in front of her and wrapped his arms around her neck.

'I'm sorry for making you cry.'

Harry laughed, brushed her tears away and kissed Bertie's cheek. 'These are happy tears, Bertie, not sad ones.'

'You cry when you're happy?'

'Yes,' said Harry, 'all the time.'

'Weird.'

Harry laughed again and blew out her candles to cheers from her friends.

'Can we do presents now?' asked Bertie, impatient to get to what he considered the most important part of the celebrations.

'Go on then. Who's going to go first?'

'Me,' said Bertie. He took a parcel wrapped in tissue paper from my bag and handed it to Harry. 'I made it myself.'

'You did?'

Bertie nodded, pushing back his shoulders and puffing his chest out in pride. Harry carefully peeled back pink tissue paper to reveal a misshapen clay pot with primary-coloured flowers painted around its sides.

'Wow, I love it!'

'Mrs Grange said these pots can be used for all sorts of tat.'

'She said that?' asked Harry, trying not to chuckle.

'Yes, well, actually she said crap, but then changed it to tat, thinking we hadn't noticed, but we all did. There's a hole in the bottom so you can't use it for cereal.'

'I'll bear that in mind.'

'Shall I go next?' I asked. Harry nodded, and I pulled a squishy parcel from my bag, wrapped in the same pink tissue paper as Bertie's.

When Harry opened the knitting set with extra large needles and unusually thick wool, she grinned. 'Are you trying to tell me something about my knitting skills?'

'No, but I thought thicker wool might help disguise some holes.'

Harry reached across and gave a good-natured punch on my arm.

'There's something else in there,' I said, helping Harry find a small package hidden among the tissue paper. Harry unwrapped two delicate silver earrings shaped like a woman about to dive into the water. 'I couldn't find any naked swimmers,' I said as she hugged me.

Pat gave Harry a beautiful hard-back copy of *Persuasion*, its pink-fabric cover home to an intricate gold-leaf design. Stephan handed over a bottle of expensive wine, and Maggie produced a shoebox filled with treats ranging from dark chocolate to scented candles. 'To give you a chance to look after yourself,' Maggie explained.

Despite leaving two weeks previously, Elaine and Christine had left a package for Harry containing more wine, a book about walking the coast path, and a guide to Cornish wild swimming spots.

'My turn,' said Seb. He left the room and returned with a large square object.

Harry opened Seb's package to reveal a beautiful oil painting of the lake. The artist had captured the multitude of greens and the way the light hit the water perfectly.

'I know you see the lake all the time, but I thought this would be a nice addition to your living room.'

'I love it,' said Harry, bursting into tears again. 'Who painted it?'

'The planning officer from the council.'

'What?' Harry stopped crying, her mouth wide with shock.

'Yes, he was admiring the lake and mentioned he paints as a hobby. I asked if he took commissions. It was a bit of a risk. He may have been an awful painter, but I thought it would sweeten him up a bit and thankfully, the risk paid off.'

'It certainly did,' said Harry. 'Thank you, everyone. I was dreading turning thirty, but you've made it so special. Are you sure you boys don't mind if us girls leave you at home tonight?'

'Of course not,' said Stephan. 'I, for one, would rather have a quiet night with a beer and a film. We're looking forward to our boys' night, aren't we, Bertie?'

Bertie nodded, unable to speak due to the large slice of cake he'd shoved in his mouth.

'Yes, I'd rather stay here too,' said Pat. 'An evening with Big-mouthed-Beryl isn't my idea of fun.'

'I'll tell her you said that,' said Bertie with a grin.

'Can I bribe you with a second slice of cake to keep your mouth shut?'

Bertie nodded, and Pat ruffled his hair.

'Come on then, ladies, let's get going.'

We said our goodbyes to the men, and headed into the night, Maggie linking arms with me and Harry, excited at the thought of a night out. I no longer worried about leaving Bertie. The residents of Lowen Farm had become as good as family, and it was important for Bertie to have such lovely male role models in his life. He was due to spend his first night with Rob the following weekend. I was dreading it as much as Bertie, though I kept my feelings hidden.

The pub was quiet when we arrived, few people heading out on a weekday evening. Aside from our group and a couple of local farmers, the only other drinker was a man I'd not seen before. In his dark jacket and tight black jeans, he looked like he'd be more at home in a city wine bar.

Beryl waved us over to a table in the corner. Beside her sat Mrs Grange, and a pretty redhead I'd not met before.

'Happy birthday!' they chorused as Harry walked over.

'Thank you,' she said, hugging each in turn. 'Liv, I don't think you've met Zoe. Zoe's local gentry.'

'Oi, don't introduce me like that. Nice to meet you, Liv. I actually live in a little cottage in the village, but my parents live at Crow Hall, which backs onto Harry's land. I've known Harry all my life.'

'Lovely to meet you. Hello, Beryl, hello Mrs Grange.'

'Good God, don't be calling me Mrs Grange all evening, it will put me off my beer. Mel, please, we're not at school now.'

I laughed and went to the bar to get the first round. As I ordered our drinks, I felt like I was being watched. I looked behind me and saw the black-clad man had his eyes boring into my back. He gave a slight jerk and turned his eyes back to the phone in his hand. The way he'd been looking at me sent shivers down my spine, but not the shivers Seb created. His lips had been drawn into a snarl, but given I'd never met him, I couldn't think what I could have done to offend him.

'Does anyone know that man over there?' I asked the others, setting the tray of drinks on the table. 'No, stop staring. Try to be discreet.'

There was nothing discreet about my friends as they craned their necks to see who I was talking about. They all agreed they'd never seen him before, and he definitely wasn't a local.

'He probably fancies you,' said Maggie. 'Take it as a compliment.'

'Maybe.'

Beryl began discussing the latest shop gossip in a voice that was both hushed and dramatic all at once. As she told us about Mavis's neighbours who since the weather warmed had moved their night time gymnastics into the garden, we forgot all about the dodgy man and his cold stare.

'*Naturists*, they call themselves,' said Beryl. 'I thought Sir David Attenborough was one of those, but according to Mavis, I'm getting muddled again. It seems the only nature Mavis' neighbours are interested in is the human kind.'

'I think I need another drink,' said Mel.

I offered to help her carry the drinks, and as we walked to the bar, I noticed the dodgy man had gone and only an empty pint glass showed he'd ever been there.

It was after the fifth round of drinks that events took a turn for the worse, or better, depending on your opinion. Harry announced her birthday wish was to go skinny dipping in the lake with her friends.

'God no,' I said. 'Have you any idea how cold it will be at this time of night? Not to mention the fact Pat might see us out of his window.'

'It will be nothing he hasn't seen before,' said Harry.

'In your case, maybe. Not for the rest of us.'

'I'm up for it,' said Zoe.

'Me too,' said Maggie, throwing her remaining wine down her neck.

'Well, if you're all game, so am I,' said Mel, 'but absolutely no photography, or phones, for that matter. The last thing the local headteacher needs is photos of her naked carcass being spread around the village.'

'I think I'll have to give it a miss,' said Beryl, her words slightly slurred. 'It's not the skinny dipping I object to, but the walk to the lake. My legs couldn't take it, not after five G and Ts.'

'I'd better give it a miss too,' I said. 'I should get back to Bertie.'

'Bertie? He's got three very capable men looking after him. No, you're coming with us.'

Harry grabbed hold of my wrist, pulling me out of my seat and towards the door. It looked like I had no choice in the matter.

Chapter Thirty-Four

We staggered through the forest, the effects of all the alcohol we'd consumed only hitting us once we were out in the fresh air. It was pitch black, and we relied on the torchlight from our phones to help us on our way.

'Ow!' My foot caught on a tree root, and I went sprawling flat on my face on the forest floor.

'Oh, God, Liv, are you hurt?' Maggie rushed towards me. I felt something on my face and reached up and pulled a leaf from my cheek. Maggie giggled.

'It's not funny,' I said.

Harry shone her torch light on my face, spluttering into her hand. I felt my face again. My fingers came away brown. I sniffed the brown substance, relieved as the smell of earth and rotting leaves reached my nose.

'Help me up.'

Maggie's giggles were infectious, laughter leaving our muscles weak. Zoe heaved me to my feet, only for me to fall into her, pushing us both to the ground once again. We all collapsed in a drunken huddle on the earth, lying on our backs, trying to stop laughing. As soon as one of us gained composure, someone else would giggle, setting us all off again.

'I'm too old for this,' said Mel, flinging her arms above her head before attempting to make snow angels in the dirt of the forest floor.

A flash of light pierced the darkness. 'What was that?' I said, sitting up and looking around.

'Dunno,' said Harry, 'probably one of our phones.'

'It couldn't have been,' I said. 'We were all lying down. No one had their phones out.'

'Don't worry, Liv,' said Mel. 'It was probably a flash of lightning or something. Come on, ladies, let's get to that lake. We can't stay here all night.'

We pulled ourselves to standing, but my laughter had left me. The night was clear and still, not a cloud in the sky. I felt certain the flash wasn't lightning and couldn't shake the feeling we weren't alone.

By the time we reached the lake, my fears were forgotten. Harry's enthusiasm was infectious, and we stood on the jetty, peeling off our clothes. The phone ban Mel had implemented meant that despite being naked, the whole experience was a very modest affair. We could barely see each other's faces, never mind anything else.

'Right,' said Harry. 'On the count of three, we go for it. Ready?' We all nodded. 'OK, one, two, three, GO!'

We stepped off the jetty, holding our noses, screaming. Just before we hit the water, the surrounding air lit up. I emerged spluttering, brushing water from my face.

'There was the light again,' I said, as the others bobbed around me, squealing from the cold.

'It's probably just climate change,' said Maggie. 'It's doing strange things to the weather.'

'It couldn't be Pat or Seb taking photos, could it?' asked Zoe.

'No, definitely not,' said Harry. 'They wouldn't do something like that.'

'Besides,' I said, 'they're both still up at the farmhouse.'

'Come on,' said Harry, 'let's have a race to the pontoon.'

We began splashing our way through the lake. I tried to enjoy the experience but couldn't shake the feeling of being watched. What if one of Beryl's much discussed *peevs* had followed us down to the lake?

At the pontoon, the others climbed up, lying on their backs panting after all their exertions.

'If you don't mind, I'm going to head back now,' I said, treading water.

'Are you sure?'

'Yes, I'm working in the shop in the morning so need to get some sleep, and I want to get back for Bertie.'

'All right, see you in the morning.'

'Night.'

I turned and swam back to the jetty. Before I'd even put on my clothes, I crouched down and pulled my phone from my pocket and called Seb.

'Liv? Is everything all right? I wasn't expecting to hear from you tonight.'

'Everything's fine. I was wondering if you're at home?'

'No, I'm on my way back, though. I'll be there in about five minutes.'

'OK. Look, I know this is a pain in the arse, but would you mind taking me back to the farmhouse?'

'Of course not. But has something happened?'

'No, I don't think so. I've just got a weird feeling, like someone's watching me. I've probably just had too much to drink.'

'I'll be there as soon as I can. Do you want me to stay on the line till I get there?'

'No, I'll be fine. I'll see you soon.'

I heard Seb rev the engine and smiled at the thought of my knight in shining armour racing to my rescue. While I waited for Seb, I pulled clothes onto my damp body and walked up the path to wait outside his cabin.

Three minutes after I'd spoken to him, Seb arrived at the cabin, the quad bike spewing up dirt as he skidded to a stop. He jumped off and rushed over to me.

'Are you all right? I was so worried.'

I laughed and put my arms around his neck. 'Honestly, I'm fine. I was just being silly.'

'As long as you're OK.'

I answered him with a deep kiss, revelling in his warmth as he held me tight, his hands running up and down my back. Suddenly a bright flash filled the air, accompanied by a click that sounded like the shutter of a camera.

'What the hell?' Seb spun round, trying to work out the direction the light had come from. 'Wait here.'

He jumped down from the deck and began searching the nearby woodland by the light of his torch. Five minutes later, he came back to where I stood, shivering from both cold and fear.

'I couldn't see anyone, but there was definitely someone there.'

'Well, I suppose at least I now know I wasn't going mad. I feel awful leaving the girls down here, but could you take me back to the farmhouse? I hate thinking of Bertie being there without me if there's some dodgy guy prowling around. Then maybe you could come back and give the others a lift home?'

'Yes, of course. I'll drop you home, then come back for the others. By the shrieks and giggles, I'd say there'll be fine here for a while. It wasn't the most sensible idea, you know, going swimming after you've all been drinking.'

'I know, sorry.'

'Don't say sorry, Liv. You're a grown woman who can do what she wants, I just don't want anything bad to happen to you.' Seb leaned forward, kissed me, then took my hand and led me to the quad bike. Unlike our first trip, this time I relished the feeling of my arms around his waist, feeling safe so long as he was with me.

Seb dropped me at the farmhouse, swapped the quad bike for the Land Rover, and turned straight back to find the others. I crept into our bedroom to check on Bertie, then went downstairs to wait for the others to return. I'd agreed with Seb that we wouldn't say anything to the others about the intruder tonight. It would be a shame to spoil Harry's birthday, and given how much they'd had to drink, goodness knows how Harry and Maggie would react. But first thing in the morning, Seb would have a good look around the grounds, and promised to get to the bottom of things.

Chapter Thirty-Five

All week I'd felt like I was being watched. It could have been my mind playing tricks, but whether on my early morning swim, on the school run, during my meetings with Seb or when I was working in the shop, it felt as though someone was there, just out of sight. A couple of times I thought I saw a shadow, or glimpsed a boot, but it could have been a trick of the mind.

It was coming to the end of my shift when the bell rang on the shop door. 'Be with you in a minute,' I said, reaching up to replenish the cough and cold medicine on the top shelf behind the counter.

Beryl appeared beside me, two cups of coffee in her hands. 'She doesn't look like the usual type we get in here,' she whispered, jerking her head toward the door.

I turned to look at the mystery customer and dropped the boxes of flu relief I'd been holding.

'Hello, Olivia.'

'Marion? What are you doing here?'

'Who's this then?' asked Beryl.

'My m... my soon to be ex mother-in-law.'

'Oh, I see.'

'Olivia, I wondered if we could have a little chat? In private.'

'Use my flat if you like,' said Beryl.

'Are you sure?'

'Yes, go on up. Help yourself to tea for your guest. Here's your coffee,' she said, handing me a cup.

We climbed the stairs to Beryl's flat. I'd only been up once or twice and wondered what Marion would make of the chintzy furniture and surfaces crammed with photos of Beryl's grandchildren.

'Take a seat,' I said, as Marion followed me into the living room. 'Would you like a cup of tea?'

'No,' said Marion, scrunching her nose, as though she thought drinking from one of Beryl's cups would poison her.

'What is it you wanted to see me about?'

'It's about this foolish notion you have that you're going to divorce my son.'

'Marion, it's not a foolish notion, and besides, Rob agreed to it. We've filled out all the forms online, now we're just waiting for the twenty week cooling-off period to be up.'

Marion huffed and pulled a large brown envelope out of her bag.

'What's that?'

Marion drummed her fingers against the envelope. 'A few things have come to my attention that I've found very alarming.'

'Sorry, I don't understand?'

Slowly, Marion peeled open the envelope and pulled out what looked like a stack of photographs. 'The way you've been conducting yourself lately, Olivia, is most concerning. We feel it would be in Bertie's best interest if he came to live with us.'

I spat out my coffee, spurting brown liquid all over Beryl's soft furnishings. 'Are you joking? Is this some weird practical joke?'

'I assure you, Olivia, there is nothing amusing about this.' Marion held up the pile of A4 photographs, waving them in the air.

'Can I see?'

She handed me the photographs, my hands shaking as I looked through. It was me, in the pub on the night of Harry's birthday, tipping a glass of wine down my neck. Me, flailing around on the forest floor, having fallen over. Me, jumping into the lake completely naked. Me kissing Seb. Me pushing Bertie through the school gates (as a joke when he'd been running late). Me hugging a man in the shop (Pat, on the anniversary of his wife's death). Me, walking down the street carrying two bottles of wine (a thank you present for Stephan and Pat's babysitting).

'You... you've had me followed?' I could barely force out the words, so incensed was I by Marion's actions.

'And just as well I did. It's clear from these photos you've been living a debauched lifestyle, leaving Bertie in the care of strange men, and behaving like the village whore.'

'Wh.. What? There are innocent explanations behind all these photographs.'

Marion let out a cold, hard laugh. 'I'm not sure a court would see it that way.'

'A court?'

'Oh, stop gaping like a goldfish, Olivia. All we want is what's in our grandson's best interest. You've got him living with a group of drop-outs, going to a second-rate school, and being left alone while you flaunt yourself around the village. I'm not sure any judge would look kindly on that style of mothering.'

'Judge? What are you talking about?'

'We've instructed our solicitor to secure us guardianship of Albert.'

I stood up, throwing the photographs to the floor. 'His name isn't Albert. It's Alberto. How dare you threaten me like this? This is all... all...' I pointed to the photographs strewn across the carpet. 'It's all a pile of horseshit, and you know it. Is this about money? Do you think I'm going to come after your money? Because I'm telling you, I want nothing to do with you or your wealth. If I never see you again, it will be too soon.'

Throughout my rant, Marion had sat calmly on the sofa, her hands clasped in her lap, her legs crossed elegantly at the ankles. 'Have you quite finished?' she asked when I flopped back down on the sofa.

'What does Rob think about all this?'

'Rob is in agreement with me that Albert moving into the family home would be in his best interest.'

'But he hasn't seen Bertie for weeks! Every visit I've arranged, he's pulled out of. You want to go to court? Fine, there's plenty I could say about your son's parenting if we do.'

'Well, of course, you've every right to fight us over this. Although, the last time I looked, it seemed lawyers were rather pricey. Do you have access to funds I don't know about?'

I struggled for words as the full horror of what Marion was saying sank in. There was no way I could fight a custody battle in the courts. I'd been doing my best to save since I began working, but I'd started paying Harry rent and the few hundred pounds in my bank account wouldn't stretch to even a consultation at a law firm. I stood up, but my legs gave way and I clung to the seat of the chair, fighting the tears that strained to break free.

'Now now, there's no need to get upset. There is a way out of this that will make everyone happy.'

I looked up at Marion like a stray dog who'd just been kicked but was still prepared to accept a bone from its attacker.

'Yes, this could all be sorted out simply.'

'How?'

'Well, you could forget all this ridiculous divorce business, for starters.'

'What?'

'Go back to Rob. Forget all about this silly farm nonsense. You could be a proper family again. Albert could have a mother and a father. Surely that would be the best option all round?'

'But you hate me. Why on earth do you want Rob to stay married to me?'

'Better the devil you know, dear. You should see some of the women he's been carrying on with since you abandoned him. Pff, I wouldn't allow them across my threshold. No, better the devil you know.'

Tears broke free and carved their way silently down my cheeks.

'Anyway, dear, there you have it. The choice is yours. I'll give you a week to think things through, but I'm sure you'll come to the right decision for everyone concerned. I'll be in touch.'

Marion stood up, dusting off her skirt as though she'd been sitting in a squat rather than Beryl's tidy flat. 'I'll see myself out.'

The door clicked shut behind Marion. I pulled myself to my feet, reaching the bathroom just in time to throw up. I was rinsing out my mouth when Beryl appeared in the doorway.

'I've closed the shop. I guessed something was wrong when that old witch marched out of the shop without saying a word. What on earth's happened?'

I fell to the floor, leaning against the toilet bowl.

'Come here, maid,' said Beryl, grabbing a handful of tissue from the roll and wiping my face. 'Let's get you over to the sofa and I'll fetch you something for your nerves.'

I leaned on Beryl as she guided me back to the living room.

'Oh my word, what are these? That's me that is!' Beryl's finger jabbed one photograph in outrage. 'Who's been taking these photos without consent?'

'My mother-in-law hired someone. I think it must have been that strange man who was in the pub when we went out for Harry's birthday.'

Beryl flicked through each photo in turn. She paused and stared at the photograph of me and Seb locked in a passionate embrace.

'Beryl, please don't tell anyone about this. No one has any idea about me and Seb, and I don't want it getting back to Bertie before I've talked to him.'

Beryl surprised me with a laugh. She sat beside me on the sofa, patting my knee. 'You think you've kept that a secret?' She laughed again. 'It's been blindingly obvious for weeks.'

'How?'

'The smile on your face in the mornings, the faraway look in your eyes, not to mention the way you blush every time a certain gentleman comes in for a pint of milk.'

'So, everyone knows?'

'No, not everyone. I know I can be a terrible gossip, but you'll be surprised to hear I can keep a confidence, if the secret belongs to someone I care about. I have a feeling Harry and Maggie have guessed, but we've not discussed it, so I can't be sure. Anyway, what was the purpose of all this spying?'

'They want to take Bertie from me.'

'What? But you're an amazing mother. Surely you can fight them?'

I shook my head, tears dropping from my cheeks onto the cushion I was hugging.

'I'll get you a brandy.'

When Beryl handed me the brandy, I downed it in one, despite hating the taste. It burned my throat and stomach and I wondered if I'd throw up again.

'Beryl, I'm not sure I can come back to work today.'

'Of course you can't. I wouldn't expect you to. You get yourself off home. You're going to need all your strength for the fight on your hands.'

I thanked Beryl, collected the photographs and let myself out of her flat and onto the street. My brain was a fog of confusion, my legs disobeying my mind. I made it as far as the churchyard before realising I could walk no further. I found a gravestone at the far end and collapsed against it. Everything I'd worked so hard for was about to be taken away, and I was powerless to stop it.

Chapter Thirty-Six

'Liv? Liv?'

'Cass...'

'Oh my God, what's happened? Have things gone wrong with Seb?'

I managed to laugh through my tears. 'No.'

'OK. Bertie?'

I let out a loud sob and wiped my eyes on my sleeves. 'They're going to take him away.'

'What? Who's going to take who away?'

'Marion and Hugo. They're going to take Bertie from me.'

'Liv, calm down. How are Marion and Hugo going to take Bertie? It doesn't make any sense.'

After a series of deep breaths and several false starts, I explained my meeting with Marion.

'The total bitch. The complete, utter arsehole weasel of a bitch. She can't do that.'

'She can. They have money. I don't.'

'Yes, but anyone with half a brain can see you're an amazing mum to Bertie. I bet he'd stand up in court and swear to it if he was allowed.'

'I'd never put him through it.'

'What about Rob? What does he say about all this?'

'God knows. All our communication so far has been through Marion. Either he doesn't have a mobile phone or won't share the number, so I have to call his parents' landline, and Marion screens all the calls.'

'Bitch face bitch. Liv, let me go to the bank. We'll fight this together.'

'I won't let you do that. The amount of money we're talking about is too much. If we try to fight it, you can guarantee Hugo and Marion will use all means at their disposal to drag the process out for as long as possible in order to make it as expensive as possible. It would leave you bankrupt, and we can't have two siblings bankrupt.'

'I'm sure Dad would help.'

'Dad needs to keep his money for his care. I'd never see his quality of life compromised over something like this.'

'Then what are you going to do?'

'I don't know. Everything's such a mess.'

'I'm coming up there.'

'No, Cass, you don't need to do that.'

'You can't stop me. I'll have to arrange cover at work, but Jasper's just finished his four on, so he's got the next few days off. He can watch the kids while I'm away.'

'OK, but don't say anything to anyone except Jasper. I don't know what I'm going to tell Bertie.'

'Nothing for the moment. Marion gave you a week, yes?'

'Yes.'

'Right, so you've got a bit of breathing space.'

'Barely.'

'OK, go home, have a bath, straighten yourself out. I'll try to get there in time to do the school run with you. You're not going through this alone, OK?'

'OK.'

'When you get home ask Harry if I can stay for a couple of days.'

'Will do. Love you.'

'Love you too.'

The usual twenty-minute walk from the village to the farm took me the best part of an hour. I dragged myself along the track, exhausted from the emotional shock of Marion's announcement. Every hundred metres, my emotions would swing violently from anger, to hope, to despair. I turned my situation round and round in my head, trying to find a solution I knew deep down didn't exist. It was a David and Goliath situation, only in this case, David didn't even have a sling, and his hands were tied behind his back.

When I reached the farm, I assumed everyone was out, until I saw a pair of booted feet poking out from beneath the Land Rover. Harry must have heard my feet on the gravel, for she slid back on a trolley, her face covered in oil.

'You're back early.'

'Yes, I wasn't feeling all that well.'

'You look a bit peaky.'

'What are you doing?'

'This old girl's got an oil leak. Yet another thing slowly breaking around the place. Why don't you have a lie down?'

'Yes, I think I will. I'll give you a hand with some cleaning later.'

'Wait and see how you feel. You don't want to overdo it.'

'I'm sure I'll be fine. Oh, is it OK if Cass comes to stay for a couple of days?'

'Of course it is. Liv, are you sure everything's all right?'

Tears filled my eyes, but I blinked them away. It would have been easier to lie, but I owed Harry more than that. 'I had a visit from my mother-in-law today while I was at the shop. Let's just say it didn't go well.'

'Want to talk about it?'

'No, if you don't mind, I'd like to get things straight in my head first.'

'Sure, but you know where I am if you need me.'

'Thank you.'

I walked through the farmhouse, stopping to make a cup of tea before heading upstairs. It was a relief to know Seb had gone to Plymouth for the day to pick up a piece of machinery for the farm. I couldn't face the thought of seeing him. What would I say? *I think I'm going to have to leave you for my ex husband or risk losing my son?* It wouldn't be fair to him. He'd want to help, but there was nothing anyone could do.

As I climbed the stairs, Maggie was on her way down. 'Did Harry tell you we've got some new guests arriving?'

'No?'

'Yes, a married couple. I'm afraid it will mean sharing your bathroom.'

'That's fine, I'll have to remind Bertie not to pee all over the toilet seat, though.'

'Yes, you do that. I've no idea what they're like. Harry's only spoken to them on the phone, so fingers crossed they fit in.'

'I'm sure they will.'

Maggie carried on her way, and I heaved myself onwards, using the banister to support my weight. I'd always known there would be comings and goings at Lowen Farm, but now was the worst possible time to welcome new guests. I'd have to be friendly when what I really wanted to do was curl up in a corner and hide.

I must have fallen asleep as soon as I lay down on my bed, for I was still wearing my shoes when a gentle voice stirred me into consciousness.

'Liv?'

I sat up and rubbed my swollen eyes. 'Cass? How did you get here so quickly?'

Cass looked at her watch. 'Not that quick. You called me at eleven and it's now half past two.'

'Half past two? Crap, I need to get Bertie from school.'

'You're not going anywhere looking like that.'

Cass pulled her phone from her pocket and held the camera up to my face. She handed me the phone and I could've cried again seeing my reflection. My curls had tangled into knots, the skin around my eyes was red and puffy, my eyes themselves bloodshot.

'I'll pick up Bertie. You have a bath and splash some cold water on your face to bring down the swelling. I'll tell Bertie you have a headache, so you'll have plenty of time to straighten yourself out.'

'Thank you,' I said, taking Cass's hand.

In the end, I had plenty of time to myself. When Bertie got back from school, he insisted on showing Cass how much all the animals had grown since her last visit. I'd told Cass I didn't feel up to going downstairs for dinner, so she brought me up a plate of food for me to eat alone in my room.

There had been several messages from Seb, but I'd not yet replied to any. Instead, I'd closed the curtains in my room, and once I'd finished eating, I'd burrowed down beneath the covers, trying not to cry.

At half past six, there was a knock at the door.

'Come in.'

Seb opened the door and walked over to my bed. I snuggled further down beneath the duvet, knowing if he saw my face, he'd want to know what was wrong.

'Are you OK? Cass said you're not feeling well?'

'Yeah, I think it's a migraine.'

Seb sat on the edge of my bed, running his hand over my hair and down to my forehead. 'You don't seem to have a fever.'

'No, I'm fine. Honestly, it's just a nasty headache.'

'Is there anything I can get you?'

'No, thank you. I've eaten and have plenty of water.'

'Would you like me to sit with you for a while?'

'No, I think I just need to sleep.'

'I can stay with you while you sleep.'

'No, please, I think it's best I'm by myself.'

'All right,' said Seb.

I felt awful. I could tell from his voice I'd hurt him by not wanting him around. If only he knew what was coming. I closed my eyes pretending to sleep, but really, it was to hide the tears which were about to pour from my eyes.

Chapter Thirty-Seven

All week I'd been walking around in a daze. I'd only slept in snatches of one or two hours each night, pacing our bedroom floor while Bertie snored away, oblivious to the change hurtling towards us.

I'd expected Beryl to want to discuss the ins and outs of my situation, but much to my surprise, she didn't mention it once. The only reference she made to my breakdown in her living room was telling me she was there if I needed anything. I'd never imagined the hardened gossip could display such sensitivity.

Seb knew something was wrong and I couldn't keep the pretence of a migraine up all week. I found excuses not to spend time with him, only attending meetings about the project when I knew Harry would also be there. At mealtimes, I kept catching him watching me, trying to figure out what it was I wasn't telling him.

Harry had asked a few times if I was ready to talk, but each time I'd put her off. I knew if I admitted what was happening to anyone at Lowen Farm, they'd try to come to my rescue. The work they were trying to achieve was so precarious; putting any time, energy or money into me was a distraction they couldn't afford. An announcement was due from the planning department any day now, and if we got the go ahead for our ambitious plans, it would be full steam ahead.

Knowing I wouldn't be around to see the project through broke my heart. Over the two days Cass had been at the farm, we'd looked at my mess every which way. We'd even consulted a solicitor Cass knew, but the outcome of that meeting was much as I'd expected. I would qualify for legal aid, but there was a waiting list, and besides, any lawyer I got access to for free was unlikely to compete with whoever Marion could afford to hire.

I wished Marion and Hugo had lost more when Rob's business went under. It turned out they'd quickly bounced back from the initial financial shock, moving investments around and calling in debts until their bank balance was as buoyant as it had ever been.

The thought of Marion invading the shop again was horrific, so I'd arranged to meet her in the churchyard. Beryl had given me the morning off without question. After dropping Bertie at school, I walked to the church, welcoming the chance to take the weight off my feet as I sat down on a bench.

It was a dreary day, mirroring my feelings. The wildflowers in the graveyard bent their heads from the weather, as though not wanting to witness my downfall. Spits of rain mingled with gusts of wind, and I was grateful for my warm waterproof coat, despite it being early summer.

The clicking of high heels on the path signalled Marion's arrival. I listened as she looked for me, hoping exposure to the rain would frizz up her neat hair.

'There you are,' she said, rounding the corner and walking towards me. 'Why you had to choose such a ghastly place to meet is beyond me. Then again, you always were a strange one.'

And you were always a spiteful cow, I thought, but didn't say. I couldn't afford to be too honest, not when Marion held so much power over me. I stared straight ahead at the grave in front of me, wondering if the person buried there had lived a happy life.

'So, you've come to a decision?'

I nodded.

'What will it be? Are you going to fight me in the courts, or do the sensible thing and come back to Rob?'

I couldn't bring myself to say the words out loud.

'Olivia?' said Marion, tapping her foot against the path beneath her. 'I'd rather not wait all day. It's raining, if you hadn't noticed.'

'I'll come back.'

'Pardon? I didn't catch that.'

'I said, I'll come back. I'll come back to Rob. I'll cancel the divorce proceedings. If that's what it takes to keep Bertie with me, I'll do it.'

'What a sensible girl,' said Marion, patting my knee. I wanted to grab a flannel and wash the invisible imprint of her hand from my skin. 'I thought you'd make the right decision, so I've already put various arrangements in place. We'll come on Sunday to collect you and take you both to your new home.'

'New home? I assumed we'd be living with you?'

'Goodness no, we don't want to be getting under each other's feet like that. No, Hugo and I have rented you a house on your old estate. It's not as large as your last house, but big enough. Living somewhere smaller should encourage Rob to get his new business off the ground faster. We don't want to spoil him too much, or he'll get too comfortable.'

'What about Bertie's school?'

'His old school has agreed to take him back. We're covering the fees, of course.'

'Of course.'

'I expect he's excited about getting back to his friends.'

'I haven't told him anything about this yet. I assumed you'd let us stay here long enough to see out the school year.'

'Whatever for? The quicker you're out of this dump, the better. Bertie should get a proper education, not some airy fairy curriculum in a backwater school.'

If I'd had any sort of weapon with me, I can't say I wouldn't have used it on Marion. I wanted to punch the cheery, smug smile from her face. In fact, at that moment, I would have been quite happy to see her with a gravestone of her own.

'What time will you come on Sunday?' I asked, standing up but still not looking at her.

'You can expect us at ten sharp. Make sure you're ready, we don't want to be waiting around for you.'

I walked away from Marion, determined not to cry. I wouldn't give her the satisfaction of knowing she'd broken me, even if it was true.

Chapter Thirty-Eight

I couldn't face going straight back to the farm, and there was something else I needed to do. I paused beside the school gate, my hand clinging on to the metal. My heart hammered, making my ears ring and breaths come fast. *We'll come for you on Sunday.* Marion had given me next to no time to extricate us from the life we'd built, and I couldn't delay what had to be done.

I pushed open the gate and walked up to the school entrance. The pink-haired receptionist was in her usual position and today I noticed she was chewing gum.

'Hello, Mrs Simmons. How can I help you?'

'I was wondering if Mrs Grange is free for a quick meeting?'

'Hmm, let me see.' The receptionist flicked through a large diary, chewing on her pen as she ran her finger along the page. 'She has a meeting at one, but is free until then. Take a seat and I'll let her know you'd like to speak to her.'

I sat in the reception area watching a TV, which played photos of smiling children on a loop. The school was so creative in its approach to learning, and the thought of removing Bertie from its nurturing environment broke my heart.

'Liv, this is a pleasant surprise.'

'Hi, Mel. Are you free for a chat?'

'Of course. Come through to my office. Would you like a cup of tea?'

'No, thanks.'

I followed Mel into her small office, which overlooked the playground. She slumped into an old office chair and reached into a drawer, pulling out a pack of biscuits, which she threw onto the table. 'Help yourself. Is this a social call, or is it about Bertie?'

'It's not a social call, I'm afraid.'

'Oh dear, sounds serious. He's not being bullied, is he? I pride myself on stamping out bullying before it can get started. I hope I'm not losing my touch.'

'No, it's nothing like that. Mel, I'm afraid we're leaving.'

'What do you mean, leaving?'

'We have to leave Lowen Farm. I need to take Bertie out of school.'

'For how long?'

'For good.'

'What? Why? I thought things were going well for you here?'

'They were, they are.' I sniffed as tears filled my eyes. Mel jumped out from behind her desk and crouched beside me, offering tissues.

'What's happened, Liv?'

I sniffed and wiped my eyes. 'If I tell you what's happened, you have to promise not to say anything to anyone at Lowen Farm.'

'I can't promise anything if this is some sort of child protection issue.'

I shook my head. 'No, it's nothing like that.'

'OK. Go ahead.'

I spilled out my sorry story to Mel, and by the time I'd finished, I'd created a Mount Everest-sized pile of damp tissues on her desk.

'There must be a way round this.'

'Mel, there's not. Honestly, I've tried everything I can think of. I've even consulted a solicitor. They said I had a very strong case, but the legal costs of fighting my in-laws would be crippling.'

'Why don't you want anyone at the farm to know? I don't understand?'

'Because they'd want to help me.'

'Isn't that a good thing?'

'Not if it would drag them down with me. The vision Harry and S... the vision Harry has for the place is amazing. I can't let my personal problems get in the way of that.'

'Then what are you going to tell them? That you've had a sudden, out of the blue change of heart? They're not going to buy that, Liv.'

'Maybe not, but it's the only option I have.'

Mel sighed and went back to her chair, spinning back and forth, deep in thought. 'If only there was a way we could help you…'

'I promise you, Mel, no one can help me. The only option I have is to go back to my old life and stick it out long enough until Bertie's old enough to decide what he wants for himself.'

'Does he know you're leaving?'

'Not yet. I'm going to tell him this evening.'

Mel reached across the table and took my hand. 'Whatever the future holds for you, Liv, there will always be a place here for Bertie, should you need it.'

This brought on a fresh onslaught of tears. Mel picked up her office phone. 'Linda? I wonder if you could bring two cups of tea through to my office with plenty of sugar. Yes, thank you.'

A bell rang, and the sound of children's laughter and squeals reached us.

'Break time,' explained Mel. 'You don't want Bertie seeing you in this state. Linda's bringing us tea, so I suggest you wait in here until the children are safely back in their classrooms.'

'Thank you.'

I watched through the window as children streamed out onto the playground. I tried to swallow the lump in my throat as Bertie ran outside, carrying a football under his arm. He was with his usual gang, all laughing as they began passing the ball to each other. Mel followed the direction of my gaze.

'There's no way you could persuade your mother-in-law to let Bertie see out the term here?'

'No, I've tried.'

'That is a shame. In that case, I wonder if you could bring him back for the end of term concert? I was hoping he could do a solo as he's taken to the cornet so well.'

'I'll see what I can do.'

'Good. Ah, thank you, Linda,' said Mel, as the pink-haired secretary came in carrying a tray. I saw the question in her eyes as she took in my tear-stained face, but I trusted Mel to keep my confidence.

Bertie's hair was flying up at strange angles as he chased after the football. It was as though I were watching him in slow motion. His face spread into a smile as he scored a goal, running up to his best friend and jumping up and down in each other's arms. Deep down, I knew I wouldn't bring him back for the concert. How could I? It would amount to rubbing his face in all he'd lost.

Chapter Thirty-Nine

The farmhouse was noisier than usual. As I opened the front door, I could hear laughter, raised voices and the clink of glasses.

'She's here,' I heard Seb say. 'I'll tell her the good news.'

I hung my jacket on the end of the banister, and Seb ran into the hall. He grabbed me by the waist, lifting me off my feet and swinging me round and round before laughing and kissing me deeply.

'What's going on?'

I noticed Seb's eyes darken as he took in my red puffy face, but even the bedraggled sight of me couldn't dampen his enthusiasm. 'We did it,' he said, grabbing my hands and jumping up and down like an excited child. 'Liv, we bloody did it.'

'Did what?'

'The council has granted planning permission. We can build the treehouses, we can get the lake project off the ground.'

'Wow, that's amazing. Congratulations.'

Seb let go of my hands and took a step back. 'Hang on, why aren't you as excited as I am? It was you who did most of the work. Liv, what's going on?'

'Let's go through to the dining room,' I said. 'There's something I need to say, and it's best you all hear it together.'

'Liv, what's going on? You're scaring me.'

I ignored Seb and walked into the dining room. The table was covered with plates of cake and glasses of champagne. Harry, Pat, Stephan, and Maggie cheered and clapped when I walked into the room. I made my best attempt at a smile as Harry handed me a glass of champagne.

'Thank you.'

'It's the least we owe you. We couldn't have done this without you, Liv. Now we've got planning permission, we can move full steam ahead with our plans. God, when I think about all the possibilities for this place.' Harry brushed a tear from her eye. 'This would make my grandparents so proud, and I've got you and Seb to thank for it.'

I took a long sip of my champagne. 'I'm so pleased it's worked out for you all.'

'Worked out for *us*, Liv. You're as much a part of Lowen Farm's future as any of us.'

Exhaustion hit me, and I pulled out a chair, no longer able to hold up my own weight.

'Liv, is everything all right?' asked Pat. 'You look a little peaky. Is it hay fever? Mine's terrible at this time of year.'

Seb pulled out a chair beside me and tried to catch my eye. 'Liv? What's wrong?'

I hiccupped and fought back tears. 'There's something I need to tell you all.'

One by one, my friends pulled out chairs and sat down. A stray balloon bumped its way across the table and Maggie knocked it to the floor. The celebratory atmosphere of moments ago had been replaced by a thick air of tension.

'I...' Unable to speak, I took a deep breath and lifted my wine glass to my lips with shaking hands. 'I'm so sorry everyone, but I'm afraid Bertie and I are leaving Lowen Farm.'

'What?' Harry jumped up, knocking her wine glass over and sending sticky liquid rolling across the table. Maggie grabbed a tissue from her pocket and began mopping up the mess. 'Leaving? Why? The project is only just getting started. Aren't you happy here?'

'Harry, I've been happier here than at any time in my life.'

'Then why go?' Seb's voice was hard, cold, his body rigid as he stared down at the table.

'I have to consider what's in Bertie's best interests.'

'And staying here isn't?' asked Pat, his voice catching.

'My husband has asked if I'll give our marriage another try. It's the right thing for Bertie.'

'Couldn't he move in here with you?' asked Stephan. 'You could take on an extra room, so you have more space.'

I almost laughed at the thought of Rob moving into Lowen Farm. Almost, but not quite. 'My husband has rented a house on the estate where we used to live.'

'I can't believe you're doing this,' said Harry, her voice quiet, her hands shaking. 'There's got to be more to it.' She stared at me, but I avoided her gaze.

'There's nothing more to it than wanting to create a proper family for Bertie. It's for the best, I'm sure of it.'

Seb pushed his chair back and stormed out of the room.

'I'll go after him,' said Harry.

'When do you leave?' asked Maggie.

'My in-laws are coming to fetch us on Sunday morning.'

'Sunday? But that's only three days away.'

'I know. I'm sorry.' I ran out of the dining room and up the stairs to my bedroom. Railing against the cruelty of life, I took my anger out against my pillow, thumping it with my fists as hot, angry tears streamed down my cheeks.

Half an hour later, a knock came on my bedroom door. I opened it to find Harry, her cheeks flushed and her own eyes red-rimmed. 'Can I come in?'

I stood aside to let her pass. She walked through the room and sat down on Bertie's bed. 'I'm sorry,' I said, sitting down on my own.

'Liv, you owe me the truth.'

'I've told you the truth.'

'No, you haven't. You've been acting strangely for a couple of weeks now. There's more to your leaving that you're not telling me. Why won't you trust me?'

I played with the corner of the duvet cover, twisting and folding it between my fingers.

'Liv? Talk to me.'

'I can't.'

'You're scaring me, Liv. What's going on?'

'Please, Harry, don't push it.'

'Liv, I'm your friend. You can tell me anything.'

I shook my head, not trusting myself to speak. It was better for everyone that I took my problems elsewhere.

'Fine, if that's how you're going to be, I don't suppose there's much I can do about it. But, Liv?'

I looked up at Harry.

'I know there's more to this. You'll learn soon enough that shutting people out never helps anything.'

Harry was right, of course, but what she didn't understand was that I had no choice.

Harry stopped at the door and turned back to me. 'Oh, and Liv? You owe Seb one hell of an explanation.'

Chapter Forty

Bertie was in a bad mood. He wanted his friends to come over and play, but the atmosphere in the farmhouse had been strained since I broke my news, and I had to tell Bertie what was going on. We walked most of the way home in silence, Bertie kicking loose rocks along the path. When we reached the farmhouse, he went to put the TV on in the living room.

'Not right now, Bertie,' I said, taking the remote control from his hand. 'I need to talk to you. Let's go up to our room.'

'But I want to watch TV.'

'And you can, as soon as we've had a little talk.'

Bertie grabbed his school bag and stomped up the stairs. Once in our room, he pulled out his iPad and flicked it on to a game. I took the device from his hands, laying it on the bedside table. Bertie frowned and crossed his arms.

'Bertie, there's something important I need to tell you. It's about Dad.'

'Does he want to see me?'

'Yes.'

'Great, can I go at the weekend? He won't cancel again, will he?'

'Bertie, this isn't about a weekend visit. Your dad wants us to be a family again.'

'You mean, like, live together again?'

'Yes.'

Bertie blew out air from between his lips. He looked around the bedroom we shared. 'I can't imagine Dad here.'

'No, neither can I. In fact, your dad doesn't want to live here with us. He wants us to go back to Exeter and live with him there.'

Bertie laughed. 'We can't go back there, don't be silly.'

'Bertie...'

The smile dropped from Bertie's face. 'You haven't said yes?'

'It's the best thing for all of us. You'll get to spend loads of time with Dad and you'll get to see your old friends again.'

'At weekends?'

'No, at school.' I was trying hard to make my voice cheery, but it came out more like a doped-up kids' TV presenter.

Bertie stood up, glaring down at me. 'You're not sending me back to my old school. I hated it there.'

'Bertie, it's for the best.'

'No! I won't go!'

'I'm afraid that's not your decision to make. Grandma and Grandpa are coming to collect us on Sunday. You can take some sweets into school and perhaps have a sleepover with your friends tomorrow evening, so you have a proper goodbye.'

'No,' said Bertie, a lone tear breaking out and trickling down his cheek. 'I won't go.' He tried to walk past me, but I grabbed his wrist.

'Get off me!' he shouted. 'I hate you!' Bertie yanked his hand free and ran out of the room.

It took me a few seconds to collect my thoughts, then I raced out of the room in hot pursuit of Bertie. There was no one in the living room, no one in the dining room, but I found Maggie making a start on dinner in the kitchen.

'Have you seen Bertie?'

'No. I heard the back door slam, though, so maybe he went outside to play or feed the animals?'

'Thanks.'

I slipped on my shoes and ran outside. There was no sign of Bertie by the pigpen, goat enclosure, or chicken coop. I ran across the lane to the field where the sheep grazed happily, but Bertie wasn't among them.

After searching the outbuildings, I ran across the field towards the woods. I fought against the memory of the first time Seb had shown me around. It wouldn't help to think like that. In the woods I called Bertie's name, but no reply came other than the flapping wings of birds who I'd scared from the trees.

At the lake, the water lay undisturbed, the rowing boat bobbing gently against its mooring. I ran my hands through my hair. Perhaps I shouldn't have chased after Bertie at all and left him to calm down.

Outside Pat's cabin, I noticed the old bike Harry had loaned Bertie resting against the far wall. I knocked and Pat came to the door.

'Is Bertie in there with you?'

Pat stepped outside his cabin and pulled the door closed. 'He is Liv, but he's very upset. It might be best if you leave him here with me for a while. As well as being upset, he's also extremely angry. He doesn't understand what's going on.'

'I tried to explain things to him.'

'Hmm, well, I'm not sure he's alone in not understanding. Why are you doing this, Liv?'

I wanted to tell Pat that it wasn't my doing at all, but I kept quiet.

'Why don't you leave him here, and I'll bring him back to the farmhouse at dinner time?'

'Thank you.'

Pat returned to his cabin, and I leaned against the wood, steeling myself for my next house call. I walked the short distance to Seb's cabin and paused outside his door.

'Liv.' Seb opened the door before I'd knocked. 'What do you want?'

'I wanted to come and apologise.'

'For what? Lying to me, leaving me, or not even having the decency to tell me when we were alone?'

'I didn't lie.'

'Really? So, when I told you I didn't want to get involved with you unless you had moved on from your husband, you weren't lying when you said you'd never go back to him?'

'I wasn't lying when I said it.'

'Oh, right, that's OK then.'

'Seb, I really am sorry. If there was any other way...'

'From where I'm standing, you're not being forced back to your husband at gunpoint. It seems to me you're going back of your own free will.'

If only you knew. 'I'm sorry.'

'Yeah, well, thanks for the apology. Now, I think it's best you go.'

'Seb.' I placed my hand on his arm and he jumped back as though burnt by a hot poker.

'Get out of here. Go on, go.'

I turned and walked away from the only man I'd ever truly loved. Seb hated me, Bertie hated me, everyone at Lowen Farm probably hated me. Whoever said *it's better to have loved and lost* was a total liar. I wished I'd never met

Seb, never set foot on Lowen Farm, for the pain in my heart of having loved and lost was more than I could bear.

Chapter Forty-One

Just as she'd promised, Marion turned up at ten on the dot. Bertie hadn't spoken to me since I'd announced our move, and whilst polite, the other residents at Lowen Farm seemed uncomfortable around me, avoiding lengthy conversations and sticking to practical topics if they spoke.

The only positive I could find from the past two weeks was that the new residents hadn't yet arrived. For their sakes, it was better they didn't land at the farm whilst me and my black cloud were still there.

I looked out of the window, wondering if Marion and Hugo were going to get out of their car. It seemed not, so I went outside, and Marion wound down her window.

'I hope you're ready.'

'I just need to bring our suitcases down. Would you like to come and wait inside?'

Marion scrunched up her nose and shook her head.

'Hello, Hugo.'

'Hello, Olivia.' My father-in-law seemed unable to look at me, keeping his eyes fixed beyond the windscreen. I wondered how big a part he had played in this scheme. My guess was Marion was the instigator, her husband and son too pathetic to stand up to her. Or perhaps I was giving them too much credit.

'Right. I'll get our bags.'

Bertie was in the living room playing chess with Pat. I ducked my head around the door. 'Five minutes till we leave, Bertie.' Bertie refused to acknowledge me, but Pat nodded to show he'd heard.

Stephan found me wrestling with suitcases on the staircase. 'Liv, Maggie asked if you could nip upstairs before you go. Why don't you pop up there now and I'll take these down to the car for you.'

'Thanks.' I ran up to the top floor, knocking on Maggie's bedroom door.

'Come in.'

I walked in and found her sitting in an armchair, looking out of the window.

'Stephan said you wanted to see me?'

Maggie beckoned me towards her. 'Look,' she said, pointing out of the window to where my in-laws were waiting in the car. 'Something's not right about all this, Liv. They've been sitting out there since they arrived, po-faced and unsmiling. This isn't a happy family reunion. We're not stupid. We all know there's more to your leaving than you're telling us.'

'Maggie, I can't...'

Maggie reached across and gripped my hand. 'I understand. Well, at least I'm trying to. But I'm worried about you, Liv. You and Bertie have become like family to me, and I know something isn't right with all this. So, I'm going to call you every Friday at lunchtime. If you don't answer or send me a message letting me know you're OK, I'm going to come and find you.'

'Maggie, you don't need to do that.'

'I do and I will. I'm afraid I'm not giving you a choice.'

I bent down and hugged her. 'I'm sorry, but I have to go.'

Maggie nodded and turned her attention back to the window. 'Stephan won't linger to say goodbye. He's got a thing about goodbyes, but know that he'll miss you as much as I will.'

'Bye, Maggie.'

'Goodbye, love.'

Downstairs, I walked over to where Pat and Bertie were in the middle of their chess game. 'I'm sorry to interrupt, but Grandma and Grandpa are waiting for us outside.'

'I'm not going until I've finished my match.'

'Bertie...'

'Tell you what,' said Pat, pulling out his phone. 'I'll take a photograph of the board, then the next time we see each other, we can pick up where we've left off.'

Before Pat had a chance to take the photo, Bertie's arm swept across the chessboard, sending wooden pieces scattering across the carpet.

'Bertie!'

'No, Liv, I understand,' said Pat. He crouched down beside Bertie's chair. Bertie had his face in his hands and Pat gently pulled them away. 'Bertie, we will see each other again, and we will resume our game. Now you need to be a brave boy and do as your mother tells you.' Pat looked up at me. 'Perhaps once you're settled, you could give me your address? I'd like to write to Bertie if that's all right?'

'Of course it is.'

Bertie flung his arms around Pat, his shoulders heaving up and down with sobs. 'There there,' said Pat, rubbing his back. He pulled Bertie's arms off and nodded to me. 'Go with your mother now, Bertie, there's a good boy.'

I took Bertie's hand in mine. As soon as we had left the room Bertie snatched his hand away, rubbing it against his trousers as though my touch had tainted him.

'Liv.' Harry stood leaning against the doorway of the dining room, a misshapen cardigan covering her shoulders.

'Goodbye, Harry.'

'Come here.' Harry pulled me into a tight hug. 'You know you are welcome back here any time. Just say the word and you can have your old room back.'

'Thank you.'

Harry let me go and I walked out onto the drive, Bertie by my side. I looked around for any sign of Seb, but I knew in my heart of hearts he wouldn't come to say goodbye. Why would he? I'd broken his heart. He owed me nothing.

'At last,' said Marion with a sigh.

'Hello, Albert,' said Hugo.

'My name's not Albert,' said Bertie with a scowl. He climbed up into the four by four, yanking on his seatbelt so hard it caught.

Hugo started the engine and turned the car towards the track. I looked behind me through the back windscreen. All my friends had gathered to wave us off. At the far side of the building stood Seb, leaning against a wall and staring at the car. I lifted my hand in a wave, but he didn't respond.

As we drove away from the village Bertie made no effort to hide the tears streaming down his face. I kept my composure, not wanting to give Marion the satisfaction of seeing how upset I was inside. Hugo attempted some small talk, but I kept my answers monosyllabic, and Bertie ignored his grandparents completely. I had no idea what they hoped to achieve by their masterplan, but if it was family harmony, they were failing miserably.

Chapter Forty-Two

After a tense journey punctuated by terse snippets of conversation, Hugo finally pulled his car onto the housing estate, which, though once familiar, now felt like a totally alien landscape. We drove past our old house, and I turned my head away.

'Here we are,' said Hugo, pulling into a street made up of new-build terraced houses. Each house was identical, built from ugly orange brick. Several had baskets of plastic flowers hanging from either side of their front doors. 'Number twenty. This is us.'

Hugo pulled into the driveway, and he and Marion climbed out. No mention had been made of Rob, but I assumed he would be waiting for us inside the house, and I wanted to put off the moment I'd have to see him.

'Come on, hurry along, we haven't got all day,' said Marion, opening the back doors of the car for me and Bertie to get out.

'Come on, Bertie,' I whispered. 'It won't be as bad as you're imagining.'

Bertie scowled at me, undid his seatbelt and climbed out of the car. The front door opened, and Rob forced a smile onto his face. He had bags under his eyes, suggesting he'd got as much sleep as I had over the past few weeks.

'All right, mate,' he said as Bertie walked up the path. 'Long time, no see.'

'Whose fault's that?' asked Bertie, scowling up at his father.

Rob laughed and ruffled Bertie's hair. 'As lively as ever, I see. Hello, Olivia.'

I ignored Rob's greeting and pushed past him into a house as bland as I'd been expecting. It wasn't hard to guess who'd chosen the décor. Everything gleamed white and my first impression was that I'd stepped into an operating theatre dressed up as a house. It was sterile, devoid of character, and felt nothing like a home.

'Are you staying for a coffee?' Rob asked his parents as Hugo removed our suitcases from the car and deposited them in the hall.

'No, we'll leave you alone for some family time,' said Marion, kissing her son on both cheeks. 'Goodbye, Albert.'

No answer came from upstairs, and Rob let out a nervous laugh. 'He's probably up there settling into his new room.'

Marion huffed and left the house. The door closed and Rob turned to me.

'Just don't,' I said, running up the stairs to find Bertie.

The first door I tried opened onto a family bathroom. A free-standing bath stood on a marble effect floor, while the walls were covered in rectangular white tiles, which reminded me of a public toilet, but which were now the height of fashion. The next door I opened led into a master bedroom, a tiny ensuite shower room squashed into one corner. The room was like a show home, pressed grey bedding, dusky pink throw strewn casually on top of the duvet. A grey velvet accent chair was tucked beneath a white dressing table, and generic prints of flowers were the only artwork on display. When I pushed the last door, I found Bertie lying on a *Spider-Man* duvet cover on a narrow bed. To call it a bedroom felt generous. It was more like a cupboard. No amount of white paint could enlarge the tiny space.

'It must be nice to have your own room again,' I said, sitting down on the bed. Bertie rolled over, his eyes fixed on his iPad. 'Can I get you anything?'

'Go away.'

'Please, Bertie.'

'I said, go away. Are you deaf or something?'

I stood up with a sigh and closed the door behind me. Downstairs, I found Rob in the kitchen diner making coffee from a fancy machine. 'Is he settling in OK?'

'What do you think?'

'I know his room's a bit on the small side, but we'll get a bigger place soon, and it was really generous of Mum and Dad to get this place for us.'

My mouth hung open as I watched Rob pottering about like it was a normal family Sunday. 'Generous? GENEROUS?'

'All right, Liv. There's no need to shout.'

I didn't want to shout. I wanted to scream. 'I assume you know how your mother persuaded me to come back to you?'

Rob had the decency to blush. 'I don't agree with her methods, but she's got our best interests at heart.'

I placed my hands on the breakfast bar and leaned forward, taking deep breaths. 'Right, I think we need to get a few things straight. Number one, you need to understand I'm only here with you because your witch of a mother blackmailed me into it. Number two, please give me prior warning if a man with a camera is going to be following me around again. Number three, I'll play your stupid game of happy families, but it's just that. A game. While Bertie's around, I'll do my best impression of a loving wife, but when he's not, I don't want to even be in the same room as you. You can sleep on the sofa and clear away your bedding before Bertie gets up. You can forget me pandering to your complex dietary needs. I'll cook for me and Bertie and save you some. If you're hungry enough, you can eat it.'

'Anything else?'

'You remember the conversation we had when I said I'd like us to be friends?'

'Yes.'

'Well, you can forget it. I don't want to be friends with a spineless excuse for a man who goes along with his mother's blackmail, using his son as leverage. Oh, and one last thing. I'll be applying for jobs, so you'll need to do your share of the housework. I'll take care of mine and Bertie's washing, but you can do your own. Or perhaps your mother would like to take care of that, like she's taken care of everything else?'

I grabbed the coffee Rob had just made and stormed into the living room, spilling drops on the new white carpet as I went. I couldn't remember ever feeling so angry. Upstairs, the person I loved most in the world was grieving for the life and friends he'd left, and I'd done that to him. Marion had done that to *us*. But Rob had done nothing to stop her, and I could never forgive him for it.

Rob walked into the living room and I wondered if he had a death wish.

'I want to be on my own.'

'Liv, we need to talk.'

Liv? Since when did he call me Liv? 'There's nothing to say.'

'There is. There are things you don't know that I think you're going to want to hear.'

Chapter Forty-Three

Rob sat in a white leather armchair opposite me, and I glared at him. 'Go on then. Spit it out.'

'I know you're angry with me, and I get it, but you need to understand I had as little choice in this situation as you did.'

'Really? I find that very hard to believe.'

'It's true. You weren't the only one who was spied on.'

'What? You mean...'

'That same guy followed me, too. Well, I suppose there could have been two of them. But yes, I was photographed in what could be construed as compromising positions.'

'Such as?'

'Drink, light drug use, women.'

'The usual then.'

Rob sighed and took a sip of his coffee. 'Like with your photos, there's more to them than what it looks like at face value.'

'Someone forced you to take drugs?'

'No, but I was set up. Dad announced that one of his friends was looking for a new business partner and arranged for me to meet him for dinner. The last thing I wanted was to go into business with one of Dad's mates, but given I was unemployed and living at home, I didn't feel I could say no. Anyway, I went to the dinner and this guy plied me with booze. He drank like a fish, and I felt I had to keep up. When the bar closed, we went up to his hotel room for a nightcap. That's when he brought out the drugs. I hadn't done anything like that since my uni days, but I was so wasted I wasn't thinking straight and went along with it.'

'But how did they get photos if you were in someone's hotel room?'

'Hidden cameras. Dad's mate was in on it from the start. The whole thing was a setup.'

'Hang on,' I said, trying to wrap my head around what Rob was telling me. 'Why the hell would your parents want to set up their own son like that? I don't get it.'

'It's about control. It always has been with them. They've controlled everything I've ever done: where I went to school, who I was friends with, where I went to uni, what I studied at uni, what business I went into. Everything. The only thing they couldn't control was you getting pregnant. I knew if I didn't marry you and they found out, they'd try to pay you off, get you to some private clinic to end the pregnancy. I may be an arsehole, but I wanted our son from the second you told me you were pregnant.'

'I've always wondered if you married me just to piss them off...'

Rob's lips twitched in something resembling a smile. 'Maybe a bit. OK, maybe a lot. I was worried about the baby, that's true, but they'd been lining me up with suitable women every time I went home for the holidays, and I suppose I wanted to see what would happen if, for once, I went against their wishes.'

'And what did happen?'

'They threatened to disinherit me. Looking back, I probably should have let them do it and cut all ties.'

'But you went ahead with the wedding, and they didn't disown you.'

'Yes, by then we knew you were expecting a boy, so I had my own bargaining chip. The family name was always so important to them. I told them if they disinherited me, they'd never get to meet their grandson. Not only that, we'd both take your surname and lose Simmons altogether.'

'God, Rob, I didn't think you had it in you. But I still don't understand why your parents needed to get dirt on you. It doesn't make any sense.'

'It's not just about control, it's also about money. They're terrified of a messy divorce and the prospect of you going after their money.'

'But I'm not remotely interested in their money.'

'I know, but they don't believe you. There's something else you should know, but before I tell you, I'm going to need something stronger than coffee.'

Rob left the room, returning minutes later with two glasses of wine. He handed me one, then carried his own back to his chair. 'Right, so the other thing I need to tell you is that I've met someone.'

'Who?'

'Nicola, my former secretary.'

I choked on my wine, and Rob visibly squirmed.

'I know,' he said, 'I'm a walking cliché.'

'When did it start?'

Rob clinked a fingernail against his wine glass.

'Oh, come on, Rob, what does it matter now?'

'I'm really sorry, Liv. I didn't mean it to happen.'

'When did it start?'

'A year ago.'

This time I didn't choke on my wine. I spat it out, all across the new white sofa.

'I'm so sorry.'

'And your parents don't approve of the match?'

'Nicola grew up in a council house and her education doesn't stretch beyond GCSEs, so what do you think?'

'That she's their worst nightmare?' I threw Rob a smile, which he returned. 'What's she like?'

'You don't want me talking about the woman I cheated on you with.'

'Actually, I do. I'm curious.'

'OK. Well, she's really funny, and I mean hilarious. She does stand-up comedy in her spare time and she's bloody good at it. She's smart too. She may not have the certificates I do, but she's ten times cleverer than me.'

'Pretty?'

'Of course. If my parents could look past their snobbery, they'd see how happy she makes me.' Rob screwed up his face. 'Sorry, this is really weird, isn't it? I shouldn't be saying all this stuff to you.'

'Why not? We may be married, but it's only a piece of paper. Besides, I met someone too.'

'While we were together?'

'No, sorry, you don't get off the hook that easily. It's someone I met at Lowen Farm.'

'What's he like?'

'He's...' my eyes filled with tears. I couldn't talk about Seb. Even thinking about him broke my heart. 'There's no point telling you, because thanks to your mother, I'll never be able to see him again.'

'Maybe you could still see him? Mum wouldn't need to know.'

I shook my head. 'Even if he accepted that scenario, which I'm telling you now he wouldn't, I couldn't take the risk. Can you think of any way out of this?'

Rob swilled his wine around his glass. 'I'm so sorry, Liv, but I can't. Neither of us has any money to fight my parents in court. We could make a stand and say we won't go along with this charade, but then what would happen to Bertie?'

'You haven't seemed that interested in Bertie these past few months,' I said, some of my old resentment resurfacing.

'I didn't have a choice. Mum said it would muddy the waters if I spent time with him. I thought she was doing it for Bertie's benefit, but I should've known better.'

'Then we're stuck in this bizarre limbo forever?'

'Not forever. I intend to work my arse off until we've got enough money of our own that mum can't threaten us anymore. Once we're financially independent of them, we'll be free to do as we please.'

My heart sank as I considered how long achieving financial independence might take. It could be years before I was able to fight Marion, by which time Seb would be long gone. I was trapped in a gilded cage and would be an old woman before I ever found the key.

Chapter Forty-Four

True to his word, when I woke up at six, Rob had already packed away his sleeping bag and there was no evidence he'd slept on the sofa. After our heart-to-heart the night before, I'd softened towards him and come to the compromise that we'd take turns with who got the bed.

Bertie hadn't spoken a word since we arrived at the house, eating his dinner in silence, hiding up in his room with the door closed. We'd agreed to let his rudeness slide for a couple of days while he came to terms with our drastic change in circumstances.

I found Rob making coffee in the kitchen. 'Want one?' he asked.

'Yes, please.' I took the offered cup and leaned against the kitchen counter. 'What are your plans today?'

'Dad's rented me a new office, so I'm going to see about finding some new clients. It will be the first test of how far news of my downfall spread. I know he pulled all the strings at his disposal to keep the bankruptcy hush-hush, but these things have a habit of getting out. How about you?'

'I'm heading to the job centre first thing, then I thought I'd call in on Cass. The one silver lining to moving back here is I'm closer to her and Dad.'

'A positive attitude, I like it.'

I smiled, putting on my best pretence of optimism when inside I felt like I was drowning.

'Liv, this is a bit awkward, but I wanted to run something by you.'

'Go on.'

'Would you mind if I had lunch with Nicola? If you do, I'll honour your wishes and stay clear of her.'

'No, I have no problem with you meeting her. The one rule I'd like to impose is that you don't bring her back here to the house.'

'That's fair enough. And if you want to meet up with your bloke, that's fine with me.'

'Thanks,' I said, knowing I wouldn't even attempt to contact Seb. I'd dreamed about him the previous night, waking up to a pillow soaked with tears and a feeling of longing mixed with despair.

We ate our breakfast in companionable silence. The unexpected friendship developing between us was a blessing. At least I wouldn't need to find ways to avoid him in our new shoebox house.

'I'd better wake up Bertie. We've got used to a short walk to school. It will be a shock having to get him ready so early.'

I left Rob reading the paper and climbed the stairs. 'Bertie?' I said, knocking on his door. 'Bertie, are you awake?'

'Go away.'

'Bertie, you have to get up for school. I'm coming in.' I pushed against the door, but it wouldn't open. 'Bertie, have you locked this door?'

'It doesn't have a lock.'

'OK, so why can't I get it open?'

'I don't want you to come in.'

'Right, well, I'm afraid I have to.'

'No.'

'Let me in this minute or you won't have your iPad back until Monday.'

I heard a creak as Bertie climbed off his bed and walked across to the door. Next came the sound of something heavy being pushed across his carpet. The door opened a crack, Bertie's scowling face poking through the gap. 'What do you want?'

'You need to get ready for school. Let me in.'

'No. I can get ready by myself.'

'What don't you want me to see?'

'Nothing. I just want to be left alone.'

Bertie's ears had turned pink, a sure sign he was lying. I pushed gently against the door, and he stepped back. The door jammed on what looked like the corner of a dresser.

'iPad,' I warned. Bertie sighed and pushed the dresser out of the way. I opened the door and was confronted by a sight that made me want to both laugh and shout. As I struggled to untangle my emotions, Bertie ran back to his bed and threw himself under the covers.

'Oh God, Bertie. What have you done?'

Bertie didn't answer, so I sat down on his bed and pulled the duvet away from his face.

'I hate this house; I want to go back to the farm.'

'I know, but that doesn't excuse what you've done.'

'I thought if I made my room look like Jake's, I might like it more.'

I stood up and walked to the far wall. No wonder Bertie had been so quiet the previous evening. He'd attempted to colour the wall black, with a thick felt tip by the looks of things. He'd only managed a small section before the pen must have run out, the remainder of the white wall covered with faded scribbles.

'Please, Mum, don't tell Dad.'

'Don't tell Dad what?' Rob stood in the doorway, a cup of coffee in his hands.

'Um, Rob, I'll repaint the walls.'

Rob walked into the room and over to the defaced wall. He ran his hand over the black smudges. From his face, it was impossible to tell his reaction. He turned to Bertie, making us both jump as he let out a loud laugh. Bertie looked over at me, but I just shrugged.

'Fancy yourself as an artist, do you?' Rob sat down beside Bertie on the bed.

'I wanted my room to look like Jake's.'

'And Jake has black walls?'

Bertie nodded.

'I'll paint over it today,' I said.

'Why?' asked Rob, turning to me.

'I don't think this would impress your mother.'

Rob shrugged and took a sip of his coffee. He walked over to me and lowered his voice to just above a whisper. 'She's got us where she wants us, Liv. But I don't remember her making any stipulations about wall colours.'

'Can I paint my whole room black?' asked Bertie.

'Don't push your luck.'

'No,' said Rob, 'Bertie's got a point. What do you think, Liv? Should we let him do it?'

'If we paint this entire room black, it will look like a cave.'

'One wall?' asked Bertie.

'We'll see. But I'm much more likely to agree to this if you've got yourself ready for school nicely.'

Bertie flung back the duvet and grabbed his school uniform from the back of a chair. He still hadn't smiled since we left Lowen Farm, but his scowl had smoothed out slightly and this seemed like a good start.

Chapter Forty-Five

Now that we were down to one car and living on an estate with no access to public transport, the school run took even longer than usual. We had to leave the house at seven in order to make it to school for half past eight. After navigating the city centre traffic to drop Rob at his new office, I turned the car around and drove in the opposite direction towards Bertie's school.

Bertie turned the radio up and stared out of the window. The way his fists sat clenched in his lap told me he placed his misery firmly at my door. The closer we got to the school gates, the more agitated he became, his legs jiggling, his fingers tugging at the tie around his neck.

'It will be OK,' I said as we drove into the car park. Bertie didn't reply. I turned off the engine, and he jumped out, striding up to the entrance without waiting for me. I ran after him, but became caught in a mass of parental drop-offs and by the time I reached the front door to the school Bertie had long since disappeared.

'Olivia, darling.'

I turned to find Cressida Jamison tottering towards me on leopard print heels. 'Hello, Cressida.'

'Long time no see. You should hear the dreadful rumours that have been circulating about your disappearance. We must go for coffee so you can tell me all about it.' She linked her arm in mine, but I pulled away, making the excuse of a busy day and *maybe another time*. Cressida Jamison wanted to be my friend as much as I wanted to be hers. Not at all. She was just looking for some juicy nuggets of gossip she could pass on to her minions.

Somehow, when Beryl gossiped away in the shop, it felt harmless. As much as she loved to discuss other people's business, it was never with any malice. Cressida Jamison was a different story. I'd heard how she tore other people's lives to shreds with her acid tongue. She could gossip about me all she liked, but I wouldn't willingly give her any ammunition.

'Mrs Simmons?'

Mr Kieling was pushing through the gathered parents. 'I wonder if we could have a word in my office?'

'Of course,' I said, trudging behind him as the heavily made-up eyes of other mothers followed me.

I found myself back in the office I'd hoped never to visit again. It was the opposite of Mel's: tidy, grand and uncomfortable. I wondered if Mr Kieling kept a box of tissues to hand for weeping parents, but thought it unlikely.

'I wanted to check in with you, given Bertie has had so much time out of school.'

'Oh, I assumed my mother-in-law would have told you when she enrolled Bertie. He hasn't been missing school. In fact, he's only missed a few days of schooling since he left.'

Mr Kieling cleared his throat. 'She did appraise me of your situation. It doesn't sound like Alberto's education has been up to the same standard we expect from teachers here.'

'Really? That surprises me, given my mother-in-law didn't step foot inside Bertie's school. She must have a wonderful imagination to have come to that conclusion.'

'Yes, well, you'll quite understand, I'm sure, that we can't let Alberto fall behind his classmates.'

'I assure you, Mr Kieling, Bertie has not fallen behind.'

'Yes, well, in consultation with Mrs Simmons Senior, we've agreed that it would be best if Alberto receives some additional tutoring.'

'You have, have you? And what gives *Mrs Simmons Senior* authority to make that call?'

A sheen of sweat had appeared on Mr Kieling's top lip, and he fussed with the papers on his desk. 'I believe your in-laws are paying for Alberto's school fees.'

'Yes.'

'Very generous of them. Although, understandably, they'd like you and your husband to fund the extra tuition Alberto will require.'

'Right.' Anger and resentment fought against a deep feeling of despair. I couldn't fault Marion's intelligence, she must have realised Rob and I would try to work our way out of her influence, and I felt certain an additional tutor would be the first of many extra expenses designed to keep us financially insecure and therefore dependent. 'And if I refuse this extra tuition?'

'It could jeopardise Alberto's place at the school. Mrs Simmons Senior assured me you would come round to her way of thinking.'

Without replying, I stood and walked away from Mr Kieling before I could say anything I'd regret.

'My secretary will email you a tuition timetable and an invoice,' said Mr Kieling to my departing back.

I ignored the group of women loitering by the school entrance and walked as quickly as I could to the car. My priority was finding a job, preferably one I could keep hidden from Marion and Hugo. If they knew I was working, it was only a matter of time before they found other ways to siphon off my income.

The job centre was less depressing than I'd feared. Having never stepped foot in one before, I was expecting something stark and utilitarian, like I'd seen in films. Instead, the building was newly furnished, purple armchairs huddled around coffee tables, discreet booths for appointments, and exhibition boards advertising the latest opportunities.

A cheery young woman dressed in jeans and a floral shirt assisted me. She ran through my qualifications, previous experience, and potential for references. Harry was the only person I could think to name as a referee. I hoped she'd be generous with her reference, despite the fact I'd upped and left the job she'd given me with next-to-no notice.

'Hmm, there really isn't a lot about at the moment,' said the young girl, scrolling down her computer screen. 'We have some great training opportunities and apprenticeships.'

'I really need to be earning now,' I said. 'Preferably something I can fit around school hours.'

'Right, that could be tricky.' The girl chewed on the end of her pen, scrunching her eyes as she clicked her mouse. 'I think the only thing that might meet your requirements is this.' She turned her computer screen around so I could study the advertisement. My heart sank. It was the cleaning job at the football club I'd seen when Rob first left me. But, as my mum used to say, *beggars can't be choosers*.

'What are the hours?'

'Four a.m. till six a.m. six days a week. We've been advertising this job for a while now, but not many people like the idea of an early start. The pay goes some way to compensate for the antisocial hours.'

'How much is it?'

'Twenty pounds an hour. Unheard of for this type of job.'

'And why is it six days a week? I thought matches were only once or twice a week?'

'The football ground is used for a range of events. They hold concerts there, school groups rent it out, businesses. All sorts really.'

'And it's an immediate start?'

'Yes. If you're interested, I could arrange an interview, possibly as early as this afternoon if you're free.'

'Thank you.'

The girl directed me to a purple armchair, where I filled out an application form. Two hundred and forty pounds a week wouldn't go far when it came to fighting Marion, but it was a start, and better than a poke in the eye with a sharp stick, another of my mum's favourite sayings. Given I was starting from zero, it felt like a step in the right direction.

Chapter Forty-Six

I sat fully clothed on the toilet, taking deep breaths. I couldn't afford to let my mask slip and had to keep pretending to be content with a life I hated. Marion had taken to dropping round on a whim, usually when Rob was at work. Goodness knows what she hoped to catch me doing, but every time she appeared she seemed disappointed to find me engaged in a mindless housework chore.

A couple of times over the past week, I'd felt as though I was being followed. As much as I resented the intrusion, it gave me some pleasure knowing my stalker would be just as bored as I was. And my stalker was not an early riser. Clearly, whoever Marion had hired didn't think it was worth watching the house before eight a.m. which was just as well.

I stifled a yawn with the back of my hand, flushed the toilet, and ran my hands under the tap. Marion probably thought I had something wrong with my bowels, the amount of times I hid in the toilet during her visits.

When I emerged from the bathroom, I found Marion nosing around the living room. That was fine by me. She'd find nothing of any interest there. I doubted she'd start rooting through the understairs cupboard, and even if she did, it was a logical place to store camping equipment and sleeping bags, given we had no garage or attic space.

'How is Albert getting on at school?'

'Fine.' A lie. He was miserable.

'And the extra tuition?'

'Fine.'

'No luck with finding a job?'

'No.' Another lie. 'I went to the job centre, but they tried to sign me up to training courses and I wouldn't be able to fit those around Bertie.'

'Quite right. A mother's place is in the home looking after her family.'

'Would you like another cup of tea?'

'No, I must be on my way. I just wanted to check in, see how you were getting on.'

I showed Marion to the door. At least she never went upstairs. If she did, she'd see one wall of Bertie's bedroom covered in black chalk paint. He'd decorated it with a range of colourful faces, all with their mouths turned down at the corners. My son was not exactly subtle.

Once Marion's car disappeared from view, I lay down on the sofa and flicked on the TV. There was only half an hour before I'd need to leave on the school run, not enough time to risk a nap. My early starts left me zombie-like for most of the day. Sleepless nights followed by three a.m. starts were playing havoc with my health. My skin was covered in pimples, my hair had lost all its shine, and no amount of makeup could hide the bags beneath my eyes. I suffered from brain fog, forgetting where I'd left my keys, what day it was. One day I'd even tried to let myself into my old house, confused why my keys weren't working.

I pulled out my phone and flicked on the messages. This was a daily form of torture I subjected myself to. It was guaranteed to make me cry, but I feared that without it, I'd forget my true self. As I scrolled through the messages from Seb, I let the tears flow freely. There had been no communication from him since I'd left Lowen Farm and I couldn't blame him. I turned my attention to my photos, reminding me of faces which had grown so familiar and who I now missed so much it physically hurt.

My alarm went off, and I picked up my bag and car keys. Bertie was struggling enough without me being late. I'd promised him a trip to Cass's house on the way home hoping to cheer him up, but even the thought of seeing his cousins hadn't raised a smile.

Outside the school, I waited a safe distance from the other parents. It only took a few days before Cressida realised I wouldn't divulge any secrets and went back to her familiar barbed comments and laughing behind my back. At Bertie's last school, there had been a mixture of mums, dads, and grandparents at the school gates. At this school, the waiting parents were almost exclusively female, either mothers or nannies (as in the au pair variety, not the grandparent or goat sort).

Bertie was one of the last children to leave school. He trudged towards me, his head bent, kicking up gravel as he shuffled his feet. As he got closer, I noticed a red streak travelling from his lip to his cheek.

'Bertie,' I said, tilting his chin so I could get a good look. 'What's happened to you?'

'Nothing.'

'Tell me now, or I'll have to speak to Mrs Bright.'

Bertie's eyes filled with tears. 'Don't, Mum, it's nothing.'

'It doesn't look like nothing.'

'They were just messing around.'

'Who?'

'Jack Jamison and his mates.'

'What did they do to you?'

A tear trickled down Bertie's cheek and he brushed it away with an angry swipe of his sleeve. 'They were saying mean things about you and Dad. That we had no money, that Dad doesn't love me. Then they started hitting me with branches.'

'Branches? Where were you?'

'They dragged me into the woodland area at lunchtime.'

'And did you tell anyone what happened?'

'I tried to tell Mrs Bright, but the others said we were just playing, and she told me to stop making a fuss.'

'She what?' I began marching up to the school, but Bertie chased me, yanking my arm to stop me.

'Please, Mum, don't. You'll just make it worse.'

'I won't stand for you being bullied.'

'But they'll bully me more if they think I'm a snitch.'

'Fine. But I want you to think about it tonight, and I want you to let me take a photo of your cut for evidence.'

After much protesting, Bertie relented and let me photograph his face.

'Come on, let's go and see Aunt Cass.'

'Can we just go home?'

'Are you sure? You love seeing Jake.'

'I don't want him to see this,' said Bertie, pointing to the cut on his cheek. 'I'm really tired, Mum. I just want to go home.'

'All right, but wait in the car while I call Aunt Cass. I need to let her know we won't be coming over.'

'OK.'

Bertie climbed into the car, and I dialled my sister's number.

'Hi, Liv. Are you on your way over?'

'No, sorry, I'm going to have to cancel. Bertie's had a bad day at school and wants to go straight home.'

'What's happened?'

'Bullying, I think. He's made me promise not to speak to his teacher, but I'm going to speak to the headteacher about it tomorrow.'

'You poor thing. As if you don't have enough to be dealing with.'

'Are you still OK to pick me and Bertie up tomorrow to visit Dad? Rob needs the car.'

'Of course. I'll be at yours by eleven.'

'Thanks. Love you.'

'Love you too.'

Chapter Forty-Seven

'All right ladies, that's us done.'

I wiped my brow with my gloved hand and stretched out my aching back. I'd cleaned fifteen toilets that morning, which had to be a record. There'd been some famous pop star or other performing at the football ground the night before and the toilets were as disgusting as I'd expected them to be. Mind you, they were never as bad as after a match. The things I'd had to fish out from toilet bowls didn't bear thinking about.

I packed my cleaning equipment away in its box and washed my hands in the staff changing area. Once my uniform was hanging in my locker, I joined the queue of women waiting for Carla to hand out our wages.

Among the long line of workers, I was the only Brit prepared to do this kind of work. All the others were migrant workers, the very workers lambasted in British papers by the kind of guys who couldn't flush their own crap, never mind clean up someone else's.

I reached the front of the queue and Carla handed me my two twenty-pound notes with her usual smile, jotting down my hours in her small notebook. Being paid in cash was a godsend. I stored my earnings in my sock drawer, counting them out each night and calculating how long I'd need to save before being able to take on Marion.

The coffee van outside the stadium was doing a roaring trade, but despite being dog-tired, I headed to the car, saving myself for cheaper coffee at home. The city roads were quiet, most commuters were not even awake yet, and I made it home in record time.

'Coffee?' asked Rob, as I walked into the kitchen.

'Silly question.' We'd not spent that much time together over the past few weeks, but the time we had spent had been amicable enough. I resented how private he was with his business and finances, but appreciated the effort he'd been making with Bertie.

'Is Bertie awake yet?'

'No, still sleeping, I think.'

'OK. I'm going to have a shower, then I'll wake him up.'

I spent longer than usual under the hot water. My shift had been particularly gruelling, and despite the rubber gloves and protective uniform, I felt covered in grime that needed to be cleaned away.

At seven I went to wake Bertie but found his bed empty. At least Rob had managed to drag him from his bed, and I wouldn't have to deal with the usual morning grump. Once dressed, I went downstairs to find Rob eating alone at the breakfast bar.

'You've not let Bertie watch TV, have you?'

'I thought he was upstairs getting dressed.'

'No, he's down here with you.'

'Liv, I've not seen him yet this morning.'

I ran into the living room, but there was no sign of Bertie. He wasn't in his bedroom, or in the bathroom brushing his teeth as I'd hoped.

'Everything all right?' called Rob.

I ran back down the stairs. 'When did you last see Bertie?'

'The same time as you. When we took him up to bed.'

'You've not seen him at all this morning?'

'No, why? What's wrong?'

'He's not here.'

'Of course he's here. He's probably hiding somewhere, not wanting to go to school.'

While Rob looked all around the house, I ran back to Bertie's bedroom, searching under the bed, looking through drawers. 'Rob! Rob, come here.'

'What is it?'

'His backpack's gone, along with a load of pants and socks.' I opened the wardrobe and began rifling through. 'There are two pairs of trousers missing and one of his hoodies.'

'You think he's run away?'

'What other explanation is there? We need to call the police.'

'Hang on a minute. Let's ring round his friends first.'

'Friends?' I rounded on Rob. 'What friends? He was beaten up at school yesterday lunchtime. All the kids know about you going bankrupt. He's miserable. I'd go as far as to say he's depressed. This is your fault. If you'd stood up to your mother, or not been stupid enough to go bankrupt, he wouldn't be this miserable. We were happy, Rob. HAPPY. If anything's happened to Bertie, I'll never forgive you, or your nasty, cruel, spiteful witch of a mother.'

I thundered downstairs, grabbing my coat.

'Where are you going?'

'To Cass's. He might be on his way there.'

'I'll come with you.'

'No, stay here in case he comes back. And don't even think about calling your parents. Marion will only add this to her collection of ammunition. In fact, she'll probably ring round her friends to have a good laugh.'

I slammed the door behind me and screeched out of the driveway, breaking all speed limits until I finally pulled the car to a stop outside Cass's house.

'Is he here?' I asked as soon as Jasper opened the door.

'Is who here?'

'Bertie.'

'Bertie? No, why, should he be?'

I burst into tears, and Jasper put an arm around me, pulling me into the house. Emmy walked into the room, took one look at me, rolled her eyes and walked back through to the kitchen.

'Jake?' called Jasper, easing me into an armchair.

Jake walked into the room, a piece of toast hanging out of his mouth.

'Jake, Aunt Liv's looking for Bertie. Do you know where he is?'

Jake shook his head. 'No. Has he run away?'

'We don't know.'

'Well, good on him if he has.'

'Jake!' Jasper looked at his son, open-mouthed. 'That's a horrible thing to say.'

'No, it isn't. She's the horrible one,' said my nephew, pointing at me. 'She's the one who made him leave his school and all his friends. It's her fault he's so unhappy. If I was her son, I'd run away too.'

Jake stormed out of the room and, rather than chasing after him, Jasper ran upstairs, returning with a bleary-eyed Cass following behind. 'Jasper told me what Jake said,' said Cass, propping herself on the arm of the chair. 'I'll speak to him later.'

'He's right, though. I am a horrible mother. It's no wonder he ran away.'

'Don't be stupid,' said Cass. 'None of this is your fault. Marion put you in an impossible situation. You were doing what you thought was right for your son.'

'But now he's missing. What if he... what if he...'

I collapsed, sobbing into Cass's arms. She stroked my hair, holding my trembling body tight until I could breathe again. I jumped as my phone vibrated in my pocket.

'Is it Rob?'

'No, it's not.' I answered the call. 'Pat?'

'Liv, hello. I'm calling because we have something which belongs to you. I assume you're looking for your son?'

Chapter Forty-Eight

'Bertie's with you?'

'Yes,' said Pat. 'He arrived ten minutes ago. Beryl found him.'

'Found him where?'

'Outside the shop. It seems he stole your husband's bank card and got himself on a train to Liskeard last night. I'm surprised they let an unaccompanied minor travel by himself, but I suppose it was late, so perhaps there weren't that many staff around to notice.'

'How did he get to the village from Liskeard?'

'Walked. All night. The poor chap's exhausted. We've given him something to eat and drink and put him to bed. I suspect he'll be out for the count for a while, so there's no need to rush over here.'

'Thank you for calling, Pat, and for looking after Bertie. I'm leaving now.'

'You found him?' asked Cass when I put down the phone.

'Yes, he's at Lowen Farm. I'm going over there now.'

'I'll come with you.'

'No, Cass, you've only had an hour's sleep since getting in from work. This is something I need to do alone.'

I made a call to Rob to let him know Bertie was safe, then set off through the busy city streets. I bashed the steering wheel in frustration as the car crawled along. Eventually, I'd reached the outskirts of the city and could pick up the pace. An hour and a half after leaving Cass's house, I pulled onto the track leading to Lowen Farm.

It was with a mix of emotions that I drove along the uneven track, the car jolting each time I went over a pothole. I'd not expected to see the farm again, and my stomach churned with nerves, shame and excitement. As traumatic as the morning had been, and as worried as I was about facing everyone after leaving them in the lurch, I couldn't shake the feeling that I was going home.

The farmhouse came into view, and I slowed my speed. What kind of welcome would greet me? Would Bertie even speak to me? Was he all right? The thought of him walking all night alone in the dark horrified me. How had I not noticed him sneaking out of the house?

The front door of the farmhouse opened, and Harry stepped out. She wore her usual shorts and tank top, but her hair hung in a long braided rope down her back. The sight of her caused my breath to catch, and I pinched myself to distract from the emotions threatening to overwhelm me.

I climbed out of the car and leaned against the door. Harry folded her arms, then her face spread into a wide smile, and she ran towards me, her hair swinging behind her. She flung herself at me, wrapping me in her arms and rocking me back and forth.

'It's so good to see you,' she said.

I couldn't answer, the lump in my throat blocking the words.

Harry stepped back and held me at arm's length. 'God, Liv. You look awful.'

My laugh came out as a choke. 'Thanks. And thanks for the warm welcome. I wasn't sure you'd be very pleased to see me. Is Bertie OK?'

'Bertie's fine. I've just been up to check on him and he's fast asleep. Now, I'm sure you're desperate to go to him, but what he really needs is rest. And we'd like to talk to you.'

'We?'

'All of us. We want you to be honest with us, Liv.'

'I...'

'Beryl brought Bertie up to the farm. She was surprisingly discreet, but she dropped some very strong hints that there was more to your leaving than you led us to believe. Of course, we all knew that already. She also hinted that you need our help and told us in no uncertain terms we weren't to let you leave again until you'd at least been honest with us.'

Harry took my hand in hers, and we walked into the farmhouse. I was both terrified and desperate to see Seb, and felt relieved and disappointed to find he wasn't waiting in the dining room. The *we* Harry had mentioned included Pat, Stephan and Maggie. Each hugged me by way of a greeting before taking their seats around the table.

'Thank you for looking after Bertie,' I said, as Harry poured me a cup of tea. 'I really think I should check on him.'

'He's sleeping,' said Maggie, reaching across the table and squeezing my hand.

'OK.' I stirred my tea with a spoon, despite not taking it with sugar. 'Harry says you want to know the real reason I had to leave?'

'Only if you're comfortable telling us,' said Pat. Maggie scowled at him. 'But of course we'd like to know.'

'You deserve the truth,' I said, launching into my tale of woe. I barely took a breath, my friends making no attempt to interrupt or stop me as I poured everything out. 'And so you see, I really didn't have a choice. I couldn't risk having Bertie taken away from me. What else was I meant to do?'

'Dear God,' said Pat, leaning back in his chair and blowing out his lips. 'Why on earth didn't you say something sooner?'

'I knew you'd all want to help me, and I didn't want you taking resources from the work you do here, be that time or money.'

'Silly girl,' said Maggie. 'Even if we couldn't help you financially, we could have supported you emotionally. What a thing to go through alone.'

'How much does Bertie know?' asked Harry.

'Nothing. That's why he hates me.' I let out a laugh that held no joy.

The dining-room door creaked open, and we turned to see Bertie, his hair messy and sleep clogging eyes that were fixed on me.

'How much of that did you hear, Bertie?' I stood up, unsure whether to go to him, scared he may run from me. Instead, Bertie flung himself across the room, wrapping his arms around my waist and squeezing hard.

'I don't hate you,' he said. 'Well, maybe I did a bit, but I thought you wanted us to leave.'

'No, Bertie. I never wanted to leave. I didn't have any choice.'

'Why couldn't Dad have stopped Grandma?'

'He was in the same position as me. You know how things went wrong with his business?'

'Yes.'

'Because of that, Dad doesn't have any money of his own and has to rely on Grandma and Grandpa to help him.'

'I hate Grandma.'

We'd always tried to stop Bertie using the word hate, but on this occasion, I felt it was justified. 'Did you manage to get some sleep?'

'A bit. Mum, can we stay here?'

'No, I'm afraid we can't, Bertie. Now you know why, I hope you'll understand. You know how I go out to work while you're still asleep?'

'Yes.'

'The reason I'm doing that is so we can start again somewhere new, even come back here if that's what you want. But, Bertie, it's going to take me some time before we can do that. So, until then, I'm going to need you to be brave for me. Brave and patient.'

'Do we have to leave straight away?'

'Well...'

'I could do with a hand with the animals,' said Harry. 'Perhaps you could stay for an hour or two?'

I looked down at Bertie. He was pulling his cute face, the one he always put on when he needed to get his own way. I laughed and hugged him. 'I can't see what harm a couple of hours can do. If you're sure?' I asked Harry.

'Of course. I've missed my little helper. Liv, if Bertie's going to be giving me a hand, I wonder if you could see to something down by the lake?'

'Of course. What is it?'

Harry glanced at Bertie, then mouthed silently, 'Seb.'

I nodded. The thought of seeing Seb made me nervous, but he deserved an explanation more than anyone. As much as I wanted to drink in every part of Lowen Farm, I was reluctant to stay too long, so decided to drive to the lake rather than walk.

Seb wasn't at home, so I made my way past the cabins toward the water. I'd forgotten how beautiful the lake was, or perhaps it was that in the full strength of summer, it had reached its peak. The surrounding trees had exploded into green, wildflowers clung determinedly into rock crevices and the water sparkled like the contents of an aristocrat's jewellery box.

Seb had his back to me, sitting in the rowing boat not too far out from the jetty. I removed my sandals and walked along the worn, warm boards, sitting down at the far end and letting my feet dangle in the cold green water. For a moment I just watched him, the way his neck craned at a twitch in his fishing line, the way his hand brushed hair from his eyes.

'Seb?'

Seb turned at my call. His beard had grown longer, dark crescents sat below his eyes. His hair looked greasy and matted and his clothes dirtier than usual. I smiled and gave a small wave, but Seb turned his head away from me. 'Don't bother jumping in this time,' he called. 'I don't want to speak to you.'

'That's fine,' I said. 'I only want you to listen.'

Seb began packing up his fishing gear and I knew I only had a few minutes before he picked up his oars and rowed as far away from me as he could get.

'Fine,' I said. 'I'll go. I just need you to know that I never wanted to leave, and I certainly never wanted to get back together with Rob. Seb, my mother-in-law threatened to take Bertie from me if I didn't go back to my marriage. What was I meant to do? I don't have the power or wealth to fight her, and I couldn't risk losing my son. I'm working hard to get out of my mess, but it's going to take me years. I'm not asking you to wait for me, but I felt I owed you the truth.'

Seb stopped packing up his fishing gear, but didn't turn to look at me. Instead, he sat still and straight-backed, his hands on his knees, his face turned up to the sky. I pulled myself up from the jetty and walked away.

Chapter Forty-Nine

Since Bertie's escape and subsequent return, we had made it through another month unscathed. After finding out the truth, Bertie had been attempting to put a brave face on things, but he was just as miserable at school, and we all breathed a sigh of relief each time the weekend rolled around.

On this particular Saturday, I had a visit to Dad to look forward to. Whilst Bertie loved visiting his gramps, the offer of a trip to the swimming pool with Jake, Emmy and Jasper was more tempting.

When Cass arrived to pick me up, she was quiet, which I assumed was down to the long hours she'd been putting in at work. We pulled up outside the nursing home, but as I began walking towards the entrance, Cass stopped me. 'Dad's not in there,' she said. 'He's waiting for us in the garden.'

'Oh, OK.'

I followed Cass along a path lined with well-tended flower beds. Early summer was in full swing and bursts of colour spilled over onto the wide gravel path. The warm sun made me sleepy, my early starts leaving me with a tiredness I never seemed able to shift.

Dad was sitting in his wheelchair beside a bench which overlooked a fountain. The nursing home had once been a stately home, and as we approached, I imagined women in beautiful silk dresses gliding along the path, parasols in hand.

'Hola, Papa.' I reached down and kissed Dad on both cheeks. His face lit up with his best impression of a smile and he waved his good hand to show he wanted us to sit down. In Dad's lap lay a piece of paper, the gentle summer breeze teasing one of its edges.

As Cass greeted Dad, she picked the piece of paper up.

'What is that?'

'Dad asked one of the nurses to help him get some of his thoughts down on paper.'

'Thoughts about what?'

'You.'

'Me?' I looked at Dad. He reached out his good arm and took my hand. His brown eyes filled with tears and his furrowed brow spoke of his frustration at not being able to express himself without the aid of others.

'Dad's asked me to read this out to you.'

'OK.'

Cass cleared her throat and held the paper tight. 'Dear Liv, I wish I could talk to you with speech, but my written words will have to do. You are unhappy. I see it. Bertie is unhappy too, and this breaks my heart. I know what happened with Marion. Cass told me.'

I looked up at Cass, who shrugged and continued reading.

'I cannot stand by and watch you throw your life away. Your mother would never have forgiven me if I let that happen. Life is too precious to live in the shadows. Half a life, half a person. This is no good, Liv. When we went out on the rowing boat, I saw my Liv for the first time in years. Beautiful, full of life, happy. That is the Liv I want to see again. But I cannot get you back to that person alone. Which is why I have asked some friends to help. Please don't be angry, and know everything I do is with your best interests in mind.'

'I don't understand.'

Cass stood up, put her fingers in her mouth and let out a loud whistle.

'Cass, what are you doing?'

I shielded my eyes from the sun, squinting at the two figures walking through the garden towards me.

'Dad arranged this,' said Cass.

I got to my feet, too stunned to speak. Harry and Seb stopped beside Dad's wheelchair. Harry bent down to kiss Dad's cheek and Seb rested a hand on Dad's shoulder.

'Your Dad asked a nurse to call Cass, and Cass called us,' explained Harry.

'I don't understand what you're doing here?'

'We're here for you, Liv,' said Seb. His eyes held mine as he stepped towards me and pulled me into him. With his arms wrapped around me, I pressed my head into his chest and breathed him in.

Seb released me from his arms, and I sat back on the bench, wiping my eyes on my sleeve.

'I'm sorry to spring this on you,' said Cass, 'but you've been so stubborn about asking for help and this seemed the only option. Besides, if you're pissed off with us, blame Dad.'

'I'm not cross. But I can't ask for your help. It wouldn't be fair. You don't understand what I'm up against. The resources Marion has at her disposal...'

'You're right,' said Harry. 'Even if we pooled all our resources, we couldn't match Marion for wealth. But as my grandmother used to say, there's more than one way to skin a cat.'

'For starters,' said Seb, sitting beside me on the bench and taking my hand, 'Marion has no way of knowing how much money we do or don't have access to. I was an investment banker once, remember? For all she knows, I could have vast sums squirrelled away somewhere.'

'Do you?'

Seb laughed. 'Unfortunately not. I squandered it all on fast living. But thankfully, you're not just relying on me. We've drawn up a document, stating all the people who are prepared to back you.' Seb pulled an envelope from his pocket and opened it. 'Right,' he said, folding out the paper it contained. 'On our list we have: Cass and Jasper, Maggie and Stephan, your dad, of course, me, Harry, Beryl, Mel and Pat.'

'I wouldn't take money from any of you.'

'I don't think you'll have to,' said Cass. 'It was Dad who got me to see it. Liv, what's the one thing your in-laws care about, even more than money?'

'Rob?'

'No, reputation. I, we, suggest you take this list of backers to your in-laws and let them know it won't just be you they're fighting if this goes to court. They may call your bluff, in which case you tell them in no uncertain terms, that if they proceed with using Bertie as a pawn in this terrible game they're playing, their scheme will find its way into a national newspaper. Dad still has contacts from his days at the university. The vice-chancellor's brother happens to be the editor of a well-known tabloid. Oh, and you can also let Marion know Jasper would be delighted to arrest her for blackmail, should you decide to press charges.'

'You really think it could work?'

'Yes,' said Cass. 'I do.'

'B... but,' said Dad, 'th... this is... R... Rob's problem t... too.'

'Yes, Dad's right,' said Cass. 'We need to speak to Rob first. The way I see it, there's no time like the present.'

Chapter Fifty

Rob was sitting in front of the TV, his feet on the coffee table, watching the cricket. 'Oh, hi, I wasn't expecting you back so soon.'

'I've got a few friends with me. I hope that's OK? They'd like to talk to you.'

'To me?'

'Well, both of us.'

'OK.'

I went to the front door and gave a thumbs up to my rescue party, who were waiting in the car. Cass, Harry and Seb filed through the front door, and I showed them into the living room.

'Harry, Seb, this is Rob.'

Rob stood up and shook their hands. I noticed Seb sizing Rob up, taking in the toned physique beneath Rob's Ralph Loren polo shirt. Seeing Seb and Rob side by side highlighted just how different they were. Seb looked even scruffier beside my well-groomed husband, but he was just as handsome, even more so with his kind eyes and easy smile. I wanted to take Seb's hand, reassure him this wasn't a competition, but it wasn't the place or time.

'Hello, Rob,' said Cass, kissing his cheek. Despite having told Cass about Rob's recent openness and our fledgling friendship, I could see Cass still felt suspicious around him.

'I've heard a lot about you,' said Rob, as Seb and Harry sat down on the sofa.

'And I've heard a lot about you,' said Seb, his tone less than friendly.

'Ah.'

'Don't worry,' said Harry. 'Liv's explained you're as much a victim in all this as she is.'

I threw Harry a grateful smile. There was something very unnerving about my husband sitting opposite the man I loved.

'What was it you wanted to talk to me about?'

'They've come to our rescue,' I said. 'But before we get into all this, there's someone missing who I think should be here.'

'Bertie?' asked Rob.

'No, Nicola.'

'Nicola? I thought you said you didn't want her in the house?'

'She's as much a part of this as anyone. I didn't want Bertie meeting her out of the blue, that's all. Speaking of Bertie, Cass, do you think Jasper could keep him out of the house for a couple more hours? I need to explain all this to him, but it's best I do it later, once we've formed more of a plan.'

'Sure,' said Cass. 'Let me call him.'

'Sorry,' said Harry. 'Who's Nicola?'

'Rob's girlfriend.'

'His girlfriend?' asked Seb, leaning forward in his seat. 'So...'

'Me and Rob are just friends,' I said.

'This is all so modern,' said Harry with a shake of her head. She turned to Seb. 'And you wonder why I'm still single?' She laughed, breaking through some of the awkwardness in the room.

'I'm the boring one,' said Cass with a smile. 'I've been with the same man since I was eighteen. There are no evil grim-laws, no lovers, no secrets. Like I said, terribly dull. Jasper's fine to keep Bertie longer, by the way. They're currently eating burgers.'

'No offence, Liv,' said Harry, 'but I hope if I ever do meet someone, it follows your sister's path, not yours. Boring sounds amazing after witnessing all this.'

'I agree,' I said. 'But Cass is being modest. There's nothing boring about her and Jasper, they just work.'

'Work hard,' laughed Cass. 'We're not perfect by any means.'

'Nicola's on her way,' said Rob.

I was curious to meet Rob's new partner, however strange the situation was. And it was strange. In fact, it was probably the most unlikely gathering the house was ever likely to witness. While Seb and Rob sat eyeing each other with suspicion, Harry launched into a long monologue to fill the awkward silence, telling us all in great detail about her favourite goat's latest health complaints.

'Would anyone like tea or coffee?'

'I'll help you make it,' said Seb, following me into the kitchen.

'So, this is weird,' I said, filling the kettle.

'Just a bit. When I tried to picture your life before Lowen Farm, I never thought it would be somewhere like this. It's all a bit...'

'Bland?'

Seb nodded.

'Well, we've not lived in this house long, but our last one was much the same, but bigger. My mother-in-law decorated that house too.'

'I don't get it, Liv,' said Seb, leaning against the kitchen worktop and fiddling with his beard. 'You seem so capable and interesting. I don't get how you could live like this for so long.'

'I suppose it's different once you have a child. My priority has always been Bertie. And when he was little, well, there wasn't much time to think about anything except meeting his needs. Trust me, when it comes to caring for a baby, you're happy for anyone to take over any decision making. In those days, I thought Marion was just being kind. I suppose she was, in her own way. It was a relief when she took over decorating our home. The last thing I had time for was deciding on paint colours and soft furnishings. And she talked me into being a stay-at-home mum, a decision I was more than happy with at the time. It was only as Bertie grew older and more independent that I began to question things.'

'Yeah, I guess I don't have much experience with kids. And you must have been really young.'

'I was twenty-one, so not that young. More of a problem was not having Mum around. There were so many times I wished I could have asked her for advice. I don't think I ever let myself grieve properly when she died. I wanted to make things better for Dad, and the only way I could think to do that was to not cause him any stress. I threw myself into trying to be perfect at everything: school, university, motherhood. When I accidentally fell pregnant with Bertie, marrying Rob seemed the obvious thing to do. It meant Dad didn't have to worry about me. Someone else was taking care of me.'

'And now?'

'Now I see that what Dad really wants is for me to be happy. Bertie's growing up fast. He doesn't need me in the way he used to. Being his mum will always come first, but now there's a bit more space for me to be me.'

The doorbell went, and I left Seb making tea. I opened the door to a young blonde woman with a stud in her nose and a sleeve of tattoos on her arm. 'Nicola?'

'Yes. Are you Liv?'

'Yes.'

'Look, I'm so sorry about what happened with Rob. We should have waited until he was divorced. It was a shitty thing to do to you.'

'In the light of what I've just been through, it isn't the end of the world. You clearly make Rob happy, and I'm glad.'

'Really? I thought you'd greet me with a punch in the face.'

'Maybe under normal circumstances...' I smiled at Nicola. She was nothing like I was expecting. Whilst Rob having an affair with his secretary was the ultimate cliché, there was nothing clichéd about the woman herself. She must have hidden her tattoos under long sleeves at work, and I supposed the nose piercing would be easy enough to remove. 'Sorry, come in. You can't stand there on the doorstep all day.'

'Cool place,' said Nicola, as she followed me into the house.

'You think so?'

'Nah, I'm just being polite.' Nicola laughed. 'I'd destroy this place in five minutes. I'm too clumsy for white. I pretend my dark green walls are a statement, but really, they're to hide stains. I can't walk from one side of a room to another without chucking my coffee everywhere.'

'Well, don't worry about making a mess here. We shan't be living in this house for much longer.'

'I guessed as much. I didn't think this was a social call, unless you're into weird threesomes which, in case you're wondering, I'm not.'

I laughed. 'Given the number of people currently in my living room, it would be more like an orgy, but don't worry, I'm not into those any more than I am threesomes. No, my friends have come up with a plan that should benefit us all, and I thought you should be here to hear it.'

'That's very generous of you.'

'Maybe. But I also wanted to size you up. If you're going to be part of Rob's life, that means you'll also be part of Bertie's.'

'And have I passed the test?'

'So far,' I said with a smile. 'Come on, I'll introduce you to the gang.'

Chapter Fifty-One

I turned to look at Bertie, who sat quietly on the back seat. 'Ready?'

'Yes.' Bertie clutched his backpack. I had no idea what was in there, but he'd promised it wasn't an iPad, so I'd let it drop.

Rob's hands still clutched the steering wheel, despite us having been stationary on the drive for several minutes. 'I'm not sure I can do this.'

'I know it's hard, but you're a grown man. At some point you need to cut the apron strings.'

'That's easier said than done when the woman wearing the apron is my mother.'

I placed a hand on his and gave it a squeeze. 'It will be OK. Remember, we're not in this alone.'

Rob rolled his shoulders, cracked his knuckles, and stepped out of the car. My first act of rebellion that day was in the clothes I was wearing. Cut off denim shorts, a loose-fitting shirt and Converse trainers were not Marion's idea of appropriate lunch attire. I'd also binned my hair straighteners, enjoying the feeling of loose curls swinging against my back.

Bertie knocked on the door and took my hand as we waited for it to open. When it did, Marion's eyes narrowed as she took in my casual attire. 'Running late this morning, were you?' she asked, looking me up and down.

'No.'

'Hmm, well, we're eating out on the patio today.' She kissed Rob on both cheeks, then led us through the house and onto the patio overlooking the gardens and pool. A sail-like canopy shaded us from the fierce sun, and Hugo had set up an electric fan to provide some respite from the humidity.

'I've prepared a cold lunch for us today,' said Marion. 'I couldn't bear the thought of spending hours by a hot stove in this heat.'

We took our positions at the table and Hugo poured out cold glasses of champagne. 'Are we celebrating something?' I asked.

'Marion wanted to mark our first lunch together since the two of you got back together.'

'I see.'

'How is school going?' asked Hugo, turning to Bertie.

'I hate it.'

Hugo laughed. 'That good, eh? I'm sure you'll settle in soon.'

Bertie looked at me and winked. I winked back.

'And you, Liv? How are you settling back into your normal life?'

'I'm struggling a little with the three a.m. starts.'

'Three in the morning? Goodness, whatever are you doing getting up at that time?'

'It's so I can be at work by four.'

'Work?' Marion appeared, carrying a large tray with an assortment of china dishes on it.

'Did you know anything about this, Marion?' asked Hugo.

'Know about what?'

'That Olivia has got herself a job.'

'But you can't have. You're at home every time I call round.'

'Yes, I know. I start work at four and I'm home by seven. It seems you can't get the staff these days, Marion. I thought the chap you've had watching me might have cottoned on to the fact I go out to work each day, but it seems not.'

'What nonsense,' said Marion, fiddling around with a potato salad. 'Of course I've not had anyone watching you.'

I took a large sip of my champagne. Bertie unzipped his bag and began removing items onto the paving slabs.

'Whatever is that child doing?' asked Hugo.

We watched as Bertie removed his T-shirt and hung it on the back of a chair. Next, he took off his shorts, then wrapped a towel around his waist and took off his pants, replacing them with a pair of swimming shorts.

'It looks as though Bertie fancies a swim,' I said, picking a cherry tomato from a salad bowl and popping it in my mouth.

'Young man, you know that pool is out of bounds.'

Bertie stuck his tongue out at Hugo, then ran down the grass verge, whooping and hollering as he dive-bombed the pool. Water sprayed up in the air, Marion's mouth hanging open as she watched him.

'Robert, you need to do something. Your son is running wild!'

Rob shrugged, grabbing the bottle of champagne and topping up his glass. 'There doesn't seem much point having a swimming pool if no one's going to use it.'

'You know the pool rules. What is going on? You're all behaving very strangely today. Is the heat getting to you?'

'No, Marion, it's not the heat. In fact, my mind is clearer than it has been for a long time. Rob has something he'd like to say to you.'

'Robert? What is all this about?'

'We're here to put a stop to your bullying. I can't stand by and take it anymore. Liv and I are getting a divorce. She is going back to live at Lowen Farm with Bertie. I'll see him every other weekend, and at least once during the week, depending on work commitments.'

'Stop talking nonsense,' said Marion. She pointed a bony finger in my direction. 'Has she put you up to this? You're making a big mistake, young lady. I've warned you what will happen.'

I reached into my handbag and smoothed a piece of paper out onto the table. 'This is a list of all the people who are prepared to support me if you pursue a custody battle, both financially and as character witnesses. In addition, if you do decide to go down the legal route, I'm afraid I can't guarantee my friends' discretion. It is highly probable news of your blackmail, and yes, what you're doing is blackmail, will end up in the national papers. I'm sure your friends at the bridge club would be fascinated to read about how you treat your nearest and dearest.'

'You wouldn't dare.' Marion's wrinkled skin had turned purple. Her hands shook. Hugo seemed to be drowning his shock under several glasses of champagne, downing each glass in one, before topping it up again.

'I would dare. Also, you may have forgotten, but my brother-in-law is a police officer. It was silly leaving me copies of those photographs, Marion. I think you'll find they count as evidence should I choose to report you for blackmail. Jasper has offered his help in creating a case against you.'

'Robert, stop your wife saying such hateful things. I won't be spoken to like this in my own home.'

'I agree with every word Liv has said.'

'We'll cut you off,' spluttered Hugo, his cheeks mottled as the alcohol took effect.

'Do it, I don't care anymore. There's more to life than money and reputation. It may have taken me a long time to realise that, but better late than never.'

'If we cut you off, you'll be destitute. No house, no car, no office. You wouldn't last five minutes without our support.'

'Actually, I don't need a house. I'm moving in with Nicola.'

I worried Hugo was about to have a heart attack. He spluttered into his champagne glass, his eyes bulging.

'I expressly forbid you to see that trollop again,' said Marion. A lock of hair had come loose and flopped about in front of her eyes. Her mouth was pinched so hard her lips had almost disappeared into her gums.

'Nicola is a wonderful woman, and I won't have you calling her names. We're in love. We're going to get married.'

'You're already married!' shouted Marion. A piece of potato flew off her spoon, landing with a plop in her champagne glass.

'The divorce shouldn't take too much longer. Obviously, you'll be invited to the wedding. In fact, perhaps we could hold the reception here?'

Rob's nerves had vanished, and if I weren't mistaken, I'd say he was enjoying himself. He piled salad and cold meats onto his plate, tucking into his food with gusto.

'You can forget about getting another penny from us ever again if you go down this foolhardy route.'

Rob shrugged. 'Fine by me.' He pierced an olive with his fork and popped it into his mouth.

'And you can hand back the keys for the office I'm paying for,' said Hugo.

'Sure. I'm folding the business, anyway. It's never really got off the ground. Nicola and I have other plans. Her agent has got her a season at a ski resort in Switzerland. Apparently stand-up comedy is the latest trend in entertainment. I'll work as a ski instructor. You know that's what I'd planned to do straight after school?'

'I remember talking sense into you.'

'Well, anyway, this is all a few months away. In the meantime, I'll find some sort of temp work. It will be hard being away from Bertie, but Liv's going to bring him out to visit at Christmas, aren't you?'

'Yes,' I said. 'Bertie can't wait.'

'Mum!' We all turned to where Bertie stood waving at the side of the pool.

'What is it, Bertie?'

'I couldn't hold it.'

'Hold what?'

'I peed in the pool.'

'GET OUT!' screamed Marion, picking up dishes of salad and smashing them down on the patio. By now, all her hair had escaped its pins and flew around her face in an angry halo. 'GET OUT GET OUT GET OUT!'

I picked Bertie's clothes off the back of the chair and as he reached me, I wrapped a towel around his shoulders. 'You seem a bit angry, Grandma,' he said. 'I'm sorry about the pee. It really was an accident.'

Marion let out a scream that reminded me of the foxes I sometimes heard at night. I bundled Bertie through the house, Rob following close behind. We climbed into the car in silence. Half a mile down the road, Rob pulled into a lay-by and turned off the engine.

'Are you all right?' I asked. 'That must have been really hard. They're still your parents, however badly they may have behaved.'

'Do you know?' said Rob. 'I've never felt better. And don't worry about Mum and Dad, they'll get over it.'

'Aren't you worried about them disowning you?'

'No. They're old, I'm an only child. If they cut all ties with me, they will only be hurting themselves. I'll take Nicola to meet them once they've calmed down.'

Rob's relaxed attitude surprised me almost as much as the faith he had in his parents. From what I'd just witnessed, I thought it would take a long time for their anger to subside, if it ever did. But they were no longer my problem. I laughed.

'What's so funny, Mum?'

'I don't know,' I said, wiping tears from my eyes. 'Maybe it's the peeing in the pool, maybe it's the memory of your pet toad, or maybe it's relief that I never have to eat Marion's overcooked cabbage ever again.'

'Mum, shall I tell you a secret?'

'Go on.'

'I didn't really pee in their pool. I just wanted to see the look on their faces when I told them.'

'That's my boy,' said Rob, turning the engine on and heading for home.

Chapter Fifty-Two

'Woah, hi, Emmy. You look... different.'

'Hi, Aunt Liv. Mum's in the kitchen.'

'Thanks.' My niece went back to her position on the sofa, pulling her headphones back on and picking up a magazine. The missing eyebrow had been consigned to the history books, as was the green hair. In fact, her entire goth phase seemed to have been binned, replaced by silver leggings, a Taylor Swift T-shirt and bubble-gum pink lip gloss.

'Emmy looks different,' I said, walking into the kitchen and kissing my sister on the cheek.

Cass rolled her eyes. 'I can't keep up. She's now saying she hates her black walls and wants them repainted mint green. Unfortunately, Jake's still firmly stuck in goth, so we're going to end up with a bedroom that resembles a cross between a mint humbug and a mint Aero. I can't keep up. Wine?'

'Please. Did I tell you Bertie tried to achieve the same black look?'

'No, you forgot that vital piece of information.'

'He coloured in his walls with a black felt-tip pen.'

'Oh God.'

'Hmm, I salvaged it with chalk paint in the end.'

'Does Marion know?'

'No, thank God. But I expect she'll find out when the letting agency refuses to hand back her deposit.'

'At least you'll be out of the firing line by then. Have you heard anything from her?'

'No. I think she's tried calling Rob, but I'm not sure he's answered.'

'Do you really think he can keep it up, this protest?'

'Who knows? If it were down to him, I'd guess he'd be running back to Mummy and Daddy as soon as his money ran out, but Nicola doesn't seem the kind of woman to give in that easily.'

'Yes, she was a bit of a turn up for the books, wasn't she?'

'I know. I really liked her.'

'Me too.'

'Who are you talking about?' asked Bertie, walking into the kitchen and helping himself to a can of Coke from the fridge.

'Bertie, you need to ask Cass before helping yourself.'

'Sorry. Can I have a can of Coke please, Aunt Cass?'

'Of course you can.'

'So, who were you talking about?'

'Nicola. I was saying she seems nice.'

'Yeah,' said Bertie. 'She's cool.'

'You've met her?' asked Cass.

'Her and Dad took me to the park yesterday. She let me have a double cone ice cream. You'd best not let Emmy meet her, Aunt Cass. She might get ideas about piercings.'

Cass contained her laughter until Bertie had left the room in search of Jake. 'He seems to be coping with all this remarkably well.'

'Yes, but I suppose me and Rob were never a very couply couple. And Rob was always at work, so I think Bertie will actually see more of him now we aren't together. I've spoken to Mel at the school about getting him access to a counsellor, though. He seems completely fine, but there have been so many changes, it would be good for him to talk to someone outside the family.'

'And you? How are you coping?'

'OK, I think. I'm just so relieved to be moving forward at last. The thought of going back to Lowen Farm is scary, though. New residents have arrived since I left, and we were so happy there before. I've built it up in my mind as some kind of paradise, which, of course, it isn't. I just hope we can make it work.'

'It will be fine. And Seb? What's happening on that front?'

'Nothing much. We're on friendly terms, at least. That's better than I could have imagined a few weeks ago.'

'Give it time.'

'Where's Jasper?'

'Picking up a VIP.'

The front door banged, and I heard Jasper swear.

'You might want to give him a hand,' said Cass.

I walked through to the living room to find Jasper trying to navigate an unwieldy wheelchair through the small, cluttered room. 'Dad!' I bent down and wrapped my arms around my dad's neck.

'There's a reason Alberto doesn't come round very often,' said Jasper, heaving an armchair into the middle of the room to create a clear path to the kitchen. 'We need a bigger house.'

'Let me help you.' As hard as we tried, the doorway was just too small for the wheelchair to fit through. I helped Dad to his unsteady feet, his arm wrapping around my shoulder for support as I helped him shuffle his way to the dining table. Jasper collapsed the chair, unfolding it at the table and helping Dad back in.

'Alberto insisted on being here,' said Jasper. Dad looked up and smiled at me, taking my hand. He pointed to the bag hanging on the back of his chair. 'Oh yes,' said Jasper. 'He brought someone else with him.' Jasper pulled out the framed photograph of my beautiful mother, causing tears to well in mine and Cass's eyes.

'She... w... would be... p... proud of you,' said Dad. 'S... so proud... of... both of... you.'

Cass joined me by our father's side. 'I suppose we've not turned out too badly in the end,' she said.

Bertie, Jake and Emmy rushed into the room, beside themselves at the sight of their Gramps, Bertie climbing onto his lap despite my protests.

Cass pulled a lasagne from the oven, and we squashed ourselves around the small dining table in my sister's messy kitchen. It wasn't so long ago that I'd been sitting in this very spot bawling my eyes out as my life spiralled out of control. Now here we were, about to embark on a new chapter that felt more exciting than at any other time in my life.

Jasper raised his glass, and we all followed suit. 'To new beginnings,' he said.

'To new beginnings.'

Chapter Fifty-Three

All I knew about Nicola's flat was that it was above a shop in a run-down area of the city. I'd have happily never laid eyes on it and left Nicola and Rob undisturbed in their love nest, but given Bertie was due to spend every other weekend there, I needed to picture where he was when not with me.

The charity shop below the flat had an unloved look about it. I imagined it would smell musty and, if the window display was anything to go by, would be packed with clothes belonging to the recently deceased. The building which housed the shop, and Nicola's flat, was a different story. A white-rendered Georgian frontage housed large, curved windows and what looked like four floors.

Beside the shop front was a small blue door. I pressed the buzzer to Flat 2, and a click signalled the door unlocking. The lobby was nothing to write home about. A threadbare blue carpet stretched up a staircase that had once been white, but which now held patches of exposed wood where many palms had worn through the paint. A battered mountain bike was chained up against some rusting pipework, and the area smelled of a curious mix of dust and oil.

'Up here.'

Nicola's face leaned over the wide staircase, and I climbed slowly towards her, dubious about what I might find.

'You found it OK?' she said as I reached her.

'Yes, no problem.'

Nicola was dressed in a floral maxi dress which skimmed her sandalled feet as she walked. The scooped back showed off a large tattooed vine which crept from her neck to goodness knows where. She pushed open a heavy oak door and beckoned me to follow. 'Don't worry,' she said, 'I know the first impressions aren't great, but I can't be bothered to waste my time on the communal areas.'

'Mum!' Bertie sprinted down a long, bright corridor, skidding to a stop on the exposed wooden floor and flinging his arms around me. 'This place is so cool. Nicola has said I can paint my bedroom whatever colour I want, and she says I can have a TV of my own.'

'I said only if your mum agrees.'

'You'll say yes, won't you, Mum?'

Before I had a chance to feel annoyed, Nicola placed a hand on my arm and apologised if she'd overstepped the mark.

'I'll think about it,' I said as Bertie grabbed my hand and pulled me deeper into the flat. At the end of the corridor, we entered a light-filled open plan space. As Nicola had promised, the walls were a rich forest green. The exposed floorboards and white window frames looked like something from a home décor magazine.

'It's handy living above a charity shop,' said Nicola. 'I got all my furniture from there.'

The furniture might be secondhand, but Nicola clearly had a good eye, the unusual mix of antique and modern giving off an air of cool rather than chaotic.

'I love your flat.'

'Thank you.'

'Come and see my bedroom, Mum.'

In the end Bertie gave me a tour of the entire flat. Even the bathroom was stylish, one wall covered in lush green plants which trailed down to the Victorian floor tiles. By the time we arrived back in the kitchen Nicola was making a pot of fresh coffee and Rob was propped on a bar stool, wearing a dressing gown, his hair wet from a shower. Despite having no desire to be married to Rob, the strangeness of seeing him so comfortable in another woman's home left me feeling like I'd stepped into an alternate reality.

'Have you got time for a coffee, Liv?' asked Rob.

I looked at my watch.

'Do you have to?' asked Bertie. 'I want to get to Lowen Farm.'

The insecurity I'd been failing to repress ebbed away. Yes, Bertie may love Nicola and her funky flat, but it was a relief to know he hadn't totally switched allegiance. 'Bertie's right,' I said. 'We'd better get going. But thank you for the offer.'

'Any time,' said Nicola. 'You know where we are now, so if you're ever in town, feel free to drop by.'

'Thank you.' As much as I liked Nicola and her flat, and it was an enormous relief that Bertie hadn't acquired a wicked stepmother, I didn't intend to become bosom buddies with Rob's mistress. In another life Nicola was exactly the kind of woman I'd have wanted to befriend, but the situation was too strange for any sort of close friendship. 'Are you still all right to meet Bertie from school on Wednesday?'

'Of course,' said Rob. 'I thought we could have a trip to the park, then we'll take him out for dinner before dropping him home. Does that work for you?'

'Perfect. I'll see you then.'

I packed Bertie and his overnight bag into the tiny amount of space left in the car. Now I knew our move to Lowen Farm would be a permanent one, I'd raided Cass's loft the night before and packed up pieces of artwork and knick-knacks my mother had left me but which had never fitted into Marion's minimal design standards. The car was new, too. Well, in as much as an old banger could be counted as new. New to me, paid for by the money I'd saved thanks to the cleaning job I'd been delighted to say goodbye to.

'Ready for the off?'

'Go go go,' shouted Bertie, turning the radio up and beginning to sing.

Chapter Fifty-Four

'Who's that?' asked Bertie, as I turned off the engine.

'I don't know.'

Outside the farmhouse, a couple were busy washing all the windows on the front of the house. 'I'm going to ask them.'

Bertie jumped out of the car and ran over to where the man was busy wiping a rag across one of the windowpanes. I walked over to where Bertie seemed to be spilling our entire life story to the bemused-looking stranger.

'Hello, I'm Michael,' the man said, holding out a damp, soapy hand. 'Sorry,' he said, wiping his hand on his jeans.

'I'm Liv. Pleased to meet you.'

'This is my wife Carly,' said Michael, as a pretty redhead abandoned her window cleaning apparatus and walked over to us.

'Are you living here now?' asked Bertie.

'Yes, we are for a while,' said Carly, giving us a shy smile.

'I'm Liv, and this is my son, Bertie.'

'We've heard all about you,' said Michael. 'Harry said you'd be arriving today.'

'How long have you been here?'

'Not long,' said Carly. Her voice was so soft it came out as a rushed whisper.

'How are you finding it?'

'Wonderful so far,' said Michael.

'I see they've put you straight to work.'

'Oh, we're happy to help,' said Carly. 'Actually, I'd better get back to it. Harry asked us to send you down to the lake when you arrived.'

'The lake? I hope she doesn't expect me to join her for a swim before we've even unpacked.' I laughed, and Carly flashed me another smile, before scampering back to her bucket of soapy water.

'Let's drive down there,' I said to Bertie. 'Then we can come back and unpack our things.'

We climbed back into the car and followed the track down to the lake. After parking, we walked through the woods, which were now teeming with life and colour.

'There they are,' said Bertie, pointing to a group of figures sitting out on the veranda of Pat's cabin.

I waved as Bertie sprinted over to Harry, Pat, and Seb.

'You're here,' said Harry, jumping down from the veranda and swinging Bertie around. She put Bertie down, and he giggled, stumbling like a drunkard over to Pat, who reached down and shook his hand.

'It's wonderful to be back,' I said, hugging Harry. Seb smiled at me as I approached the veranda, causing butterflies to flutter their wings in my stomach. 'I was expecting you all to be at the house.'

'There's been a bit of a change of plan,' said Seb, standing up so I could take his seat.

'Thank you.' I sat down in the wicker chair.

'You're probably expecting to have your old room back,' said Harry. 'But I'm afraid it's not available.'

'Oh.'

'Yes, we've given it to the new couple who've moved in, Michael and Carly. You may have met them?'

'Yes,' said Bertie. 'They were cleaning windows. Will we have to sleep outside?'

'Good Lord, no,' said Pat. 'Actually, I'm responsible for this turn of events. You see, all this walking back and forth to the farmhouse is getting a bit much for me. Old legs, you know.' Pat tapped his knee with his hands. 'Luckily for me, Harry has kindly made a couple of rooms available in the farmhouse. So what I propose is that you two move in to my cabin.'

'But this is your home, Pat. We can't take your home from you.'

'Ah, no, my dear. It's just bricks and mortar, or logs, in this case. Don't think I'm offering charity. I mean it about my legs. Seb's tried getting me on that damned quad bike, but that sets off my hip. Not much fun, this getting older lark.'

'We'd be neighbours,' said Seb, his hand brushing against mine, sending tingles up my arm.

'And there'd be no excuse not to join me for a swim each morning,' said Harry, glancing down at the lake, which sparkled in the hot summer sun.

'I don't know, Pat. It feels like we'd be kicking you out of your home. It doesn't sit right with me.'

'Listen, Liv. If I'm to continue living independently at my age, I have to be sensible about these things or, before you know it, I'll be stuck in an old folks' home.'

'We'd have to come to some sort of financial arrangement.'

Pat waved my comment away with a flick of his wrist. 'What use is money at my age? You can't take it with you, as they say.'

'I'm afraid I insist.'

Pat let out a dramatic sigh. 'Fine. But not today. Today, you need to settle into your new home. And once you've done that, I wouldn't mind a game of chess with Bertie up at the farmhouse.'

'Deal,' said Bertie with a grin. 'But watch out, Pat, I've been practising. I found an app on my iPad where you can play against a bot.'

'You've been playing against a bottom?'

'Not a bottom,' said Bertie with a roll of his eyes. 'A bot.'

'I'm afraid I have no idea what you're talking about, dear boy. But I have been practising too, or trying to.'

'He's roped me into a few games,' said Seb, 'but I'm not up to Bertie's standards.'

'No,' said Pat, 'I think young Seb could do with that practice bottom of yours, Bertie. Right, if you don't mind, Harry, I'd like to be getting back to the farmhouse. I need to get a good rest before facing such a fierce opponent as Bertie.'

'Of course,' said Harry. 'Take your time settling in, Liv. There's quite a lot we need to update you on with the Lake project, but that can wait until tomorrow. We'll see you at dinner later, though.'

'I'd better get going too,' said Seb. 'I've got a local builder arriving any minute to plan out the treehouse build.'

'Do you want me there?'

'No, it's fine. We can talk about it tomorrow. Like Harry says, you need time to settle in.'

It was only once our friends had left that we ventured into our new home. It was similar to Seb's cabin, but a little larger. Just like Seb, Pat had whitewashed the pine, painting the kitchen units sage. I'd never been inside Pat's cabin and was amazed at the amount of light flooding in from the sliding doors that enjoyed uninterrupted views of the lake. Beyond the open plan kitchen and living area was a small bedroom containing bunk beds.

'This is my room,' said Bertie, climbing up onto the top bunk and pretending to snore.

'Fine by me,' I said.

Next to the bunk room was a small, functional bathroom. A staircase rose from the middle of the living room. I climbed the stairs, trying to shake the feeling I was invading Pat's personal space. He had removed all of his belongings and there was no reason to feel like an intruder, but I still struggled to believe all this space was ours.

At the top of the stairs, a mezzanine area looked over the living space and I decided it would make a perfect office space. Beyond it was the second bedroom, a simple room containing a bed, chest of drawers and writing desk. Light flooded in from two skylights and the bed looked so tempting I could've curled up in it there and then.

Bertie was still lying on his bunk when I came downstairs. 'Come on, let's go to the car and start bringing our things in. The sooner we unpack, the sooner we can start living our new life.'

Chapter Fifty-Five

'Wow, this is quite the gathering!' The dining room was bursting at the seams. As well as the residents of Lowen Farm, we were joined by Beryl, Mel, and Zoe, who rushed to greet us with open arms.

'Oh, maid, it's good to have you back,' said Beryl. 'I've been storing up so much of the customers' news to tell you I feel like I may burst. You can start back at work on Monday, can't you?'

I disentangled myself from Beryl's arms and laughed. 'That depends. Do you have the latest gossip on Mavis's naughty neighbours?'

'Do I heck!'

'Then yes, you'll be seeing me bright and early on Monday morning.'

Mel had bent down to talk to Bertie and was engaged in what looked like a serious conversation.

'Good,' she said, standing with her hands on her hips. 'Bertie tells me he's been keeping up his cornet practice, which is fortunate as we're working on a very special piece for the grand fundraiser and need him up to scratch.'

'Hello again,' I said, sitting down opposite Michael and Carly. 'Those windows are looking good.'

'Thank you,' said Michael with a wide smile.

I thought arriving home to new residents would feel strange, but Michael and Carly seemed to slot in just as well as Andrea and Christine had all those months earlier. In fact, it felt good not to be the newbies, a sentiment Bertie seemed to share as he gave a monologue on animal care like he'd never been away.

With so many dinner guests, there wasn't much room around the table, and a shiver of nerves went through me as my leg pressed against Seb's. We hadn't yet talked about where things stood between us, and I was itching to get the conversation out of the way. Part of me suspected he'd struggle to take me back after all that had happened, but there was a kernel of hope deep inside me I couldn't ignore however hard I tried.

'Ladies and gentlemen,' said Pat, making us all laugh as he appeared in the doorway wearing a chef's hat. 'Dinner is served.'

Pat and Harry came out carrying trays of pizza.

'My favourite,' said Bertie.

'I know,' said Pat. 'That's why I moved my cooking night forward by a day. I wanted to welcome you back properly.'

Bertie climbed off his chair, walked around to Pat and gave him a big squeeze. As Bertie released him and walked back to his chair, I noticed Pat pull a handkerchief from his pocket and dab his eyes.

'It's so good to have you back,' said Maggie. 'The place hasn't been the same without you.'

'And our boys' nights have been extremely dull,' said Stephan.

'Can we have a boys' night next weekend?' asked Bertie. 'I want to watch *Spider-Man*.'

'Sounds wonderful,' said Pat.

'Count me in,' said Stephan.

'My favourite film,' said Seb, giving Bertie a fist bump. 'Michael, are you up for a boys' night?'

'If it involves *Spider-Man*, just try stopping me.'

'What is it you do, Carly, if you don't mind me asking?'

'I'm an accountant,' she said with something between a smile and a grimace. 'Not the most glamorous profession, I know.'

'I've recently left a job as a toilet cleaner,' I said. 'Accountant sounds wildly glamorous by comparison, and your skills will come in useful here.'

'Carly's already offered her services,' said Harry. 'She'll make an excellent addition to the Lowen Farm team.'

Carly's smile spread wider as she looked across at Harry.

Sitting around the table enjoying the busy hum of conversation, it felt as though we had never left. Beside me, Seb reached under the table and squeezed my hand. I wasn't sure I'd ever felt so happy or relieved.

'Back in your happy place?' he whispered.

'Yes, I think I am,' I said, tears of relief filling my eyes.

After dinner I was looking forward to a quiet evening settling into our new home, but it took a lengthy game of chess before I could prise Bertie away. By the time we reached the cabin, the excitement of the day had caught up with him and after giving him a piggyback from the car to the cabin, Bertie fell into bed and was asleep in seconds.

I took my glass of wine out on the deck and lit one of the paraffin lamps Pat had left behind for me. Within seconds, an influx of fluttering moths dulled the lamp's light. I lit a citronella candle as a precaution against mosquitoes and pulled a blanket across my legs. Beyond the deck, the lake lay still, like an emerald, its smooth surface caught by the light of a waning moon.

'Do you mind if I join you?'

I jumped as Seb stepped out of the darkness. 'Sorry, you scared me.'

'If you'd rather be alone, that's no problem.'

'No, of course not. Take a seat. I'll get you a drink.'

'How does it feel to be back?' asked Seb, as I handed him a glass of wine.

'Amazing. Leaving here was the hardest thing I've ever done. Coming back is a dream come true, not to mention the bonus of living in Pat's cabin.'

'Well, I for one am happy we're neighbours.'

'You are?'

'Yes.' Seb reached over and clinked his glass against mine. 'Cheers.'

'I thought you might hate me after I left the way I did.'

'Hate you?' Seb laughed. 'I could never hate you, Liv.'

'We should probably talk about us.'

Seb took a sip of his wine. 'Yes, we probably should.'

Between us, a silence developed, interrupted only by the beating wings of insects and the gentle lap of water against stone. It became a battle of wills, who would break first. Inevitably, it was me. 'I understand if you'd rather just be friends.'

'Hmm.'

'I wouldn't blame you after the way I behaved.'

'Right.'

'And of course, being in a relationship could be complicated given we're now neighbours.'

'Yes.'

'And then there's Bertie to think about. Although he's taken to Nicola amazingly well, and at least we know he already likes you.'

'Liv?'

'Yes?'

'Stop talking.' Seb got up from his chair, took my wine glass from me, and placed it on the table. He took my hands, pulling me up from my chair. He moved my hands around his neck and placed his own around my waist. 'Dance with me.'

'What?'

'Dance with me.'

'But there's no music.'

'There is. Listen.' He rocked me back and forth to the rhythm of the lapping waves, the call of a fox, the song of an owl deep in the forest. The rowing boat played out a slow, soft bass line as it brushed against the jetty.

'Mum!'

I stepped back from Seb and turned my attention to the cabin. 'Bertie? Are you OK?'

'It's so dark in here. Can you turn the light on?'

'You'd better go,' said Seb. He leaned forward and brushed his lips against mine. 'In answer to your question about us. Of course there's an us, there's always been an us. But let's take things slow. You've been through some massive upheavals in the past few months and probably need time to process it all. But for now, go and see to your son. You know where I am if you ever need me.' Seb kissed me again, then climbed down from the deck and disappeared into the night.

'Coming, Bertie,' I said, blowing a kiss in Seb's direction before closing the cabin door.

Chapter Fifty-Six

It was an extraordinary morning: the sun warming the ground in misty clouds, the water of the lake turquoise, above it a rainbow of pink, purple, yellow and electric blue courtesy of the butterflies and dragonflies who danced through the air.

'There's a treat for you in the kitchen,' I said, as a bleary-eyed Bertie walked in to the living room. I hugged my cup of coffee, as transfixed by the view outside as I had been every morning for the past month.

'Wow, coco-pops! Thanks, Mum!'

'It's a special day today, so I thought you deserved a treat. How are you feeling about the concert?'

'Good. Did you hear me practising last night?'

Funnily enough, it was hard to avoid the sound of a blasting cornet in a small log cabin. I pitied the poor woodland creatures whose peace had been shattered since Pat moved out and we moved in. 'Yes, it's sounding great.'

'Did you know Michael's a drummer? He's going to play drums for the band today.'

'No, I didn't know, but that sounds wonderful.'

'Is Dad still coming today?'

'Yes, I think so.' Bertie had settled quickly into the shared custody arrangements, enjoying his weekends in the city, but equally happy to come home to our oasis in the woods. My relationship with Rob remained cordial, checking in regularly about Bertie, but keeping some distance when it came to our personal lives.

It had been Bertie's idea to invite Rob and Nicola to the fundraiser, and I was curious to see what they made of Lowen Farm. Six months ago, I wouldn't have been able to imagine Rob here, but he had changed so much recently I suspected he wouldn't stick out like a sore thumb as he once might have.

'Aren't you having breakfast?' asked Bertie.

'I'm too nervous to eat.'

'You always say breakfast is the most important meal of the day.'

'All right then, I'll have a piece of toast.' My stomach was fizzing with nerves. It was important everything was perfect at the fundraiser, as securing the interest of potential investors was crucial to the future success of the lake project. Pat had funded a prototype treehouse, and it was very impressive. Inside, if it weren't for the leaves fluttering against the large windows, you'd think you were in a comfortable cabin at ground level. It contained a double bed, sofa, rainwater sink and a wraparound balcony to make the most of the views.

Bertie had been begging to have a sleepover in the treehouse. I'd promised he could stay in it with his friends the following weekend. I couldn't risk them doing any damage in there before the deep-pocketed investors had seen it.

I was buttering my toast when Seb knocked on the door. The past month had been torture. He'd kept to his word about taking things slowly, and other than a few stolen kisses, our relationship had stayed firmly within the bounds of friendship.

'I've written out a to-do list,' I said, as he walked in and poured himself a coffee. 'Maggie, Stephan and Harry are coming down at ten to set up tables for the stalls. Are you OK to take care of the water sports?'

'Yes, I'll set out a dedicated swimming area using buoys, and Carly has agreed to play lifeguard for the day. She worked a brief stint at a leisure centre so has all the relevant qualifications. I'll alternate the kayaking and team building sessions throughout the day, and anyone can take out the rowing boat so long as they sign a waiver agreeing to do so at their own risk.'

'It sounds like you've got everything under control.'

'I hope so. What else is on your to-do list?'

'Harry's friend Zoe is coming to set up her face-painting stall this morning. I've left Mel in sole charge of the entertainment. Maggie's enlisted a couple of local teenagers to keep drinks topped up and make sure we don't run out of cakes. They're coming over at lunchtime so she can give them their instructions. I need to hang bunting, fairy lights, make sure copies of our business plan are strategically placed around, and give the cabin a tidy in case any investors want to come back here to discuss sensitive money matters.'

'And Pat's running a nature trail?'

'Yes.'

'And how about you, Bertie? What will you be doing today?'

'Having fun,' said Bertie, stuffing a spoonful of cereal into his mouth.

'And playing his cornet in the band,' I said.

'I'm looking forward to hearing that.'

'I've been practising,' said Bertie.

'Have you?'

'I'm surprised you haven't heard it,' I said.

Seb winked at me.

'Right, all the guests are arriving at two, so let's get going!'

'I'm having a shower,' said Bertie.

'OK, but don't be long.'

'And I need to borrow you for a moment,' said Seb. Seeing my panic, he added, 'Don't worry, it'll only take a couple of minutes and then you can get straight back to your to-do list.'

'All right then,' I said, casting one nervous glance at the long list over on the table.

Seb took my hand and, without another word, led me outside.

'Where are we going?'

'Shh.' He put a finger against my lips, then lifted my hand and kissed it. With a gentle tug, he pulled me towards the lake.

I hadn't been able to see it from my window, but now I noticed something standing up from the grass just above the shingle beach, covered in a sheet. I gave Seb a curious glance, but he simply grinned back at me.

When we reached the object, he stopped and turned to me. 'Do you remember when we first started working together, Harry said we needed a better name than *the lake project?*'

I clapped my hand against my forehead. 'I totally forgot about that.'

'Then it's lucky I didn't.' Seb's eyes flicked between me and what I now realised was a wooden sign. 'I hope you like it... maybe you'll think it's not that imaginative... obviously we can change it if you hate it...'

'Seb, show me,' I said.

He stepped forward and pulled off the sheet. Beneath it, a rustic wooden sign had a border of beautifully painted leaves, butterflies, and dragonflies. In its centre, in green lettering, read *An tyller lowen*, and beneath it, in brackets, *the happy place*.

'*An tyller lowen* is Cornish for *the happy place*,' said Seb, rubbing his palms against his shorts.

'Yes,' I said with a laugh, 'I'd got that.'

'So, what do you think? Is it too much of a mouthful?'

'It's perfect.' I ran my hands across the beautiful sign, tears of happiness filling my eyes. 'I love the design, was it...'

'The planning officer from the council, yes. His artistic talents have come in very handy lately.'

'An tyller lowen,' I said to myself, my fingers tracing the outline of a butterfly's wing. 'When did you do all this? When did you decide on the name?'

'Your dad was the first one to give me the idea, *un lugar feliz*, a happy place, remember? Then, the day you came to see me after Bertie had run away confirmed it. I knew then that whatever happened between us, this would always be our happy place, and I also knew how important it was to share it with other people. The name came to me, so I asked a friend for the Cornish translation, contacted our pal at the planning office, and here we are.'

I stepped towards Seb, almost drowning in the love I felt for him at that moment. 'Seb.' My fingers reached out to touch his face, but I pulled them away as a shout reached us.

'Cooee! We're ready and reporting for duty.'

We turned to see Maggie, Stephan and Harry appearing from the trees.

Seb laughed, put an arm around my waist and whispered, 'there'll be time for us later, but for now, your minions await.'

I smiled up at him, then turned my attention to my friends. 'Come into the cabin, the to-do list is in there.'

Chapter Fifty-Seven

By mid afternoon, the forest was a hive of activity. Just as I had imagined, the woodland scene had been transformed into something resembling a village fete and an old-fashioned fairground. Its usual residents hid in burrows and tree tops as children ran from stall to stall, parents dug into their wallets for yet more change, and Mel's brass band blasted out arrangements of pop songs that sent birds scattering from trees.

Everyone had gone to town on their stalls, with colourful banners advertising everything from a lucky dip to splat a rat. The bunting and fairy lights we'd strung up between the trees gave the forest an otherworldly feel, as though magic was in the air.

The potential investors I'd invited seemed impressed by what they saw. I'd held a series of meetings in my cabin, securing promises of further conversations, if not blank cheques. The day was warm and muggy and with relief, I finished my schmoozing and made my way back to the festivities.

'Liv, there you are.'

I looked up to see Rob and Nicola descending the treehouse staircase.

'This place is completely amazing,' said Nicola, her eyes bright, the bangles on her arms jingling as she waved in excitement. 'It's paradise. I want to move here myself.'

I laughed, her enthusiasm infectious. 'You're welcome to come and stay anytime. Bertie would love that, but as for living here, well, that may take our unconventional arrangement to a whole new level.'

'Yes,' agreed Rob, 'I've changed a lot recently, but not so much that I'd be happy using a compost toilet.'

I smiled at my ex-husband, who looked like a different man in his denim shorts and loose fitting T-shirt. He even wore a leather bracelet around his wrist, and I wondered how long it would take Nicola to persuade him to get a tattoo or piercing.

'We've got you something,' said Nicola, digging around in her bag.

'What? There's no need for any gifts.'

'There is. The way you've dealt with everything that's happened, the generosity you've shown in accepting me into your family, well, I owe you big time.'

'And so do I,' said Rob. 'We may never have been suited as a couple, but in Bertie you've given me the greatest gift a man can have, not to mention all those years you put up with my parents.'

I laughed. 'Thank you.'

Nicola handed over a square package, about the size of a large dinner plate. 'I hope you don't take this the wrong way,' she said, as I peeled back the wrapping paper. 'It's not meant to remind you of dark times. But when I saw one of those photos Marion's thug had taken, I didn't see a debauched, unfit mother. I saw a woman surrounded by friends captured in a moment of joy.'

I peeled back the last scrap of paper and swallowed the lump in my throat, unable to stem the tears snaking down my cheeks. The canvas painting was of the lake at dusk, a group of naked women jumping into the water. The artist had somehow captured the moment, whilst preserving the subjects' modesty. It was one of the most beautiful pieces of art I had ever seen. At the bottom was written *An Tyller Lowen*.

'Oh my goodness, this is incredible.'

Nicola waved a hand. 'I've got a friend who's an artist, and she did this as a favour, so it's not an expensive gift, but I'm pleased you like it.'

'Me too,' added Rob, although I suspected the gift had been all Nicola's doing.

'How did you know about the name?'

'We called Seb to check if the painting was a good idea and he mentioned the new name of the project.'

'I honestly don't know what to say. Thank you.'

'You're welcome. We'll leave you to it, as I'm sure there are tons of people here you need to speak to.'

After more thank yous and even a hug, we parted ways. I found Maggie and Stephan beside a stall selling candy floss. Stephan had patches of pink sugar stuck to his chin, but Maggie was too busy with her own sugary delight to have noticed.

'Oh, Liv, what a wonderful job you've done today.'

'It was very much a team effort.'

'Learn to take a compliment,' said Stephan.

'I'll try.'

Pat wandered over to us, munching on a toffee apple. 'I fear this will ruin my false teeth,' he said. 'Please, no one tell my dentist.'

'Your secret's safe with us,' I said.

'Bertie is doing a wonderful job with the band.'

We all looked over to the stage. Given the heat of the day, Mel had discarded her usual bow tie, slacks and braces in favour of linen shorts and a Hawaiian shirt covered in images of pineapples. As the band played, her conducting style was more like something from *Strictly Come Dancing* than *Last Night at the Proms*.

'Mel's in her element.'

'Indeed, she is,' agreed Pat. 'Harry too, by the looks of things.'

We all looked over to where Harry was installed on a hay bale, surrounded by children desperate to gain entry to her makeshift petting zoo. A floppy-eared grey rabbit sat in her lap, a goat nibbling treats from her outstretched hand. She looked up, saw us watching and gave a thumbs up with her one free hand.

'Have you been down to the lake to see what's happening there?' asked Pat.

'No, I've not had the chance yet.'

'Here,' said Maggie, handing me a bag of candy floss. 'Take this to Seb. He's been flat out all afternoon and could do with some sugar.'

Seb was helping a group of teenagers out of life jackets. 'Hi,' he said as I walked towards him. 'Could you give me a hand dragging the kayaks further up the beach?'

'Of course. How's it going?'

'Great. I even got some of the suited businessmen into the kayaks. How have your meetings gone?'

'Very positive. It's a relief to know the business plan stands up to scrutiny.'

'You should have more faith in your abilities.' Seb reached across a kayak and took my hand.

'Gross,' said Bertie, running down onto the beach. 'You're not going to start kissing, are you?'

Seb laughed. 'I think our secret's out.'

'That you have a crush on Mum?' said Bertie. 'Oh, I've known about that for ages. Mum, can I have some more money? The band's having a half hour break, so I want to make the most of it.'

'Sure,' I said, so surprised by Bertie's revelation I grabbed the first note I landed on which happened to be ten pounds.

'Wow, thanks, Mum.'

'Hang on, I only meant to give you five,' I said, but Bertie was already sprinting off toward his friends.

'So much for telling him when the time's right,' said Seb, walking around the kayak and wrapping his arms around me.

'Do you know, I don't think I can remember ever being so happy?'

The sound of sniggering teenagers reached me as Seb leaned forward and kissed me. 'That was nice,' I said as he pulled away.

'It's a taster of what's to come.'

'Really?'

'Yes. I've had enough of taking things slowly. How about you?'

'Agreed.' I leaned forward and kissed Seb again, all the noise and activity around me blurring into insignificance as I melted into his arms.

On the beach, one teenager pretended to be sick before shouting, 'Get a room!'

'We'd better get back to work,' said Seb.

'We better had.'

I walked away from the beach, then stopped and turned to watch as Seb shared a joke with the gang of teenagers. The lake glistened in the sunshine, birds shocked from the trees as the brass band struck up once more. I couldn't wipe the smile off my face as a wash of gratitude swept through me. I'd finally found where I belonged. *An tyller lowen...* The happy place. Never had a name been more fitting.

***

Thank you for reading *The Happy Place*!
If you enjoyed Liv's story please consider leaving a review, it's the best way of helping other readers find the book!

Acknowledgements

The Happy Place is my tenth published novel, and if I've learned anything over the past ten books, it's that the process for writing a book is unique to each story. This book began on a sunny walk with friends. They were telling me about a co-living house in Cornwall they had heard of. I found the idea fascinating but thought no more of it. Fast forward a month or so, and during a meeting with a publisher I was asked if I had any ideas kicking around for a new novel. Out of nowhere the conversation about the co-living house popped back into my mind. I ended the call, picked up a notebook, and the plot for *The Happy Place* came pouring out.

In the subsequent weeks I couldn't write fast enough. It was as though the story was desperate to escape my brain and I'd never experienced anything like it before or since. I was waking up early to write, staying up into the small hours, carrying a notebook around so I could still be getting the story down when away from my laptop. This book was a joy to work on from the initial idea to the final edits (something I usually find quite tedious!). I hope this sense of joy comes across in the reading of Liv's story.

Lowen Farm is a fictional location, but the lake is based on one I have visited several times. The lake at *Cornish Tipi Holidays* is a hidden gem off the beaten track in Cornwall, surrounded by lush trees and with a jetty and rowing boat just like Liv's. I hope to visit again for a swim soon (but no skinny dipping- I'm not as brave as Harry!). Thank you to Lizzie and her team from *Cornish Tipi Holidays* for the warm welcome as I took endless photos of the beautiful lake.

Big thanks to Karolina, Ivy and Franky for spending a beautiful afternoon pretending to be book characters and helping with photography/video as we tried to capture the essence of this book on camera. Thanks also to the hugely talented Tom Fosten for providing beautiful music to accompany the images.

Thank you to Jorge Garcia and Matthi Ab Dewi for your help with the Spanish and Cornish sentences in the book (although I can't blame Jorge for 'polla', that was all my own work).

It's one thing writing a book, but at some point, you have to stand back and hand it over to other people for fresh eyes and input. Thank you, Jo and Pete, for your constructive editing advice, Audrey Davis (a talented author as well as proof reader) for picking up on my many errors, and Jarmila Takač for your gorgeous cover design.

Thank you to my family and friends for your continual support and interest in my writing, and of course, to my wonderful readers who make writing these books worthwhile.

Thank you for reading Liv and Bertie's story. I hope you've enjoyed their adventure at Lowen Farm!

About the author

Author and musician LK (Laura) Wilde was born in Norwich, but spent her teenage years living on a Northumbrian island. She left the island to study Music, and after a few years of wandering settled in Cornwall, where she raises her two crazy, delightful boys.

To keep in touch with Laura and receive a 'bonus bundle' of material including the FREE eBook *The Island Girls*, join her monthly Readers' Club newsletter at lkwilde.com

Or find her on social media- @lkwildeauthor

Also by LK Wilde

Book 1 in the Cornish feel-good *The House of Many Lives* series

Kate is stuck in a rut, She works a dead end job, lives in a grotty bedsit and still pines for the man who broke her heart.

When Kate inherits a house in a small Cornish town, she jumps at the chance of a fresh start. A surprise letter from her grandmother persuades Kate to open her home and her heart to strangers.

But with friends harbouring secrets, demanding house guests, and her past catching up with her- can Kate really move on? And will her broken heart finally find a home?

People say you get one life, but I've lived three.

I was born Ellen Hardy in 1900, dragged up in Queen Caroline's Yard, Norwich. There was nothing royal about our yard, and Mum was no queen.

At six years old Mum sold me. I became Nellie Westrop, roaming the country in a showman's wagon, learning the art of the fair.

And I've been the infamous Queenie of Norwich, moving up in the world by any means, legal or not.

I've been heart broken, abandoned, bought and sold, but I've never, ever given up. After all, it's not where you start that's important, but where you end up.

Based on a true story, *Queenie of Norwich* is the compelling tale of one remarkable girl's journey to womanhood. Spanning the first half of the 20th century, Queenie's story is one of heartbreak and triumph, love and loss and the power of family. It is a story of redemption, and how, with grit and determination, anything is possible.

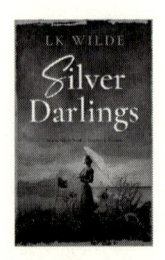

Book 1 in the Watson Family Saga

In 1895, a Northumberland island welcomes two new residents. Clara and Jimmy are born on the same night to families poles apart. Clara is an islander through and through; Jimmy longs to escape.

When tragedy forces them from their island and each other, they join the herring season in a bid to survive. As they follow shoals of silver darlings to Lowestoft, their paths are dogged by war, injury and misunderstandings.

Will they be reunited? And will they ever find their way home...?

Manufactured by Amazon.ca
Acheson, AB